Please return or renew this item by the last
shown. There may be a c
be returned
KT-169-305
1300
RUN,
RIOT

30117803370184

RUN, RIOT

NIKESH SHUKLA

HODDER CHILDREN'S BOOKS

First published in Great Britain in 2018 by Hodder Children's Books

1 3 5 7 9 10 8 6 4 2

'Man Down' from *Hold Your Own*, written by Kate Tempest,
published by Picador Poetry © Kate Tempest

Lyrics from 'Run, Riot' contains elements from 'Run' by Driving
Lolita (831 Records). Written by D. Dhanjal, A. Hafiz, G. Affinita
Cover created with images from Shutterstock.com

A CIP catalogue record for this book
is available from the British Library.

ISBN 978 1 44494 068 8

Typeset by Hewer Text UK Ltd, Edinburgh
Printed and bound in Great Britain by CPI Group (UK) Ltd, Croydon, CR0 4YY

The paper and board used in this book are
made from wood from responsible sources.

Hodder Children's Books
An imprint of
Hachette Children's Group
Part of Hodder & Stoughton
Carmelite House
50 Victoria Embankment
London EC4Y 0DZ

An Hachette UK Company
www.hachette.co.uk
www.hachettechildrens.co.uk

For all the young journalists I've worked
with at *Rife* magazine – you make me.

AUTHOR'S NOTE

This is a work of fiction that was conceived and drafted before the tragedy in Grenfell Tower. While I did my best to ensure that this remained a work of fiction, the awful events that happened in 2017 loomed large in my consciousness. I hope the residents of Grenfell get justice soon and the government takes their plight seriously.

NIKESH SHUKLA
FEB, 2018

YESTERDAY

11.42 p.m.

Sim stares at his laptop screen. He can't quite believe what he's watching. It's definitely Mr Johnson. And him. That man. With the angry voice. Unmistakeable. Sim can't focus on the words he's shouting at Mr Johnson, he's too surprised to see the man there. The blows to Mr Johnson's face, his chest, sound painful. Sim winces. He wants to look away but he can't.

He feels tears froth in his eyes.

He rubs at his newly shorn head and feels the bristles against his fingertips. He lets the tears come. How could that man do this to his mentor? That man from NextGen Properties was beating on Mr Johnson. Then, into frame comes another face Sim recognises. A copper. Inspector Blakemore.

Sim looks around the top deck of the bus that's taking him back to his neighbourhood. No one is there. Not at this time of night. Sim's head is all over the place.

This NextGen guy's supposed to be a businessman, Sim thinks. *This violence. It's just . . . it's too much.*

But it proves Mr Johnson is innocent.

Sim feels an angry burn in his chest as the bus nears his stop. He ejects the USB stick containing the video files and buries it in the pocket of his long puffa coat. He stands up, steadying himself on the back of the seat in front of him. His knees feel weak.

NextGen, Sim thinks.

He steps off the bus and looks over at Firestone House, his home since the day he was born. He hears the low murmur of people across the road. He nods when he sees it's CJ and one of his guys. Sim walks towards Firestone House, unsteady, trying to process what he's just seen. The video. He was surprised enough to hear from the sender, but never in a million years did he expect this. What does it mean? And how did the sender come across it in the first place?

And what in god's name should he do next? He has to confront Patterson, surely. Give the man an opportunity to come clean before he's exposed. Get Mr Johnson free.

Sim approaches the entrance to his tower block, looks up the fourteen floors to the top and blows a kiss, like he always does when he comes home.

'You're late,' he hears.

He spots Taran, in the shadows, leaning against a wall. She smiles and readjusts the cap on her head. She walks up to him, arms outstretched for a hug.

Sim accepts the hug, linking his fingers around Taran's back. As she rests her cheek on his chest, he stares at the ground over her shoulder, unsure what to do now, knowing that what he has just seen on the screen of his laptop is going to change everything.

DAY 1

5.40 p.m.

However it starts, it has to be loud.

Taran whispers this to herself as she pushes the door leading to the roof wide open. The door swings back on its hinges as she stomps through and then bangs shut behind her. Like a kick drum.

Whatever happens, it has to happen big. Big start, maximum repetition for effect, slow build, big chorus . . . No – scratch that – an unbelievably big anthem-like chorus and, at the centre of it, her bars.

Because she's not messing about. This is her year. Her time to shine. She's done the odd verse on the odd mixtape here and there. And there's been the odd bit of heat. And people keep telling her they're waiting. Now it's time to release things. It's all she can think about, recording. Every day, that's all she wants to do. Record bars.

Producer? Check my microphone levels, run the beat, let me loose.

Give me the stage. In fact, why am I even going to that gig tonight when I could own any of the rappers on that stage?

Except Rage. No one is as good as Rage.

Taran is going by 'Riot' now. She's settled. That's her MC name. Riot. It's because every bar is the soundtrack to a riot, every syllable is dissent and every rhyme is an exploding grenade. *Riot.* The more she says it to herself, the more she loves it. She hasn't told the guys yet.

She's keeping it close in her heart. Like that Warren Zevon song her dad used to play over and over again – 'Keep Me in Your Heart'. Damn, just thinking about that song hurts. She asked Cody to sample it but when he played her the beat she just ran out of the studio cos she couldn't breathe.

Anyway, 'Run'. That tune, the one she was working on today, it's called 'Run'. 'Run' by Riot. Sick.

Her cap is pulled down low over her eyes so she doesn't see Anna stood in front of her, staring out into the middle distance. The first sign she has of her best friend's presence is when Anna says, 'Can you see that?'

Taran looks up and sees Anna is pointing. She follows the arm to the finger to the nail to the skyline across the city.

'We can see the weather approaching from here,' Taran's twin brother Hari often says. 'We know what's coming and what's gone. We're the present.'

Hari doesn't say much. He likes to be the strong silent type. But every now and then he'll go all poetic and say abstract shit like that. Like he's competing with his rapper sister. He wrote a sonnet for Jamal to give to Anna one time for Valentine's Day, and now he thinks he's a big man of letters, like a Shakespeare or even an Akala or something. Really, Taran's the poet. Hari's the fighter. The funny thing is, Jamal never even gave Anna the poem cos it was so bad.

Anna is pointing at a helicopter. It's approaching fast. Cutting through blankets of invisible air like its blades are a scythe.

'Where's it heading?' Taran asks.

'It's either the news or some weird security shit. You know the park is gonna be rammed. It's probably paparazzi. Now he's finally coming home, they probably wanna get aerial shots of all of us coming out to support. Cos they know everyone is gonna be there.'

'Someone is always watching,' Taran says. 'Anyway, where are those fools Hari and Jamal? We need to go. It's gonna be busy already.'

'No idea.'

Pause.

'How was your day?' Anna asks.

'Good. Been in the studio since ten. Working on some heat,' Taran says, grinning. She knows Anna's gonna be annoyed she wasn't at college today. Not that anyone else notices.

'I figured. Your absence was noted. The teachers sent their TAs down to the park to make sure no one was bunking to wait by the stage. But anyway, of all the people who bunked today, your absence was noted.'

'Not by any of our teachers, I bet.'

'Nope, don't be silly. By me. I've been on my own all day.'

'What about my brother? He said he was going in today. And Jamal?'

'Ain't seen either of them all day,' Anna says, shaking her head.

Much as Taran rinses Anna for being a square, she knows Anna gets pissed off by always being the conscientious one. She knows Anna just wants her fam to take their futures as seriously as she takes hers.

'Probably just cotching in the park, innit,' Taran says. 'You know what those boys are like. Rage is Jamal's idol. I bet Jam's found us a nice spot down the front and everyone is getting irritated with him while he protects it. Hari's being all pushy and aggressive while Jamal's being all nice about it.'

Anna laughs.

'Don't pretend Rage ain't your favourite rapper,' she says.

'I know, I know,' Taran says. 'I just have to be cool about it now cos Rage's good mates with Sim, innit.'

'What?' Anna says.

Taran nods. 'Yeah, same year at school.'

'That's so cool,' Anna says. 'Anyway, where *are* those idiots?' She says it like they're naughty boys and she's their scolding 1950s mummy, resplendent in a floral dress and apron.

Taran hardens her hand into a stiff judo chop and swings at the air like she's slicing the rotary blade off the helicopter. She closes her eyes and imagines it falling from the sky.

She opens them again as Anna walks to the edge of the roof and leans on the railings. Looking down to the ground, Taran feels a little unsteady and grips a bit harder.

'Today was long. Longer-than-a-marathon long,' Anna says.

'Longer than a Long Island Iced Tea?'

'Longer than Long John Silver's long book about some long mission to find some treasure.'

'What was so long about it?' Taran asks, smashing out her judo-chop hand in the opposite direction, like she's now attacking an unseen enemy.

'You try going to college, pretending to learn stuff, eating by yourself, spending your entire day imagining your mates are having a better time than you.'

'You try going to the studio, watching your engineer get blazed on your time and money, recording the best bars of your life, then realising he forgot to press record,' Taran says. 'Well, that wasn't today. But it's happened. Trust.'

'It's a hard life, Taran.'

'It's a long life.'

'Long, not that long.'

Those words suck the breath from Taran.

Her father used to say that: 'Life is long, it's not that long.' Or, in other words, time is short and you have to deal with crap that keeps you from enjoying it, so remember life isn't long and take the time. He was filled with pidgin-English immigrant wisdom.

Taran watches as the helicopter passes over their heads. She closes her eyes again.

'Do not run riot in your own home!' Dad would shout at her and Hari when they wrestled with each other, bending and contorting the other's limbs until one shouted for mercy.

That's where her MC name comes from. It's a nod to him.

Their dad constantly made them be quiet. Whatever they were doing, they had to be quiet. If they were playing computer games, the volume had to be off. If they were roasting or rinsing each other, it had to be whispered. If they wrestled or play-fought, no one could yell for mercy. The home was a hive of quiet activity. And then, randomly, Hari got moved to the sofa and Taran stayed in their bedroom.

Both were confused. It had come out of nowhere. And when they'd asked their parents why, it had been met with an impenetrable, 'You're too old to share now . . .'

She remembers the conversation with Hari after. 'It's because I have periods and breasts now so Mum and Dad have banished me to my own bedroom. To hide my shame. I am unclean. Unclean women can't be near the pure-bred heirs to the throne.'

Hari's reply: 'It's probably because Mum thinks I'll be playing with myself all the time and you don't need that kind of hassle in your life.'

They might sleep in different rooms now, but Mum still struggles to separate them sometimes, calling them 'Taran-Hari'.

Taran looks round at her city. Occasionally, when you stand on the roof, you can feel the whole building vibrate. Like it's shaking its head at you in disgust. Occasionally, the building feels alive. And judgmental.

She breathes in the thick acrid pollution, the gaseous exhausts of cars and industry and the sighs of people whose tired feet keep them sleepwalking to and from jobs they don't care about. She breathes in the light from the cars on the motorway a mile or so away. She breathes in the recycled air conditioning seeping out of nearby concrete office buildings. She breathes in the steely tang of the cranes that loom like mechanised giraffes further out.

Dad said this place used to have such a bad reputation in the 1980s, she thinks. A comedian had joked that the pages for this area in any street-map book had a 'POLICE LINE DO NOT CROSS' sticker across them. Bad stuff still happens. Whenever the local news needs shots of urban environments with high crime rates, it's her high street that appears on TV.

She breathes in the bits they never show: the happy kids riding bikes through their estates, the old grannies and nonnies and bas sitting at bus stops with their shopping bags talking about the day, the rising damp starch of rice cooking on hundreds of stoves, the music erupting from car stereos that make passers-by shout for a wheel-up as they drive past. Nope, all they want to film is the threatening yoots with their hoods up.

She breathes in the sweet cloud of skunk and the disappointment and the dust and the pollen and the sadness and the tears and the anger and the fear, and in all those scents she tries to breathe in her mother. She knows Mum is out there, working another fourteen-hour shift, maybe an eighteen-hour if she's unlucky.

A ninety-minute commute each way to the only hospital that was employing nurses, to be racially abused on a daily basis by Leave voters who can't bear the thought of a South Asian nurse touching them to insert an IV or take their temperature or hold their hand as they spasm in pain.

'Why don't you move into her bedroom then? She's never there,' Taran had said to Hari once, knowing Mum was drinking tea in the kitchen and could hear every word. Taran's face stings thinking of the cheap shot, still to this day.

'But that's her room, innit,' he'd replied.

Mum had appeared at that moment, quietly walking into her bedroom and closing the door on them. Hari had shot a look of daggers at Taran, so deep it'd felt like she'd been jolted backwards.

'Where you at, T?' Anna asks.

'Here. Stuck here,' Taran says, shaking off her daydream. 'I wanna go to the concert. I am so hyped to see Rage.'

'Look, shall we just go? They're probably already there.'

'Along with ninety-five per cent of this entire building.'

'Even my mum wants us to go,' Anna says. 'And she hates Rage.'

'No she doesn't,' Taran says. 'She loves him. She was bumping "Family Anthem" the other day in her new car when she drove past. Head bopping, fingers gunned, shouting the chorus. Made me laugh so much.'

Anna cringes and goes red, which makes Taran laugh.

She walks to the opposite edge and looks out east, to where the weather is headed, to where the helicopter is circling.

She points. 'Look,' she says.

Anna follows Taran's gaze. The helicopter is circling in a pattern, over a spot roughly a mile away – where the big park is, where the Rage concert is happening. Taran imagines that if the helicopter wasn't there, she'd be able to hear the bass bins throbbing out raps and beats for people arriving for the show.

'Maybe that's how he's entering!' Taran says. 'Arriving by helicopter. Now that'd be sick.'

'No way. See if anyone's chatting about it.'

'Check Twitter or something.'

'I ain't got credit. You got credit?'

Taran reaches into her pocket and throws her phone to Anna, who catches it. Just. She swipes and types and swipes and scrolls.

'Nothing on Twitter. Or Facebook. Cody's tried to FaceTime you three times though.'

'He can wait,' Taran says. 'Cody probably doesn't even remember I was in the studio today. He's probably listening back to my bars and wondering how a ghost recorded two songs as me this afternoon.'

Anna joins Taran at the eastern edge, looking out towards the blocks where blue flashing lights bounce off the walls like a light show at a rave.

The faster you run, the harder they'll come.

The song's still in Taran's head. The final one she recorded before she left for the day. Before Cody chucked her out, saying he had to record some rich boy's vanity EP and didn't want her hanging around such mediocrity dressed in badness.

He keeps telling her, as does Sim, that what she's recording now is like Nas's first album – it talks of a time and a place. It tells the stories of the people all around her, the ones who walk up and down the stairs and along the corridors, the ones who say hello as she walks home, the ones who screw up their faces as she nods at them – she is building a history of this block and this area and these people, the ones who you never see or read about or hear from.

She tries not to let it go to her head. She loves Nas. Sim saying she's making things that are as important as his first album is basically saying she's as good as a lot of people's favourite music of all time. How can anyone ever be that good?

Taran smiles. The tune she did today still sounds big. And loud. However it starts, it has to be loud.

Run, you better run now.
Full force, cos the chase is on.

5.54 p.m.

Taran jumps as the fire door bangs open and Hari and Jamal spill out on to the roof, out of breath, unable to talk.

Jamal is gasping, short grunting breaths, his asthma playing up. Hari looks pale.

Jamal flops on to his front, breaking the fall with his knuckles, wincing as the coarse concrete cuts into his skin. He grimaces. Drool trails down from his mouth to the floor, a long sticky trail.

Anna rushes over and hands him the spare inhaler she keeps in her bag. He breathes in the medicine, trying to slow his panicked breaths.

'Jamal, you OK?' Taran asks. 'Where you been? We thought you were saving us space at Rage.'

'No time,' Hari barks.

'Are you in trouble?' Anna asks.

Jamal flashes her a look that seems to say, *Please don't get on my case now*.

He slowly stands up. He takes in a deep breath as if to calm himself.

'Bro, what's the matter?' Taran asks.

Hari looks at his sister. 'We came . . . back for you . . . man. We g-gotta go,' he stammers.

'Yeah, to the park – we know, we've been waiting long enough,' Taran says.

'No, no. We need to run.'

'What?'

Hari looks directly at his twin. 'Because they're coming for us,' he says.

'Who?' Anna asks.

'We have to go,' Jamal pleads.

'We're not going anywhere till you tell us what's—' Anna stops as Hari grabs her hand. He shakes his head.

'Now,' Hari says. '*Now.*'

Taran squares up to him. He's taller than her but she's hencher. Their dad's weights ended up in her room.

'What's going on?' she says. 'We're not moving. What's this drama?'

'Please, T. We ain't got time. We've gotta go.'

A siren bursts out in the distance, startling Hari.

'Why?' Taran says, as the siren fades away into the distance.

'You know Sim Francis? He's been killed.'

Taran flinches, stumbles back. She suddenly feels like she's floating. The rest of the conversation is happening in front of her body. But she's not there. She's somewhere else, lost, behind a wall of ice, screaming.

Jamal and Hari look at her like they're thinking, *What? Since when did she care about Sim?*

'Two people killed him. Police. He was unarmed,' pants Hari. 'Unarmed, and this five-oh just kicked him to death, like a dog, in the street. They both kept kicking and kicking until . . .'

Hari stops talking, as if lost in the horrific memory of what he saw.

Anna steps in closer to Taran, looking like she's seen a ghost. She's trembling.

'How do you know?' Anna says, her mouth dry. She flashes Taran a look.

'We saw it,' Jamal says. 'We have to go,' he says, urgently.

Anna pulls Taran towards the door. Taran's body is on

autopilot. She feels like she's having an out-of-body experience, watching the whole thing. Hari pulls the door open.

They run.

6.12 p.m.

Hari takes three steps at a time, Taran and Anna take two. Jamal, still out of breath, clutches the bannister and takes each one on its own terms, bringing up the rear. They make it down the first flight of stairs to the floor below the roof.

Taran stumbles, grabs the bannister and stops. Just for a second, to close her eyes. She puts her forehead on the window at the top of the stairwell in front of her and slowly opens her eyes. Looking down on to the courtyard, she sees something.

'Wait,' she says, slowly. 'Wait, look.'

She points towards the street, down fourteen flights of stairs to ground level. There is a police van arriving, screeching up outside the front of the block. Three men jump out and stride towards the main entrance.

'Hari, wait!' Anna calls. 'What now?'

She hears Hari's footsteps stop on the stairs, then climb back up towards her.

'Let's go. Don't think. Let's just go. We can think later,' Hari says, puffing out his chest.

'But *where* are we going, Hari?' Jamal wheezes.

'I don't know, man,' he says. 'I'm making this up as we go. Don't stress me.'

'Tell me a place. I need to know where I'm going,' Jamal says.

He has a thin film of cold sweat on his top lip, hanging off the hairs of his scruffy beard. Jamal is jittery, needing to bust loose, get out of here.

Jamal hates confrontation, Taran thinks, still gazing down at the courtyard. *He will want to hide till all this blows over.*

They push on down the stairs.

At the next floor, floor thirteen, Hari stops and looks down the middle of the swirl of stairs. The *clank-clank* of ambient noise from lower floors, the *flicker-flicker* pulse of the lights all around them, the concrete dull thud of the floor beneath their kicks.

'No,' he says. 'We can't just run down the stairs, that's dumb.'

'But isn't this the quickest way out?' Anna asks.

'Man, listen,' Hari says. 'We know this block. These guys don't. Let's go out the back entrance, right? Away from that van.'

'Look, if you're in trouble,' Anna continues, 'we should go to the park. We can lose whoever in the Rage crowd.'

Hari looks at his sister. Anna looks at her too, for approval. Usually, she's the one who takes the lead; they always turn to her for direction.

'Taran,' Hari says.

Taran meets his eye, confused. She is removed; she is somewhere else. She's still behind that wall of ice, screaming.

'Hari's right,' Jamal says. 'Let's get away from these stairs. They came in through the front, so we should head to the back.'

He looks at Taran. Taran shrugs.

'Come on,' Anna says.

They all run in unison down the thirteenth-floor corridor, thick rubber soles pounding on concrete.

Every tremor shudders through Taran's calves, making her feel more and more tired. She just wants to lie down. In her room. Alone.

Even thoughts feel far away, behind her wall of ice. She can hear herself breathing, hard. *You can hear every little noise in this building. You can hear iPhone alarms three floors down, kettles boiling, arguments, people coming home drunk or worse at all hours.*

Yeah, and the guy who runs a Tollywood cinema out of his front room cos he's got a sick Sonos. And the kids shouting out Stormzy lyrics as they scooter up and down the corridors.

That dull thud of kick drums from the flats that double as music studios.

The seventeen languages, forty different television programmes and five guffaws of laughter at any given point.

Sim's got a big laugh. The way he throws his shoulders back and his head cocks to one side, with each 'ha' loud and singular and filled with joy. Sim.

Taran emerges from the wall of ice.

She runs harder, catches up with Hari.

'You need to tell me,' she pants. 'What happened?'

'Not now, T,' Hari says.

'How do you know Sim is dead? I need proof. Where is the body?'

Hari stops.

'Can you just go with me? Things are dangerous out there. I'm not making you do this cos it's jokes. We need to move.'

'Seen,' Taran says.

Hari is rarely this sure about anything, she thinks. *He spends more time choosing what to eat for breakfast than eating it. He's not a decisive man.*

Jamal reaches them, Anna just behind.

'Anna's flat,' Jamal puffs, with a wary look at Anna. He's almost wincing. 'It's on this floor. Let's go there, catch our breath, maybe work out exactly what we're doing.'

'What?' Anna snaps. 'You not gonna ask me first, Jamal?'

'No time. Your mum home?' Hari asks. Anna shakes her head.

'Well, then,' Hari replies. 'That's where we're going.'

6.22 p.m.

Anna fumbles her keys in the lock, nervous. She'd hoped everyone would forget she lived on the thirteenth floor. They're her best friends, but she still doesn't want them coming in with her. Not if there's trouble behind them. She just wants to dip into her yard, take herself out of the equation. Just go to her room and her studies and close the door and not get caught up in whatever this is. Especially now the police are involved.

'Trouble follows those twins.' That's what her mum says. She's right. Not that Anna would ever tell her mum that. Or Taran. None of them ever come here. Ever. Everything gravitates to Hari and Taran's flat. Because it's *their* flat, not their mum's. Anna's flat is off-limits because of her mum's rules, her disapproving eye, her neatness. She wishes her mum were here now, to get rid of them without Anna having to feel guilty about it.

She can feel Hari's and Jamal's stress, urging her to hurry up, willing her to snap back the lock quicker. That only slows her down. She can't perform under pressure – that's another thing her mum always tells her. That's why she got a B in her Physics exam, cos she panicked and couldn't remember the equations in the right order. Or which hand you use to work out the flow of electricity currents.

Finally, Anna finds the right groove and slides her keys in. The door opens and they spill into her flat.

'We never get invited round here,' Hari says, bursting in and flopping on to the sofa.

'That's cos I live with my mum. Your mum is always at work. It's always more fun at yours. Feet off the sofa, man.'

Anna watches as Taran enters tentatively. She looks shell-shocked. Anna smiles that she remembers her manners and slips off her Timberlands at the door.

'Yeah, but your mum's cooked food is nice,' Hari says.

Anna brings Taran and Hari food in Tupperware whenever their mum is doing nights. Hari always refers to Anna as 'Mum Two', which she pretends irritates her.

Taran refused the food for months, so now Anna only brings it for Hari and his mum.

'I don't do charity,' Taran says.

Don't do cooking neither, Anna has always thought.

Hari and Taran's mum is thankful for the food. She and Anna's mum don't always see eye to eye, but they are both part of the Firestone community. A community that looks after its own. The amount of people who came to Hari and Taran's dad's funeral from Firestone House who they knew by face and not by name was overwhelming for Taran. It made her feel at home, like she had never lived anywhere else.

'Want something to eat?' Anna asks.

Taran shakes her head. Jamal watches the corridor through the peephole. Hari is on the balcony, looking down on to the back of the block. It's a mess of grass and wasteland leading down to the railway tracks.

'What's going on, Hari?' Anna calls after him.

Taran sits down on the sofa and picks up a plump cushion, holding it under her chin like a comforter.

'Careful with that,' Anna replies, plucking the cushion from Taran's arms and miming for Jamal to remove his trainers. She puffs the cushion out and places it back on the sofa.

Taran stands up. She seems back from wherever she had gone in her head.

'Sim. What happened?' Taran asks, trying not to seem too concerned – concerned, yes, but only for her brother, not for Sim. Anna can see the struggle in her friend's face. She knows the truth, after all. She's amazed Taran is holding it together.

Hari comes in from the balcony. The flat is at the back of the building so it's shaded at this time of day, but he's sweating. Anna shivers.

Hari sinks into the sofa, head in his hands.

'Tell me about Sim,' Taran begs. 'Please, Hari. Just tell me what happened.'

Hari lifts his head, sighs deep and starts talking.

4.40 p.m.

Jamal's waiting outside Shah's Cash 'n' Carry at the end of Hari's shift.

Hari spots him as he emerges from the side entrance and throws a mango his friend's way.

'One of your five-a-day,' Hari says. 'Or should that be year? Five-a-year. Underneath all that melanin, Jamal, you're probably looking malnourished, you know?'

'Man, what took you so long? Did you swipe this?'

'Nah, man. Shah can't pay me today. Cash-flow issues. So he threw me a mango and said he'll sort me out later.'

'Again? I don't understand how they can afford to keep you on. No one shops there. They get in all this fresh produce that no one buys. And they employ you to keep filling the shelves. They pay you to incubate fruit flies.'

'They don't even really pay me. Except in going-off fruit,' Hari says, laughing.

'Exactly. Bro, I worry about you,' Jamal says, putting a hand on Hari's shoulder.

'Well, at least it's cash in hand.'

'No, it ain't,' Jamal says quietly. 'There is currently no cash in your hand.'

'No. Just one mango.'

'That's jokes,' Jamal says. 'What would you have to do for a pineapple?'

'Triple shift. On a weekend, probably.'

Hari notices Sim Francis standing against a wall across the road. He's looking directly at them. Jamal nods, a curt up-nod, as if to say, *What's up?* Sim points at them both with the gun fingers on his right hand, a cigarette burning away in between the index and middle finger. He winks. Sim's only a couple of years older, he's only nineteen, and yet Hari feels like Sim's his old uncle or something.

Hari mouths, 'What's happening, Sim?' and turns away.

Hari is wary of the man, doesn't want to stay and chat too much in case he gets a rep just by association. Sim may have been helping to run the youth centre for the last couple of years, but Hari has heard all the stories about what Sim was like when he was sixteen. Sim's brother too.

Jamal whispers, 'We should go chat to him.'

'Sim? No way. He's a bad man.'

'What are you talking about? He's cool, Hari.'

'I heard he beat up some kids who were dealing on his turf.'

'From who? Anyway, that would have been years ago. My man's changed.'

'I don't know, man. Do people change?'

'Depends if they're given a chance to. Hari, what do you know about him? He ain't like that any more. What else have you heard?'

'Nothing good. At least that's the chat around the gym. He trains there. I seen him benching like, a lot. And people keep saying he's still the same old Sim.'

'You know he went school with Rage? Like, apparently they're still tight.'

'So?'

'You ever chat to him?'

'Nope.'

'Exactly. All I know is, he paid our council tax bill for a year when my uncle got made redundant and he loves Anna's mum's omelettes so much he stops round to get some every Friday morning without fail.'

'Yo, Jamal,' Sim calls from across the road. He drops his cigarette on the floor and beckons for Jamal and Hari to come over to him.

Jamal runs across without hesitation. Hari follows, slower, watching the road. Jamal fist-bumps Sim and looks round at Hari.

'You know Hari, right?'

'Yeah, of course. Taran's bro. You cool, Hari?' Sim says, smiling.

He may be smiling, Hari thinks, *but I can tell this guy's stressed from that creased brow. Something isn't right with Sim.*

'I'm fine,' Hari says without looking directly at Sim, while wondering how he knows Taran.

'But are you cool?' Sim asks, again.

It makes Hari nervous. He knows his body language is getting jittery, and he's looking around for passers-by, for police, for CCTV cameras, for anything that might incriminate him. Talking to a person with Sim's reputation . . . Imagine if his mum found out. Either way, whatever Jamal says about Sim, the man has that reputation for a reason, and it's not like his brother CJ doesn't already give Hari trouble. Hari does not need any focus being thrown on to him or his sister, especially before her mixtape drops.

Also, they're nearly done with school, and after that Hari can move away. One of his mates is moving to London for uni, and Hari was thinking of going with, finding a job in a trainer shop or something. Maybe even uni for him too. If he can decide what he wants to do. Something with business or sports, or both.

None of that gives Hari any space for hanging with Sim on the corner opposite his place of work.

'You work in there?' Sim asks Hari, pointing at the shop. 'Shah's?'

Hari nods.

'That's good, man. They are good community people, always willing to give a leg up to those round here who need it. I like those guys. You know what? They gave me my first ever job. I had to unload the delivery trucks every morning. Five a.m. starts, Monday to Friday, till seven-thirty. I went to school every morning smelling like meat and rotten fruit. That was a different time, back when they had customers.'

'Yeah, innit,' Hari says, absently.

'This area's changing, you know that, right?' Sim says. 'Soon, there won't be no place for people like Mr Shah. Not unless he's a one-man Tesco brand, you know? You know they're opening a supermarket across the road from here?'

'For real?'

'Yep, selling all the same stuff he does.'

'That's not fair,' Jamal says, looking back at Mr Shah's.

'That's city life,' Sim says, exhaling slowly.

Hari nods.

Jamal turns back to Sim. 'What's happening?' Jamal says, excitedly. 'You cool? Just hanging? You going out to the Rage concert later? You must be. You know him, right? Went to school together? What's he like? Can we get backstage? Come on, bro. Hook us up.'

Sim smiles at Jamal. He bursts out laughing.

Hari grits his teeth at Sim, as if to say, *Back off, my friend.*

'Nah, man,' Sim says. 'I'm not going. There's too much work around here to be done.'

'So that's a no to those backstage passes?' Jamal says.

Sim laughs again, the gap in his front two teeth glistening with saliva. Then he stops and there's a moment of silence so loaded Hari just wants to cut and run. He can tell Sim only called them over so he could ask something.

'Listen,' Sim says. 'I need a favour—'

Hari cuts him off. 'Nah, we're busy, Sim. We're cool. Thanks, man, but no.'

'What, Hari, my brother? You don't know what I'm about to say,' Sim replies. 'I'm not going to ask you to move a dead body or nothing.'

'What is it?' Jamal asks. 'We're cool.' He looks at Hari and repeats himself. 'We're cool.'

'I'm just intrigued,' Sim says. 'What does my man think I'm about to ask him?'

Hari sighs slowly as Sim and Jamal both look at him.

'Nothing,' Hari mumbles.

'Look, it doesn't matter, man. I know what people round here tend to think and say without knowing anything. It's cool. I understand that's how the world works. Listen, don't believe everything you hear. Especially tonight. Tonight, something's going to change.'

Sim looks around.

'Yeah, man,' Jamal says, like Sim is a prophet. 'Innit, same shit different day.'

'You think I'm some big boy around here. But the truth is worse than that.' Sim looks at Hari. 'I'm a troublemaker for the powers that be. And I'm going to bring the system down.'

Hari snorts and Sim laughs out the side of his mouth. Hari goes serious. He doesn't like Sim laughing at him, trying to show Hari he's one of them or something. It feels fake.

'Whatever, man,' Hari says, looking at his feet.

'What favour do you need, Sim?' Jamal asks.

'I need you both to be documentarians. You know what that is?' Jamal shakes his head. 'A documentarian is a person who records life, and shows it back, holds it up as a mirror to society to say, "This is your story." I need you to record my life and show it back to me, to people. You see that underpass there?' Sim points. 'In about five minutes' time, I am going to walk into that underpass and I am going to chat to some people. And I need you both to be my documentarians. You know what the most important role of a documentarian is? You do not ever get involved in your subject. Can you do that?'

'Yeah, man, of course,' Jamal says, and smiles at Hari, quickly, smoothing over the fact that the decision has already been made.

Hari sucks his teeth, like Anna taught him to. Usually, they'd all just laugh at the dry air passing over his dehydrated tongue, but today the meaning's clear. He hates when anyone makes his decisions for him. He needs to have a choice. There is no backing out once he commits; he just wants to be the one to decide to commit.

'And you, my man?' Sim says, looking at Hari, smiling at him with the side of his mouth. Almost cocky. Almost like he knows you're gonna say yes. That sort of smile always winds Hari up.

'Whatever, man, just make it quick.'

'It'll be quick. You got cameras on your phones, right?' Jamal nods keenly but Hari stays silent. 'Good, that's good. And charged batteries, right?' Jamal winks at Sim this time. Hari wants to cringe. 'Wicked, wicked. OK, so I need you to not be seen. Documentarians, not intervening – not seen, seen? Yeah? Go.'

Hari calls Jamal a chief as they run over to the underpass.

'Come on, man. It's Sim. He's cool.'

'Is he?' Hari says. 'All I'm saying is, his reputation is large. And there's no smoke without fire.'

'Hari, bruv. You always say about your boxing that no one needs to prove anything to anyone.'

Hari's cheeks burn and so does his elbow, from the last time he got dropped by CJ and his guys. They laughed at Hari, powerless, pushed him down the stairs, where he banged his elbow on the scuzzy pane of glass that separates the musty stairwell from the fresh air that makes the rest of the world go round. That was the day Hari decided to head to the boxing gym after school and train.

'I just don't know the man,' he says.

They reach the underpass. No one goes through it, ever. It stinks.

It stinks of rubbish that's been there for twenty years. Rubbish that has formed its own culture and civilisation and is slowly waging a war on itself.

You can hear the scurry of creatures clambering over the mulch of old food, cracked discarded bones, electronics that haven't biodegraded, plastics that have melted through the ebb and flow of heat and breeze, breeze and heat.

Hari unwraps the white bandana from his wrist and ties it over his face. Jamal pulls his hoodie on and covers his nose and mouth with the collar, tugging at the drawstrings urgently till only his eyes are visible, pinched from the tight grey material framing his face.

Light finds its way into the underpass in small shimmers and cracks but it is mostly dark.

'That's where he'll go,' Hari says to Jamal, and they run towards the lit part of the underpass.

Hari looks around and spies an old car. The passenger door hangs open but it's close enough to the lit area.

'What is happening here?' Jamal asks. Hari shrugs. 'What are we doing?'

'I don't know,' Hari says. 'But you said we'd do it. So that means we're doing it. We gave our word.'

Hari's hoodie is charcoal grey and it hides him well as he sneaks into the car. It reeks – of dirty pants, of vinegar, of thick filthy detritus. Hari retches. He watches as Jamal scurries back and forth, useless, until he spies a grand concrete pillar. It has a vantage point from the opposite side of the lit-up area, but it is still shrouded in darkness.

They wait.

Hari breathes through his mouth, into his bandana, which smells of sweat from when he wiped his forehead earlier. After that run, where he peeled away from the bus stop to avoid his English teacher. Because she knew he was bunking that day. Because he had to earn some money instead. Because why go school now and earn money later when it's money now and more money later. London's expensive.

He watches Jamal move out from behind the pillar and cross towards him.

'What are you doing?' Hari hisses at him.

'Bruv, I'm shook,' Jamal whispers. 'I don't know what this is. I think we bounce.'

Clip. Clip. Clop.

Sound filters into the underpass. It's Sim's boots, Hari thinks. He knows the sound of boots on concrete; he hears that sound most nights, in the corridors, thudding along. They make a distinct sound. A sound that, if you listen carefully to the core noise, it has a rhythm – *clip, clip, clop*. Like rap songs. Like *tum-ti-tum-ti-tum*; like poetry. And Sim is always rocking the tight tan immaculate Tims. He moves with a self-satisfied skip most of the time.

'He's coming,' Hari hisses.

Jamal jostles to the other side of the car and crouches. He quickly props up his phone on the bonnet and lines up the shot, pressing record. Hari does the same from inside the car.

Sim strides into the underpass. Hari watches him look around. Small refractions of light frame his creased brow and bald head, like he's glowing. His gaze settles in Hari and Jamal's direction.

He seems nervous, Hari thinks.

Then Sim takes off his long puffa coat and drops it to the ground. He steps out of his Tims, using the toes to stand on the heel of the other foot. He nudges them towards the heaped coat with his right foot. He pulls his pockets out of his jeans, so the whites hang over the stonewash denim. Then he folds his arms and closes his eyes.

Hari's confused. He raises an eyebrow, as if to say, *What is going on?* He doesn't know the man too well so he doesn't really get his ways or what that posturing means. It's confusing.

Clip-clop clip-clop clip-clop. A more regular sound erupts into the underpass. More than one person, maybe two. It's familiar – impatient, official.

Purpose.

Walkie-talkie frequency buzzing.

Police.

The noise of both of their steps combined sounds urgent. Hari hasn't had too many dealings with the police but he's had enough to feel the itch of fear on the back of his neck.

Hari looks back to Jamal and the movement shifts the car. There's a quiet murmur. He can see Jamal's hoodie bob up and then down again. He can feel his own body tensing with the urge to run.

This feels too real now.

Hari's one run-in with a copper was one more than he'd ever intended to have. Be invisible, that's what his mum had taught him – blend into the background, don't give anyone an excuse to grab you, give you shit, make you feel like you don't belong.

That time, he was stopped and searched under anti-terror laws. He was on his way back from his cousin's wedding, early because of a migraine, and he had been pulled to one side at the station. It wasn't even like they were searching a lot of people there. They grabbed *him*. And they strip-searched him. He was strip-searched, in front of everyone.

His arse was on display for everyone to see while a copper shoved two rough fingers up inside him and whispered, 'What you hiding?' as he searched every contour with his finger.

Hari can still remember the stench of instant coffee on his breath. When Hari asked why they thought he was a terrorist, the officer said that he fit the profile. When he asked what profile that was, the officer said it was obvious. When Hari asked for the officer's name and number, and a record of the search, the team had laughed at him. When he was told to go, Hari looked around, but he couldn't see anyone filming it, or even stopping to stand up for him. He felt so alone and violated.

That wasn't even the worst story of police being arseholes that he had heard. There were so many names of so many victims. People in much worse situations than him, with no justice.

And now two policemen walk up on Sim.

He keeps his arms crossed. Hari can only see them in silhouette and can't hear what's said but all three of them keep looking around shiftily. Like they don't want to be heard.

Sim gets stiffer in his body language as they speak. His posture is straight. He is still. His hands lock, gently, in front of him.

He starts talking. Smiling. Calm.

The more he talks, the more irritated the two policemen seem to get. Their body language goes from mildly aggressive to cramping Sim's space, getting their faces and their bodies too close.

Hari keeps his phone straight, dimming the brightness of the screen in case it reflects off surfaces behind him and gives up his position.

Thoughts run through his head. *Why is Sim snitching to cops? You never EVER talk to cops. Why are they pissed at what he's saying or not saying?* And most importantly, *Why does he need this documented?*

Sim occasionally flashes an eye-swipe in Hari and Jamal's direction. Hari can't see his face clearly. Is he panicked? Checking they're there? *Maybe it's a comfort*, he thinks, *for Sim to know that we have his backs. Or, at least, whatever's going down is on video.*

Hari steals a look at Jamal, just for a second, and he misses it.

SMACK.

SMACK.

SMACK.

They sound like gunshots, but when Hari focuses, Sim has fallen straight down to the ground and one of the men is punching and kicking him. Hari can't see the impact or Sim's face, but these are wild, violent punches. The kind where everything stops and you can't breathe. Hari flinches with every blow.

When they stop, for a second Hari thinks he can hear Sim whimpering. Then the man who until now has stood by suddenly joins in and kicks and kicks at Sim.

Hari feels like he's suffocating. Like he's on the floor with Sim.

Except Sim's not there any more.

The two cops are standing over an unmoving body. Hari tries to pinch in closer on his phone, tries to get a better look at their faces. A creak pings from the car, somewhere in its bowels.

One of the men grabs something from the floor – *A brick? A rock?* – and bashes it down, repeatedly, violently. Hari clamps a hand over his mouth to suppress a cry of shock and squeezes his eyes shut. He hears Jamal gasp.

The car creaks again.

One of the policemen looks up and turns in their direction. His face is now lit enough for Hari to see he has mousey brown hair and a goatee. He's white, and he has this snarl, like everything you say to him would sound like a turd falling into his lap. The other man throws the brick into the darkness of the underpass. Hari flinches with the kickback of sound, as whatever it is hits the ground deep in the tunnel. He watches as goatee cop squats to the floor, maybe to check for a pulse.

He can feel someone shuffling quietly to his left. Hari whips his head around. It's Jamal, straining to look, still holding his phone out to film.

Hari can hear his heart beat and his muscles clench; everything is making the loudest noise. He has never seen a dead body before. He cannot deal with it. He needs to get out of here. He needs to move. He can't breathe. He pulls the bandana down from his mouth, and the full force of the smell in the car makes him cough. Both cops look up, alert. Hari feels the sting of panic in his gut. They watch, wait, then return to Sim's body.

Jamal is still straining to get a better view. He's leaning on the car, which rests on its rims because the tyres are long gone; it's years since it was joyridden into the underpass and then abandoned. The car cracks, and Hari knows what's coming. He leans forward to his knees and lets himself fall out of the car as it creaks, a metallic crunch reverberating through the underpass.

'Run,' Jamal says, quietly, and Hari jumps to his feet.

The coppers whip round at the noise and one yells – not 'Stop!' not 'Oi!' but a single consonant, something more primal.

As Hari runs to the edge of the underpass, he can feel Jamal hotfooting it on his tail, not far behind, faster than him, able to catch up.

They run.

And they haven't stopped.

6.42 p.m.

'You've got a video of Sim Francis being murdered by two policemen?' Anna asks. She can't believe what she is hearing, doesn't want to believe it. She can feel her hands shaking. She saw him this morning. He came round for his breakfast. Like he did every Friday, for Anna's mum's omelettes.

Anna steals a look at Taran. Taran is still. Utterly still.

Hari nods at Anna. 'Two hours ago, I had no time for the man. Now he's gone . . . it's . . . It was the way he went. Like a dog that's been hit by a car, being put down. No one should go that way.'

He juts out his jaw and puffs out his chest. Anna looks from him to Jamal. Her boyfriend clenches his hands together inside his hoodie. Suddenly Jamal looks like a child, not some guy about to turn eighteen and leave college.

Hari whips out his phone and finds the video. Taran goes to the other side of the room. She covers her ears and closes her eyes, but curiosity gets the better of Anna and she peeks over Hari's shoulder. Jamal joins her.

Anna squints at the screen. Sim stands there. He removes his coat and his shoes. He crosses his arms. Everything looks staged now it's pixellated on the screen. Maybe Sim is still alive, and it was all just an act? The policemen enter and they start chatting to Sim. Hari makes the volume the loudest it can go, but the voices are muffled and Hari's own deep, nervous breathing obscures them.

Then Sim's body snaps back as it is struck, and a butterfly of blood bursts from his nose as a punch lands in the centre of his face. Anna cries out. Jamal steps back and rests his shoulder blades against the nearest wall. Hari does not look away.

Taran is still, her entire body tense.

Anna gently takes the phone from Hari's grip and plays the video again, slowing down the frame rate to see if she can recognise any of the faces of the men, or badge numbers, or anything at all. Scrub back and watch again, scrub back and watch again. What is Sim thinking? He looks like he's at peace. That sideways grin, that beautiful sideways grin, like he always knew something you didn't. And he was not going to tell you. Because half the fun was the learning.

In the corner of her eye, Anna can see Taran flinch with every sound of a body blow. Anna stops the video.

'You have a murder on film, man,' Taran says, weakly. 'We need to get this online. Immediately.' She stares at the floor. At her trainers. Like she doesn't want to make eye contact.

'Get it online?' Hari says. 'You crazy? The police did this! And now they're after us. What do you think they'll do to us if they know we have put it online? We need to get the hell away from here. We've seen what they can do.'

'Why did you come for us?' Anna says. 'If you knew it was dangerous?'

'Where else we gonna go?' Jamal says, offering her his hand. 'We were scared. We thought you, and T, would know what to do.'

'You need to leave,' Anna says, suddenly scared. 'You need to get out of my yard. Just get far away from here. Till things die down. Both of you, go.'

'What?' Taran says. 'Come on. That's my bro.'

'They're coming here, aren't they? They're coming here. They're going to come here. Into my home. And my mum's gonna be back soon. What do we do then, Hari? Jamal, you too. What are you bringing to my door?'

'Listen—' Hari starts, but the sound of a firm knock cuts him off.

Everything stops.

Anna can hear her heart beating through a denim jacket, a sweatshirt, a tee and a bra.

Jamal creeps to the door and looks through the peephole. He turns back to face them immediately, an expression in his eyes like he's seen the death of a loved one.

'Oh no,' he whispers. His knees buckle.

Taran pushes Jamal out of the way and looks into the peephole. She spins and is in action. She pulls Jamal by the armpit and gestures to Hari. Anna stands back to let them pass as they creep, quickly, through the flat, past her mum's immaculate white sofa pointed at the immaculate flat-screen television, her dad's pride and joy, to Anna's own room, where Taran pushes them inside.

Anna stays where Taran left her. She can feel her heart *bang bang bang* at an alarming rate.

6.55 p.m.

Taran holds the front door open. Her cap is pulled down low. Every inch of her is teeming with adrenaline and she has to fight to stop herself launching into the police with an untold hurt.

Two men stand in the doorway; one wears a police uniform, the other a suit, both looking up and down the corridor.

One has a goatee. The other has wild stubble.

As soon as they see her, she watches the veneer of fake pleasantry on their faces slip into disdain. She holds the door open but blocks the entrance with her body.

'What's up?' , she says, looking over both of their shoulders. 'Can I help you?'

She never makes eye contact with a policeman. Not least a murderer. She could let them know she knows and close the door. And get on Anna's wi-fi and upload the video to somewhere people would see it. She's not too smart when it comes to making stuff on the internet go viral but this is something people need to see.

'Where's Anna Johnson?' asks one of the men.

Taran can feel Anna, always subservient to any show of authority, edge forward, but Taran closes the door more, so that her body completely fills the door frame and she's all they can see.

'Who's asking?' she says.

The man takes a badge from his jacket pocket and flashes it at her, before quickly replacing it.

'Well, as you can see, I'm a policeman. And I'm asking.'

'Name and badge number please, officer. Surely, it's standard procedure to show proper identification. Surely you need us to trust you before we just tell you everything we know. You can buy replica badges down Poundland.'

'I'm Inspector Blakemore. And you are . . .?'

'What about him?' Taran says, pointing at the other man.

'This is Inspector Patterson,' Blakemore says.

Taran squints. 'And what about those badge numbers, Inspector Patterson and Inspector Blakemore?'

Patterson looks at Blakemore, who nods at him. Taran catches the subtle interaction.

'Four three one four,' Inspector Blakemore says, pulling at the wisps of his goatee.

'And you, Inspector Patterson?'

'Triple zero one.' Inspector Patterson is eyeballing Taran.

She knows what they're doing.

She remembers something Sim once told her about the police. 'They act like we belong to them, that's how control works. They forget that we employ them.' They were sitting on the roof at the time. It was hot. They were listening to the echo and bustle of sirens as the sun melted across the face of the earth . . .

'Cool,' she says to the men. She takes out her phone and writes the information down in the notes. 'Triple zero one, eh? You the first police officer in the constabulary or something?'

'Anna Johnson,' Inspector Blakemore says. 'We're looking—'

'She ain't here. She's busy,' Taran says.

Taran can feel her toes itching in her socks. This is the longest interaction she has had with a police officer and it's not something she likes. She feels as if her chest has expanded with hot air, like it does when you're in a swimming pool and that thick warm chlorinated smell makes you feel sleepy but also short of breath.

'And when will she be back?'

'Later,' Taran says. 'What's this regarding?'

'And you are?' Inspector Patterson asks.

'Why? Don't you need to read me my rights? Don't you need to tell me what I'm being asked all these questions for?'

'No,' Inspector Blakemore says. 'No, we don't.'

Taran pictures the fold-out card in her wallet that she got at a protest, which says what your rights are if you are stopped by the police. She hadn't ever really looked at it, thinking that when the time came she'd just whip it out and refer to it. Now, she can't get to it, and she knows that if, for a second, she shows she doesn't know what she's doing, she'll lose the power. She wishes she'd read it. Surely you have the right to ask why you're being stopped, or stopped and searched, or questioned?

'No, you need to tell me what this is about first,' Taran says.

Inspector Blakemore sighs, a deep smoker's breath, then coughs and folds his arms, cocking his head to one side, as if to say, *Stop wasting my time.*

Inspector Patterson takes a step towards her.

'We're looking for Hari Ramsaroop. And Jamal Ahmed,' he says.

Taran's eyes dry out at the mention of her brother's name. Anna rushes forward, pushing herself into the doorway.

'Jamal? Why are you looking for him?' Anna demands.

Oh, Jesus, Taran thinks. *For god's sake, Anna*, she wants to scream in her face. Why do you always jump to sticking up for your man at these ridiculous times? Taran wants to shush her, order her to the bedroom or something. *You don't need to always stick up for Jamal. He's a grown man now. He can stick up for himself.*

'And you are?' Patterson asks, smiling at Anna.

'Anna Johnson. I live here.'

Taran kisses her teeth and Anna looks at her, grimacing. Taran knows it – Anna is suddenly realising that maybe this wasn't the best time to step in.

'Why are you looking for Hari Ramsaroop and Jamal Ahmed?' Taran asks. 'And what makes you think we know them or where they are.'

'Taran?' Blakemore asks. 'Taran Ramsaroop?'

She knows Inspector Blakemore can tell from her hesitation that he's nailed her. He knows who she is. And she knows he knows who she is.

'I ain't seen them all day. I been in school.'

'And you?' Inspector Blakemore says, looking at Anna.

'I've . . . I've been . . . I've been in school too, sir,' Anna replies.

'So, neither of you know where –' Inspector Blakemore looks at Taran – 'your twin brother or –' he turns to Anna – 'your boyfriend is?'

Taran shakes her head and stares at the ground. She looks at Inspector Patterson's boot. There's a speck of red on it. As big as a bindi, claret red, dried. She looks up from it and meets his eyes for the first time. He smiles and looks at his boot then back to her.

The way he's so quiet. And then smiling. It prangs her out.

'Fair enough then,' he says. 'You know we'll be back.'

'Good to know, badge number four three one four and badge number triple zero one,' Taran says. 'And what shall I say it's regarding?'

'Tell them Sim Francis sends his best,' Patterson replies, flatly, then they turn to the corridor and walk away.

There's a shout and a bark, probably Leon mucking about with his pit bull three flats down. The noise is deafening; it makes Taran's heart beat out of rhythm, like it's starting to build to a nuclear meltdown.

She closes the door.

She rests her forehead on the cool PVC.

She shushes Anna before she talks.

She closes her eyes.

She counts to ten, slowly.

Anna puts her hand on Taran's shoulder. 'You OK?' she says.

Taran doesn't answer, just turns and heads to the bedroom. Anna follows.

7.07 p.m.

Taran bursts into Anna's room. Hari's sitting on the bed, holding his ankles. Jamal is cross-legged on the floor.

'We've done something bad, haven't we?' Jamal says. 'Oh god,' he says, cowering as Anna bends down to stroke his hair.

'What have you done that's bad? Witnessed a murder?' Taran says. 'No, bruv. Don't think like that. We need to get you guys out of here. Get that footage to someone who knows what to do with it. Like the press or something.'

'What happened?' Hari says. 'Man, they're police, right? What did they say they wanted?'

'Two policeman came to my door,' Anna says. 'They knew me, they knew Taran, they knew Jamal, they knew you. They know all our names. They know where *I* live.'

'They'll know where me and Hari live too . . .' Taran says. 'OK. We might not be able to go back to ours, but we still need to get you out of here. Somehow.'

'Fine,' Hari says.

'How do they even know it was you in the underpass?' Taran asks.

'Maybe Sim told them,' Anna says.

'Sim would never do that,' Taran says, firmly. 'How do they know?'

'They've been putting up CCTV everywhere recently. Maybe they're watching us,' Jamal says.

'Does it matter?' Hari asks.

'If they're watching us,' Taran says, 'where can we go?'

'We could stay here till Mum gets home,' Anna says.

'Nah,' Taran says, waving her hand. 'I don't like them knowing where we are. Maybe we could go to my mum's hospital. What do you think? Maybe she'll know what to do.'

She taps her foot against the carpet repeatedly, nervous.

Hari stands up and stretches out his right calf. 'OK,' he says. 'Let's go.'

'Hang on a second, guys,' Jamal says. 'Let's not run out. Let's wait, innit. They're out there right now. They're in the block. They know where we are. I imagine they know we're bullshitting. I wouldn't be surprised if they busted in here with riot police or something.'

'Into my house?' Anna says, gulping. 'My mum—'

'Screw your mum,' Jamal says. Taran can see he immediately regrets it. He throws his hands up. 'Sorry.' He chews his cheek as Anna glares at him. 'OK, so what? Shall we dress up and pretend to be old ladies or something?'

Anna laughs – angrily, but still it's a laugh. 'This isn't an episode of *The Big Bang Theory*, man. This is serious business.' Her smile drops. 'Did you see Patterson? Serious. Serious business.'

'I know,' Hari says, spacing out into the blankness of Anna's immaculate magnolia walls. 'I seen it.' He pauses and then places a hand on his sister's shoulder. She flinches but then rubs his hand. 'We need to leave the building and then we disappear for a bit. You're both right.'

'So – Mum's hospital?' Taran says. 'I know it's miles away, but that's an advantage, in my eyes.'

'But we *still* need to get out,' Jamal mutters.

'This is a crazy suggestion,' Anna says. 'But what if we go up? Like up a floor to fourteen. Then we cross over to the emergency staircase. They'll think we're going down. Down the one nearest to us. And the other staircase comes out at the back of the building. But if we go up first, we're giving them the runaround, confusing them.'

'Or we could use the lift,' Jamal says. They all laugh. The lift never works.

'Yeah,' Taran says. 'Yeah, we can do that. Except, floor fourteen, that's where CJ is. Hari, you sure you wanna risk running into him? He wasn't too kind to you last time that happened. I don't imagine he's just going to let you past like everything's OK.'

'At the rate we'll be running,' Hari says, balling his hands into fists and thrusting them into his hoodie pocket, 'man will struggle to keep up with me.' He smiles. 'We're headed that way. I'm ready for him.'

Taran looks at her brother. He's no longer spindly now he's been training. All that boxing has paid off. Still though, CJ's CJ.

'OK,' Taran says. 'It's settled.'

7.15 p.m.

Taran peers out into the corridor. Anna's place is five seconds from the nearest stairwell, but a thirty-second bolt from the one they need to hit. She can't tell which way Blakemore and Patterson walked so they have to assume they won't be going up, only down.

When there's no movement in the corridor, when it feels still, Hari and Taran burst out of the flat and run. Taran catches sight of Jamal holding his hand out to Anna, who grabs it, but fumbles her keys to the floor, concerned with locking the door behind her. Taran smiles at the intimate moment. It feels like what Anna needs right now. Something comfortable. Taran needs that comfort too.

They run.

The rubber soles of their kicks squeak on the floor, squelching and singing the high notes. Hari and Taran grip each other's sleeves. They run past two flats, a third. They can see the exit sign signalling the stairwell they need.

Hari pushes the door and they all spill out into the stairwell.

Hari takes two stairs at a time; Jamal follows. Taran drops back to Anna's pace and urges the smaller girl ahead of her.

'Oi,' they hear. At first it's quiet, incidental. Like ambient noise from another flat. Then it graduates into an intense yell. Taran looks down the stairwell – empty. Then – *boom* – through the door behind them bursts a policeman. Taran's so shocked she trips and the officer grabs on to her arm.

'Keep going,' she shouts to the others.

The copper has no grip, his grab lucky, so Taran pushes and he falls backwards with the weight and the force.

Yes, she thinks. *Yes, now go.*

Hari and Jamal pause to let Anna catch up; they climb together.

Hari looks down at his sister. 'Come on,' he shouts.

'I'm coming! Run.'

The policeman, having regained his footing, starts banging up the stairs. 'Stop!' he shouts. 'Stop, now!'

Taran turns to take a proper look at him. She knows this guy. Shorn head, long jagged scar on his neck. It's PC Roberts.

'I'm on your side,' he yells.

She stops.

It was about three months ago that Anna and Hari noticed a bigger police presence on the block. This copper, Roberts – they both saw him most days. He took to driving up to the disabled parking spot in front of Firestone House, getting out and leaning on the bonnet of his car, watching the door. Not doing anything. Just being intimidating. Watching everything. Watching everyone. Being suspicious. Side-eyeing questionable behaviour. Occasionally writing things down.

Roberts was there the day of Hari's run-in with CJ. Hari told her every detail straight afterwards.

Her twin was walking home from a shift when he saw CJ's boys, two of the henchest guys around, out the front of the block. Roberts watched them openly dealing, while he leant on his bonnet, reading the paper. Roberts then got in his car and drove away, just as CJ emerged from the front door of Firestone.

CJ always wears black, without fail – black tee, black hoodie, black sweats. Black jeans if he's out. He has a scar across his cheek. His face has a busyness to it, like all his features – his glasses, earring, nose ring, neck tattoo are all designed to take the focus away from his eyes, which are calculating, always making decisions, always capturing everything.

Hari tried to look oblivious to what had just happened, but as he approached, CJ stepped into his path.

'You're Hari, innit?' Hari nodded. 'Your sister's that rapper, innit. The one that dresses like a man. You need to watch that.'

'Why do I need to?' Hari murmured.

'What did you say, my guy?' CJ said, getting up in Hari's face, a blade glinting from his fist.

CJ grabbed the back of Hari's neck and squeezed, lifting the blade up so Hari could see it.

'Your dad's dead, your mum's never home, your sister's walking around like she's a man . . .'

Then he let go of Hari's neck, let the blade drop to his waist. 'You want to earn some money?' he said, smiling. 'Good money, man. I'm always on the look out for soldiers, you know what I mean?'

Hari looked down at his trainers and replied, 'I'm good, thank you, CJ. I have enough work. And school. But thank you. Safe, yeah?'

He started to walk to the door.

'You know I own this block,' CJ shouted after him. 'You know I run things, yeah?'

Hari shrugged.

Then – *slap, bang* – he felt something dull and hard hit his back. He stopped and turned around. The blade lay on the floor behind him. CJ had thrown the knife at him and the handle had whacked him in the back. Hari told her later how his blood turned to ice at the sight of it.

'That's your warning shot,' CJ said. 'You best be a ghost round here. I don't want to see your face, working man.'

Hari has never worked out why CJ picks on him so much. He asked them all, but none of them knew.

'Maybe you disrespected him,' Jamal said.

'When exactly did I do that?' was Hari's reply.

'He's super sweet to our mum and dad. And he's always said hello to me,' Taran herself said. 'It's literally just you.'

And Anna's advice: 'He's best avoided.'

But it's got steadily worse. From kissing his teeth every time he sees Hari, to calling him names – waste man, dickhead, wimp boy – to then throwing a knife at him, it's been clear that whatever Hari did, CJ isn't planning to let go.

Hari ran inside after the knife was thrown.

When he told Taran about that incident later, she asked him about Roberts. 'Why was this cop letting people deal in front of this building?'

Hari shrugged.

'Maybe they've all given up,' he said.

7.20 p.m.

Roberts isn't on our side, Taran thinks, and snaps back into action.

Turning away from him, Taran runs up the stairs towards the fourteenth floor. *Get away from them. Push, push, push*, she thinks. Her body is crying for rest. She needs to exercise more.

'Where's Sim?' PC Roberts calls from below.

Taran stops running and looks down at him, furrowing her brow.

'What did you say?' she asks.

PC Roberts smiles and beckons to her. His radio crackles. A voice – *Blakemore's?* she wonders – is asking for a status update.

'Run,' Roberts says. 'We'll talk later.' Then, into his radio, 'Nothing on this side.' He looks back to Taran. 'Be safe,' he says to her. 'And tell Sim that Roberts needs him to get in touch.'

Confused, Taran turns away from him and runs up the final step.

7.22 p.m.

The others are hanging back for her at the top; Anna's holding the door open. Taran bounds through after her and they run down the corridor together.

Together. Taran knows it. That's how they all have to be. *Together.* Everything they do, they do together. They look out for each other. That's how it's been since Hari and Taran moved to the block.

When Anna relapsed into anxiety and depression about exams and her mum telling her she couldn't afford to send her to university. Not with her dad in jail. Anna couldn't leave the flat, wouldn't do homework, she barely replied to the group chat, she took everything off the walls in her bedroom and painted them white, then she removed pictures of her dad. Slowly she erased every memory of him from the flat, because the thought that he had done what he had done was too much to bear. The only thing that remains is the television.

When Jamal's mum's and dad's visas ran out and both of them had to go home. Jamal had had the worst choice to make – stay, with his uncle as his guardian, with his social group, in a place he fit in and with people he cared about, or say goodbye to his parents for god knows how long. Not that his uncle was ever around. Not that Jamal ever spent any time other than sleeping in their second floor flat. Not that he ever referred to it as home.

When her dad's cancer came back. As he got weaker, Mum took on the strain of paying the bills, and she and Hari took on the strain of being his carer. Jamal and Anna were there the whole time, cleaning bathrooms, washing dishes, never judging, always helping.

Sim paid for their dad's cremation. There's no way they can survive for a long time on Taran's delusions of being a rapper, or Hari's cash-in-hand jobs. Or their mum's salary as a nurse. Which is supposed to be enough. But it isn't. Sim lent their mum money to get her car fixed so she didn't have to take three buses to get to work.

Sim.

Jamal, leading the gang, looks back to see what's keeping everyone.

Then – *blam*. He drops to the floor. Out cold.

Anna screams.

A tall hench guy wearing a grey hoodie and sweats stands there with a cricket bat. He holds it behind his head as Taran and the others skid to a halt in front of him.

Jamal is on the floor, unconscious, a bloodied graze across his ear.

'This ain't your floor, my friends,' the cricket-bat man growls.

'You,' says someone from behind cricket-bat man.

Taran places herself shoulder to shoulder with Hari. She can feel his body tense, his fists ball, then unclench beside her.

CJ steps forward, a hand in the waistband of his black sweats.

'I . . .' Hari mumbles.

'I thought I told you I don't want to see your face, working man.'

7.33 p.m.

Taran is surprised, walking into CJ's flat. If you walk into most homes, you expect to see something of the person hosting you. Like a painting or a poster or a photograph, like some furniture, just some evidence someone lives there.

CJ's flat is bare. Like no one lives there.

The walls are all magnolia. The furniture is reminiscent of an Ikea catalogue, all plain-coloured – the sofa, the table, the carpet, the chairs. There's not even a smell; no detritus from consumed food, nothing.

Two of his goons wait inside, hench, tall, wide, like the backs of vans. There is a gun on the table.

CJ smiles at Hari as he closes the door behind them all. His gold tooth glints in the soft lighting, like it sparkles all by itself.

'What do you w-want with us?' Hari stammers. 'We need to get out of here.'

'We're late . . .' Taran says, interrupting. 'Heading to the Rage concert, innit.'

'You're gonna be even later,' CJ says, baring his teeth, pressing his tongue against the back of them. 'You going to see Rage? It's good to support.'

Taran feels like she can hear the beating hearts of everyone in the room. She feels sick. Tense. And sick. All at once.

CJ and his men form a circle around her, Hari, Jamal and Anna.

Jamal places an arm around Anna.

'CJ,' Taran starts, trying to be the diplomat. 'Listen, we need to—'

'I ain't talking to you, wannabe Cardi B. Shut up.'

'Don't talk to my sister li—' Hari says, angrily, but Taran holds up a hand to stop him. It is not the time for this fight. And she doesn't need him to fight her fight.

'CJ, what can we do for you?' Taran asks.

CJ circles them, until he's standing directly in front of Hari again. He eyeballs him and smiles.

'This is certainly an interesting set of circumstances, my friends. It could have just been we ignore each other and that's that. Or it could have gone another way. Your man here could have been an employee. Done your hours. Earned some Ps. Kept the nature of my business ticking over. But no. And now here we are. In unknown territory.' He pauses for effect, and squares his chest to Hari, who drops his chin, like his boxing instructor taught him. Taran can see Hari clenching his fists. 'What did I tell you, working man?'

'You never wanted to see me,' Hari stammers, staring at CJ's black Nikes, so shiny, they act like a mirror.

'And yet here you are. In my yard. How funny, eh? This is definitely an unexpected set of events.'

CJ steps forward and breathes on Hari's bowed forehead.

'We're sorry; we were just breezing through,' Jamal says, holding up both his hands.

'No one is talking to you, bruv,' CJ says slowly, his eyes still on Hari. 'Or do you not remember how you got clocked just now?'

Taran feels Anna shift beside her. *Stay cool, sis*, she thinks.

7.37 p.m.

Anna can't breathe. The way CJ's talking slowly to Jamal, it's making her feel like everything is slowing down. Anna's leg muscles tighten. She feels like she is standing too close to Jamal. She feels like her skin is itching all over. She is feeling claustrophobic.

'How funny it is,' CJ says. 'You see, I know about you, Hari Ramsaroop. I know you got this pride complex, where you're like, I don't care about my community and how it operates, what it needs and how it evolves and moves and shakes. No, you're like, I'm not about that. I'd rather live in my dead dad's flat, while my mum is . . . well, where is she? Who knows? Have you seen her? Does she even exist? I think you're lying. You have no mum. You'd rather work for the man. Work for shops and cafes and for call centres. This honest wage you're desperate to hold on to. Where's it got you, eh?'

'CJ,' Taran says. 'Look, we don't mean you any disrespect, but we need to go. We've got—'

Anna starts edging away from what's happening.

'What are you doing on my floor, working man? After I told you I never wanted to see your face. What are you doing on my floor?'

'I—' Hari starts.

'What are you doing on my floor?' CJ says, again, almost pressing his face to Hari's, their noses nearly touching.

Hari wipes flecks of spit off his cheek.

'I . . .'

CJ steps back and slaps Hari across the face. Anna sees Taran lurch forward then stop herself.

CJ's in-turned ring cuts into Hari's cheek and Hari recoils to the left with the impact. He doesn't stumble. The slap is forceful but not enough to bring him to the ground.

Hari looks up at CJ. Hari's fists raise then drop. Anna can see her friend's angry but he knows better than to rise to it.

CJ smiles. He raises his hand again. Hari recoils.

Anna can't take it any more. She can't be in here. She feels like she's going to faint. She feels like she wants to run into the wall. Anything to make this moment stop.

'Sim's dead!' Anna says, her high voice jittery, nervous. 'Jamal and Hari, they saw Sim get killed. Beaten to death by two coppers. Kicked and punched and bashed in with a brick so he can't have an open casket at his funeral.' She babbles on, unable to stop the words flowing out of her mouth.

CJ hesitates and turns his gaze on her. He has a quizzical look on his face. Taran and Jamal try to shush Anna but she ignores them.

'They saw it. He asked them to film him. It was two policemen. And they've chased us into your corridor. They know us.'

She knows the more she talks, the more CJ can't hit anyone else. And she can feel Taran edging backwards, out of CJ's eyeline. To the table with the gun. If Anna can just keep talking . . .

'They know our names, CJ!' she says, hurriedly. 'They know where we live. They know everything about us. We're not safe. You probably aren't either.'

CJ laughs. His henchmen join in.

'Sim's dead? You're chatting shit, Anna,' he says. 'I saw him like four hours ago.'

There's shouting in the corridor. *People on their way to Rage*, Anna thinks. *Where we should be right now.*

CJ's attention turns back to Hari. He steps in closer to the teenager, grabbing his chin and lifting it up so he's looking up into CJ's eyes.

'Tell me my brother is fine, working man,' CJ growls. He smiles but Anna knows it's fake. He's not being friendly.

'I can't,' Hari says.

CJ punches Hari in his stomach. Anna watches Hari double over, gasping, so winded he can't even call out in pain. Jamal reaches out. A henchman holds Jamal back. Anna is rooted to the spot.

'Easy, bruv, easy,' the henchman says. 'OK, easy.'

'Everything my brother said is true.'

CJ whips round at the voice. Taran is standing at the door, one hand on the handle, the other holding a gun. CJ looks at the table – the now-empty table – and back to Taran. Anna's seen enough films to know there's a safety, and it is visibly off.

Anna notices CJ flinch. He's trying not to appear worried.

'We're going now, CJ,' Taran says. 'I'm sorry about Sim. You know how sorry. But now we are going to walk out of this door. Don't waste your time following us. We need to go. We don't have time for this.'

'Taran, darling,' CJ says, letting out a slow exhalation and closing his eyes. 'You of all people should not be lying to me. You of all people.'

'CJ, please,' Taran says. She wipes at her eye. 'Please, we need to go. You know we need to go.'

'Taran,' CJ says, slowly. 'Give me my gun back.'

Anna notices the gun waiver. She begins to edge towards her friend.

'CJ, we need to go,' Taran says.

CJ steps forward.

BANG.

Taran shoots at the floor between CJ's feet.

Every single person in the room jumps.

The noise is deafening in the empty flat.

Anna feels like she's going to fall over. Her ears ring from the noise.

'We're going now, CJ,' Anna whispers. 'I'm sorry for your loss. I'm really sorry.'

Jamal shakes off the henchman holding him and grabs Hari, steadying his friend as he gasps for air. Anna feels a rush of tenderness for her boyfriend. Always caring, looking out for them all.

Jamal pushes Hari towards the door, past Anna, who follows behind, out into the corridor. She watches as Taran backs out of the flat. She stumbles. Anna throws an arm around Taran to steady her as they leave. She takes the gun from Taran's hand. It feels heavy and odd. She slips it into her bag.

As Taran reaches the door, CJ calls out, 'Oh dear, oh dear, my friends, this ain't the last of it, is it? We'll catch up with you. So, best run . . .'

Taran closes the door and holds it tight. There's the sound of shuffling in the flat.

'Enough mucking about,' she says, weakly. 'We need to go find our mum at the hospital. Now. She'll know what to do.'

8.02 p.m.

They run back to the stairwell. Taran's still shaking. She can feel the imprint of the gun in her hand, cold metal against her palm. She didn't like it at all.

'It's been ages,' Anna says. 'They must have given up looking for us. Surely.'

'Let's not be sure,' Taran pants. 'Let's be gone instead.'

'Wait,' says Jamal. 'First we had those two coppers looking for us. Now CJ. What are the chances we can avoid all of them?'

'What you suggesting?' Taran asks.

'I have an idea,' Jamal says. 'Trust me.'

Taran shakes her head. 'Jamal, stop. We have a plan. Please can we stick to it? I feel . . . funny. Like I need to just get out of here.'

She can feel her hands trembling, almost like they're still reacting to the kickback from the gun.

'We can't ever come back to this floor, can we?' Jamal says as they approach the fire door leading to the stairwell. 'Even if we get justice for Sim, Taran just went and shot up his brother's yard.'

'Can we worry about that later?' Anna hisses.

'These are our ends,' Hari says. 'Ain't no one making me leave.'

'Stop being melodramatic,' Taran snaps. 'You hate this part of the city. Hell, you complain about living in this building on a weekly basis. Now suddenly you're all nostalgic?'

Taran loves this place. But she remembers distinctly the disappointment she felt when Dad said they were moving here. It was so scary leaving their childhood home, changing schools, leaving their lives behind. And it was all because they could no longer afford the house they rented; their area had become the cool place to be, and the landlord decided to double the rent with no warning. Dad had been signed off work because of the chemotherapy and couldn't work. This was even before he went into remission, and before it came back. And he was way past the time he could claim sick pay. She sat on the stairs with Hari, listening to the sadness in their parents' voices as they discussed it. She held her brother's hand tight.

The building groans at that moment. A creak in its innards. Like a furnace has been switched on. It pulls Taran back to the present. Just in time to see Jamal push open the fire door and run through.

As she passes the last flat before she reaches the door, Taran notices it's been boarded up, and has a sign saying 'Repossessed by NextGen Properties'.

She has seen that sign around the different floors a lot.

8.04 p.m.

Hari's heart is hammering against his ribcage. Two flights down, he asks to rest. He's still winded. Taran shakes her head.

'We know what's behind us; we don't know what's ahead,' she says to him.

Hari feels winded all over again. He knows exactly why she said it.

Those were the last words their father said to them before he went out for a walk, sat down on a bench to catch his breath, and his body gave up.

The morning after, they sat over breakfast, not eating, just moving things around their plates. Their mother hadn't emerged from her room yet. She was angry at Dad for never going to the doctor, no matter how much she told him about early detection of cancers and how being a medical professional made her opinion count more than his.

'You don't have to live with what comes after,' she shouted, when, over dinner, he just came out with it.

'It's back,' Dad said.

'How could you do this to your family?' she shrieked.

It didn't need any more explaining. They all knew what 'it's back' meant. They all knew that their father's health was deteriorating.

Even now Hari remembers how Dad said it – so casually, almost in passing, as he paused between two large mouthfuls of food.

The room was empty. No one had any fight left in them. They sat in silence.

This memory anchors Hari, tethers him. 'We know what's behind us; we don't know what's ahead.' It became his dad's epitaph.

Hari's stomach still aches. He still can't breathe properly, but there's something in that memory that strengthens his resolve.

He straightens up and they run.

8.07 p.m.

Jamal leads them into the corridor of floor eleven. He turns and smiles.

'Where we going, Jam?' Taran asks. She's feeling uneasy; she's never been on this floor before.

'Trust me,' he says. He walks them past three doors before he stops. He reaches up on to the lintel and picks up a key. He opens the door in front of him and lets them in.

'I can't believe the key was still there,' he says, grinning. 'Turns out you *can* go home again, Dorothy.'

They're in an empty flat.

There are old poster marks on the grotty walls. The carpet has been tugged up at its corners. Chicken boxes lie in a trail across the floor. There is a film of dust on everything.

The place smells like home, Taran thinks – the mixture of burned rubber and long-ago cooking and nicotine embedded in the carpet fibres.

'Whose place is this?' Taran asks.

'It's his mum and dad's,' Anna says, with a look at Taran and Hari to say, *Don't push this any further.*

They all know that Jamal's mum and dad aren't around any more. They know that both his parents lost their leave to remain and are back home. Jamal had the choice. 'There are opportunities here,' his mum told him. 'There are opportunities everywhere,' he said.

He wanted to stay, but he wanted his mum and dad to stay too.

He stayed. They went back.

'How is it still empty?' Hari asks.

Jamal shrugs. 'I dunno, man, but every time someone wonders where we're gonna house refugees, I'm always like, put them up in my old yard. It's empty. They can have it. From one refugee to another.'

They all sit on the floor. Hari, lying down, brings his knees up to his chest and tries to regulate his breathing.

'This is a waste of time,' Taran says. 'We need to go find Mum.'

Jamal nods. 'Yeah, yeah, I get that, but surely we need stuff to calm down first and—'

'Jam,' Anna says, interrupting. 'We agreed already – we can't just stay in the building. Why did you bring us here?'

'Just for a timeout,' he says. 'Taran fired a gun. Hari ran into his nemesis. We saw someone die. Anna's house ain't safe. Here feels like a sanctuary. Even if it's for a short while.'

Hari turns his head to Anna. 'Jamal's right,' he says. 'Why were we gonna run away like frightened kids? We need to fight.'

'Fight?' Anna says. 'We're running for our lives, not having a punch-up.'

'Fight? The police? You are both crazy,' Jamal says. 'We just need to stay put for a couple of days, till things calm down and the coppers give up, and then we can get out of here and find your mum.'

'A couple of days!' Anna squeaks. 'My mum—'

'Things aren't gonna calm down, Jamal,' Taran says. 'This is a waste of time.'

Taran looks at her hands; she's been leaning on them. They're black from the floor. She shows them to Jamal. He shrugs. There is months and months of dust clogging up the air.

'We need to move,' Taran says again, to no one in particular. She is restless. She paces the room. She walks to the window. The view from here is familiar. It feels comfortable. She remembers spending whole summer evenings sitting on the roof with Jamal and Anna, watching the sun set over the entire city, sipping sugary chai from a thermos and not worrying about anything. Everything feels so different now. So heavy.

'Why did they do it?' Anna chokes on a sob. 'Why did they kill Sim?'

Jamal wraps his girl in a hug.

Taran walks into another room. She doesn't want to talk about what happened to Sim. She was with him only hours ago.

She pictures it. She smiles. He was alive.

9.30 a.m.

The beat drops.

We're family
This is a simple and profound realisation
That I was brought to this nation
To be not seen, not heard, be patient
I'm racing, tasting tension, tercile intervention

The beat cuts out suddenly. There's a loud hiss in Taran's headphones.

'What's happening?' Taran bellows into the microphone, still filled with the flow.

Sim's voice comes into her headphones. She doesn't turn around to face the booth. She hates people being able to see her face while she spits.

'T,' he says, delicately. She can feel him holding back. He pauses. 'What are you talking about in these bars?'

She turns round. She faces the booth. Sim is standing there smiling while the engineer, Cody, actively avoids eye contact and fiddles with some knobs, turning them up and down at random.

'What did you say?' she says, aggressively.

No one questions her bars. No one. Ever. Not even him. Not even in his honey voice.

'T, seriously. You just said "I'm racing, tasting tension, tercile intervention". I know you said you wanted to drop a freestyle, but that's pushing it.'

She takes the headphones off.

'Look, you're distracting me. I ain't ever had anyone else in the studio before. Meet me for lunch. Later. One p.m. On the roof. OK?'

Cody holds out a subtle fist for Sim to dap him. Sim daps, still smiling. He holds his hands up.

'OK, OK, I'm going,' he says.

'Cool,' Taran says, putting the headphones back on. 'Run it, Cody. Hurry, Sim. Go. Lunch. Chips, yeah?'

She finds out from Cody later that Sim got up to leave, but lingered until she was facing away from him again. He listened as the beat dropped, that guttural electronic squelch of a bass, louder than a bomb, with the incessant whining droning bleeping – like a siren, chasing you through the streets you know best as you leave it in the dust. And he listened as she spat.

Four bars, rolling drums, clanking snare like a baton against railings; clanging, incessantly banging.

Kiss my arse, pig, I see you coming
You got me running, you ain't nothing
What you uphold is the white man's law
I'll eat you up with a side of 'slaw
I'll hide my paws, rip you with claws
I'll never tire, I'll never exhaust

Cody tells her Sim was beaming from ear to ear, like he was thinking, *That's the one.*

1.06 p.m.

Sim is already there when Taran reaches the roof.

He's holding a bag of chips, greasy in his hand. He puts it on the ledge as he stands up to greet Taran. He bends down to kiss her on her forehead. His nose nudges her cap off her head. She grabs it and pulls it back, wrenching her shoulders to free herself from him.

Sim smiles and snatches the cap from her hands. He lets it hover over her head, unsure of her boundaries. When she looks up at him and smiles, sheepishly, he lifts the cap away and drops it to the ground.

He takes in her unevenly shorn head and puts a hand up to his lips to stifle a laugh.

'You think it's funny,' Taran says, reaching for her hat.

He jabs it out of her reach with his toe and steps forward, clutching Taran by her temples, softly, playfully, not aggressively. He kisses the top of her head with the wettest kiss he can muster.

She smiles.

'It's drastic,' he says. 'I like it. I'm just, I dunno. It's weird. I never have to deal with your hair cos you're always wearing a cap. So it feels like a statement now. Look, it's beautiful. You look like . . . like a . . . ruler.'

'A *ruler*? You're a cheeseball, Sim,' she says, laughing. 'You wanted to say "queen" but then worried that I might call you a colonial bastard.'

'I was going to say Phil Mitchell,' he says with a sly grin.

'Who's that?'

'Come on. From *EastEnders*? Instant classic. I know you're only two years younger than me, but still . . .'

Taran is laughing harder now. 'Of course I know who Phil Mitchell is, that's what we call my Maths teacher, man.'

'Mr Cole?'

'Yeah, man. You know.'

'We just called him the Thumb.'

They both fall about, like there is nothing else happening in the world.

'That freestyle,' he says, finally stopping laughing. 'It was good. Playful. I like it when you're playful. It makes all the political stuff bang harder. All the references. Watching you, that was the closest I've felt to true love.'

'Playful, but political. OK, I hear that. But I don't feel like I think too much about whether I'm being playful or political or emotional or whatever, I just write what's in my heart. This block inspires me, y'know.'

'I just told you I love you,' Sim says. 'We just skipping over that?'

'Tell me more about what a sick MC I am. It'll help me process this subtweet declaration of love.'

'Taran, I love you,' Sim says, taking her hands and pulling them to his chest.

Taran looks at him with no expression, then her gaze moves down to his hands holding hers, then she goes back to his face and wrinkles her nose like something stinks.

'You cheeseball,' she says.

He drops her hands. 'Taran, FFS, come on . . .'

She bursts out laughing again. Sim tuts and turns away from her.

Taran puts a hand on his shoulder and pinches it lightly.

'I love you too, Sim. I love you too,' she says.

There is no one around to hear this moment. The sun is moving across the city, bathing both of them in some Instagram filter sepia wash. It feels private and intimate and Taran knows that if she were to truly write what was in her heart, it would be about Sim.

8.23 p.m.

Anna smiles at Taran as Taran walks back into the room.

Taran asks Hari for his phone. She watches the video. She can feel Anna's gaze on her the whole time. Tears bubble in Taran's eyes; her fist clenches in her jacket pocket.

She looks at Hari. She hasn't told him. How can she even start that conversation now?

'Hey, Hari, how was work today?' Anna asks, brightly.

Taran feels a wave of gratitude wash over her – she knows her friend is trying to distract the boys, give Taran a moment to herself.

'Boring,' Hari says. 'No, wait. Really boring.'

'And you, Jamal? What were you doing all day, while Hari was working?'

'Looking for work. I'm skint at the moment.'

'Find anything?' Anna asks, a small note of impatience in her voice.

'Not really,' Jamal says. 'I basically just spent all day on YouTube watching videos. Sorry. I used up all my credit too, cos my uncle ain't given me any spare cash in like three months.'

'Yeah, I know, Jamal. You remind me every day so you don't feel guilty about never replying to anything . . .'

'I'm sorry,' he says. 'I found one job. Some building company wants community artists to draw murals on the boards they're putting up to hide the new construction sites round here.'

'That sounds wicked,' Hari says. 'But you're a terrible artist.'

'Bruv,' Jamal says. 'It's community art. If it's crap, you pretend it's been done by a six year old and you call it cute.'

Anna laughs. 'Yeah,' she says. 'Hey, Jam – remember the art Dad got for the walls of the youth centre when he reopened it after he got the CAT?'

'CAT?' Hari asks.

'Community Asset Transfer, bruv, come on,' Anna says.

'Oh god, yeah, I remember that,' Jamal says. 'The stuff the Thompson twins did? Those monsters? Genuinely terrifying. And their mum was like, "Oh, no, that's just Peppa Pig."'

They laugh at the memory.

'The day we met,' Taran says, quietly, joining the conversation, 'your dad was talking about the CAT even then. Sim was there too . . . He helped us carry our boxes from the car – remember, bro?"

Hari nods, memories clearly stirring for him too. 'He had that same puffa on he wore all the time. He was wearing it when . . . Anyway, yeah, I remember. He got those other guys to stop smoking and help. No matter what I thought of Sim after, I always thought that was respectful, you know, cos of how Dad looked and all that.'

'How he looked?' Anna asks, gently.

'The chemo had done its worst by then,' Taran says. 'Dad's hair was long gone – and he used to wear it in this long plait with a handlebar moustache to match; he was so proud of it. Anyway, yeah, they must have realised it was cancer and stopped smoking out of respect. Sim was respectful, you know.'

Anna nods. Taran knows she gets it, more than Hari ever would.

'Mum kicked us out so she could scrub the flat clean, so we just ended up in the youth centre,' Taran goes on. 'Your dad met us at the door, Anna. I remember Mr Johnson saying no drink or drugs, and all food should be shared with him. Oh, and no lord's name should be taken in vain: Lord Jesus, Lord—'

'Krishna or Lords of the Underground,' Anna finishes for her. 'That's one of his favourite jokes.'

'Lords of the what?' Jamal asks.

'A rap group he loved— Loves,' Anna corrects herself.

'And then he introduced us,' Taran says, winking at Anna. 'You came out with your nerdy glasses on and a Malorie Blackman book in your hand.'

'Yeah, I didn't want to be disturbed – the book was good, man! And I hate it when I'm forced to make friends. But I didn't really mind with you lot. You looked like you could do with a friend . . .' Anna says. 'I showed you the office, didn't I?'

'And Sim was in there,' Hari mutters. 'He didn't even look up from his phone when we came in.'

Taran feels a jolt of electricity in her stomach. He'd looked at her.

'Don't sleep . . .' she whispers. 'That's what he said to me.'

She hadn't realised what he was on about at first, then she remembered she was wearing her Nas tour T-shirt, from when she went to see Nas at Wireless with Hari.

Right there, in Anna's dad's spotless, ordered office, it was like she had been seen – like, truly seen – for the very first time.

'That community art wall was jokes,' Jamal says, interrupting Taran's thoughts. 'Jules and Khadija basically did that weird tapestry that was like the plot of *The Hunger Games* . . .'

'And then your dad was like, "Spoiler alert, I've only seen the first two,"' Hari says, creasing up.

'He was so pissed,' Jamal snorts.

They fall into a contemplative silence.

'Now that wall has been painted over with that ad for NextGen Properties, innit,' Taran says soberly, sighing.

'NextGen,' Jamal says. 'Yeah, they're the ones who are advertising for the community artists.'

'NextGen is on the takeover around here,' Hari says. 'I keep seeing and hearing their name everywhere. Who in these ends gives a shit about the name of some twat property developers, innit?'

'Where are they buying up and flipping now? They've done nothing with that youth centre. Nothing,' Anna says, angrily. 'I grew up there. My dad poured every inch of his life into making it a safe place for us to go. And they buy it up and do what? Just sit on it? Yeah, great. Fuck NextGen, man . . .'

'Maybe they're buying Mr Shah's shop,' Hari says. 'They were on the phone with him earlier.'

3.30 p.m.

Hari is scrubbing the back of the fizzy drink shelf, trying to lift the sticky Coke off the murky white surface.

Nothing else is happening in the shop. Mr Shah refuses to put the radio on and won't let Hari put earbuds in.

Hari can hear Mr Shah on the phone. He can't hear the other end of the call but he knows Mr Shah isn't happy. His voice is getting louder and louder. It's a welcome distraction from the endless silence and what's going on in Hari's own head – a mixture of money worries, anxiety about CJ and doing everything he can to not think about Dad.

Hari scrubs and listens.

'What do you mean? My debt with my bank isn't for a third party. I don't understand. By the terms of the leasing agreement we have, and the financing package . . . Look, I haven't defaulted on any payments. I haven't been late with any payments. Can I speak to your supervisor please? Every month, I pay. Even when I don't have the money, it comes out of my salary. So why have you given this debt to a third party?

Who are they? . . . NextGen Properties? Who's that? I don't care if they are an American company, what do they want with my leasing agreement? This is illegal . . . No, I know what this is. This is about that coffee chain. How many letters did NextGen send me? How many? I'll tell you. I kept them all. Fourteen! This is harassment! They wanted my property, they kept telling me. Prime real estate for new luxurious apartments. And I kept saying no, and you know what, they did not like that . . .'

Who'd want to live here? Hari thinks. *Well, I do*, he reminds himself. *But why would anyone live here if they had a choice . . .?*

Though lately he's noticed the students. More of them everywhere. New blocks of posh student housing have been springing up all over the city. In Hari's head, student halls would be like army barracks, with rows and rows of bunk beds. But then he saw one of the rooms on a flyer he found on the bus. They're plush, big enough for a desk, double bed, wardrobe, shelves and an en-suite bathroom. All these old abandoned buildings knocked down and renovated for students. That's why he and Jamal, and Taran and Anna don't feel welcome in the centre any more. Cos they feel like these students are looking at them and judging. And Jamal is sick of telling people he and Hari ain't dealers.

If Mr Shah's goes, and they replace it with something else, I hope they'll be hiring, he thinks.

There'd be less time to live inside his head if this turned into a Tesco. And they'd definitely play music.

8.24 p.m.

'NextGen Properties again . . . Weird,' Taran says.

She settles down cross-legged next to Anna.

'Why weird?' asks Anna.

'Maybe it's not just weird,' Hari jumps in. 'Shah's is an institution. And it sounded like they're being threatened by NextGen. That feels shady.'

'Sim said—' Taran stops. 'He . . .' She looks at her brother. In this moment, with the sting of Sim gone, her stomach empty and aching, she actually doesn't care what he thinks. She swallows to steady herself. 'He mentioned NextGen. In the studio yesterday. Said that they were taking over the whole area or some—'

Hari interrupts: 'Taran, gimme my phone. Let's put the video online. We need justice for Sim.'

'Wait!' Anna says. 'I've been thinking. Let's not be hasty. Don't put it online. You can't . . . It might jeopardise the case . . . And we don't even know why they killed him yet.'

'What do you mean?' Taran says, suddenly tired. She hands Hari the phone and leans back till she is lying down. 'Why does that even matter? And what case?'

Anna sighs.

'Anna? What's going on?' Jamal asks.

'I saw Sim, this morning,' Anna says, looking at her hands. 'He came to our house for omelettes as usual. But he told me something important. Something about my dad.'

Taran sits bolt upright.

'Tell us,' Taran says. 'Everything.'

7.17 a.m.

The knock on the door is short and firm. Anna hears it through the sound of the toothbrush against the enamel on her teeth and Missy playing on her phone.

She feels movement in the flat and listens as her mum opens the door.

'Hey,' she hears her mum say, cooing, almost flirtatious.

'Ma'am,' comes the reply.

'I'm not an old lady,' her mum says, laughing. 'Don't call me "ma'am".'

'OK, Mrs Johnson.'

She laughs again. 'Cynthia, please.'

Anna knows who it is. Sim Francis. Every Friday, without fail, he comes round for one of her mum's famous omelettes.

She spits out her toothpaste and rinses her mouth.

She ducks out of the bathroom and, on her way back to her bedroom to dump her PJs, she peeks into the kitchen.

Sim is leaning against the kitchen counter, clutching a mug of tea and laughing with her mum. Anna walks in, forgetting she's carrying her nightclothes. She bunches them into her armpit and squeezes.

'Morning,' she says, embarrassed, then doubly embarrassed that she sounds as flirty as her mum did.

'Anna banana,' Sim says. That voice, so fluid and easy, like syrup or a smooth milkshake or something – she can't put her finger on it, but whatever it is, it makes her melt inside. Like she wants him to reach down and pick up her five-foot-one frame and smother it into himself. *I'm with Jamal*, she reminds herself. *Sim's with Taran.*

She looks up. He's smiling at her. Expectant. Like he's waiting for something.

'Sorry, what?' she says.

'You cool, Anna banana?' he says.

'My dad used to call me that,' she replies, quietly.

'He's a good man, your dad. I have a lot of respect for him, as you know. Mr Johnson gave me a lifeline, letting me work out of the youth club and do good things for the area. But anyway, you know all that. I'm just here to chat to your mum. Something has come to my attention and I reckon it can help with your dad's case. I need to get it looked at. By a lawyer or someone who knows what they're doing.'

'Barrister,' Anna says.

'What?' Sim asks.

'Like, you know, a lawyer is an American thing. Here, we have solicitors and barristers. I want to be a barrister.' Anna blushes. She's doing that babbling thing she always does.

'OK, right, right. My bad, Anna banana, my bad. That's cool. Look, I am going to get a *barrister* . . . to look at your dad's case. Get it reopened.'

Anna has had this conversation with Sim before – it's a waste of time. Why would she want to get her hopes up? Why open up old wounds? It comes with too much pain to even think about.

'Why?' she asks. 'And why now?'

'What do you mean, why? Don't you think he was innocent? He's your dad!' Sim says, looking at her mum, like Mum's going to jump in and agree.

'What do you want me to say? That my dad was set up by a bunch of corrupt police? That he was in the wrong place at the wrong time? That he's a victim of racial profiling? That his alibi, although it can't be proved, is entirely reasonable because it's in line with the everyday of his job? Hashtag "MrJohnsonIsInnocent" doesn't *do* anything, Sim. Cos he is still behind bars. And there is nothing we can do about that.'

'Mr Johnson isn't just your dad, or my mentor; he meant a lot to this community,' Sim says, turning serious. 'We owe him.'

'Isn't *just* my dad? That's unfair,' Anna says, fighting back tears. She doesn't want to cry, not in front of him, especially not in front of her mum.

'Darling,' Anna's mum says. 'Sim's got something new, something that might help your dad . . .'

Sim leans forward, putting down his cup of tea. 'Look, my sister—'

'I'm not your sister,' Anna says, suddenly angry.

All she has wanted to do since her dad got arrested is keep her head down, her nose clean and not be seen. All she has wanted is to do her work, get her grades, get the loans so she can go to university and become a barrister. All she has wanted to do. And people keep trying to drag her back to the dark place.

Cos if she can do all that, *then* she can help her dad. But that is the long road. Everything else is distraction.

'OK, what I'm trying to tell you is this: the system is man-made, not god-made, not community-made. It's man-made. And men are flawed. They get things wrong. They abuse the system. Mistakes happen. Injustices happen. Because of people. It's time for a change. I'm going to make that change.'

'What makes you so sure, hero?' Anna asks, one foot out the door.

'I have actual, physical proof your dad was innocent.'

Anna stops and turns to her mum. Mum nods. Anna walks up to Sim and jabs him in the chest.

'What are you talking about?' Anna says, curtly. 'What proof?'

'Something always struck me as strange about your dad's case. I knew it never really sat right, you know. Like, why is this man, a respected member of the community, a church-going man – why is he mixed up in that kind of business? God, he'd even raised money from local people for that CAT so the youth club could stay open – why's he then gonna get mixed up in the stuff they say he was mixed up in? Exactly how they found that bomb-making equipment in his car, exactly how they knew it was there, like, was he even under surveillance? It never made sense. I'm like, this dude, we sat with him, me and CJ, we had extra tutoring with him every Sunday. Your dad, even if he was talking about something I didn't have any time for – and believe me, I had and *have* no interest in becoming a god-fearing man – I still paid attention to his every word. You know why? Because there's kindness. And that kindness comes with no game, no ulterior motive. He's a good man, your dad. He gave me a place to work. He took me in.'

'We all know that,' Anna whispers. 'You said you had proof?'

'Yeah, I got sent some evidence. And I think there's a case to appeal the decision, you know? Either of you heard of a company called NextGen Properties?'

Anna looks at her mum. She thinks she sees her mum's eyes widen, just momentarily. But then Cynthia shakes her head, no.

'I have a video recording of a police officer saying he set your father up.' Sim stops. 'He names himself and the other guy who did it. That guy's from NextGen. I have it on video.'

Anna won't let herself smile, she won't let her heart skip a beat. She won't jump for joy. Because none of this means anything.

'It's in my yard. I can play it to you later. I've got some stuff to do. Maybe I can come round for dinner?'

Anna nods. Her mother stands up. 'Once you've done your homework.'

'Mum, this is—' Anna stops when her mum glares at her.

Mum has also been here before, so she will not smile, she won't let her heart skip a beat, she won't jump for joy either. Because none of this means anything.

Yet.

At least, that's what the little smile Anna does allow herself means.

8.37 p.m.

Anna's worried she's remembering it wrong. She's worried she's forgotten some important detail because immediately after it happened she put it out of her head and went to school as normal. Now, as she tells them about it, she doesn't want to leave anything out.

'How did Sim know all this stuff?' Hari says. 'He wasn't some detective.'

Anna looks at Taran.

'No,' Anna says, catching Taran's eye. 'But he was a good man. My mum won't have a bad word said about him.'

'Whoever he was,' Jamal says to Hari. 'He didn't deserve that. Beaten to death and left to rot, like a rat. Man. That's dark.'

'None of you knew him,' Taran says.

She stands up again and walks around the room. She is restless. A *thump-thump-thump* of shoes runs past the front door. The empty flat is an echo chamber, and each of them flinches.

'What does that mean?' Hari says, aggressively. 'You didn't know him either.'

Taran looks at her brother. Anna can feel the tension.

'He funds my studio, innit,' she says, looking away. 'I see him every session. He's funny, knows his rap, always helps out with lines and stuff. I like him.'

Anna's heart aches for her friend. For what she has lost.

'Shall we open the windows and see if we can hear Rage's gig?' she says, quietly.

'Nah, but listen though.' Jamal ignores her. 'Hari said it himself when we were catching jokes. Who now owns the youth club your dad was trying to take ownership of? NextGen Properties, innit. I'm sure that's what the sign on the door says. And then Sim is asking about them in reference to your dad's imprisonment? And now Sim's dead? It feels linked.'

'So what are we all saying? That this is all linked? That Sim was uncovering a conspiracy?' Anna says. 'Some sort of conspiracy to do with this area? Weird, when you put it all next to each other like that.'

'Why would anyone want to live here though?' Jamal says. 'There's nothing here – no decent schools, no decent youth club any more. The nearest OK football team is miles away. I don't get it.'

'What are you talking about, Jam?' Taran asks him. 'You love it here.'

'What's so good about this place that they want to encourage fancy people to live here?' Jamal continues.

'What fancy people?' Anna says.

'Look at this – it's our home, but it isn't our home, neither,' Jamal says, pulling a scrunched up bit of paper out of his pocket and handing it to Anna.

She unfolds it and reads.

It's white text on blue paper, with an image of a rooftop swimming pool and a view into the infinity of a skyscraper-strewn city in the near distance. The backs of two white people, one with blonde curly locks and the other mousey brown with a short back and sides. He has a generic tribal tattoo on his shoulder. They wade in the water and stare out over the view.

'We are invested in your city,' the flyer says. 'That's why we have five hundred new flats for sale. Buy now. More jobs. More places to live. Safer streets. Your home. NextGen Properties.'

'Oh,' Anna says. 'Well, I doubt they expect us to live side by side.'

'Yeah, I can't wait for all these bearded idiots to turn up with their expensive headphones and bikes. CJ will be sorted for life, business-wise. Nah, this sounds like hell,' Hari adds.

'Again,' Anna says, 'I don't think they expect us to live side by side.'

Anna gets up, looks out on to the city. She looks at the tower blocks, similar to the one they're in. She imagines them all disappeared. Replaced with slick glass buildings with penthouse infinity pools. It doesn't feel like her city any more—

'Oh my god. Roland!' Taran exclaims.

'Who's Roland?' Hari says to his twin.

'Roland! At the studio. Cody's big brother? Owns the flat Cody operates out of? He gave Cody notice a couple of weeks ago, said he was selling up. Been given an offer he couldn't refuse . . . I didn't really think anything of it, other than being vexed at losing my studio. But, yeah . . .'

'Shiiiiiit,' Jamal breathes. 'NextGen. Has to be.'

'This is too much,' Hari says, up and pacing now.

'I'm scared,' Taran says.

8.52 p.m.

Taran takes Hari's phone out of his hand.

'We need to upload this video,' she says. 'Anna, I'm sorry about your dad's case, but we need to make this public. We can't wait.'

Hari stands up. 'I agree, sis.'

'Got credit?' Taran asks.

He shakes his head. She looks at Jamal. He shakes his head too.

'OK. I haven't got enough data for an upload, so if we can get back to our place and get on the wi-fi,' Taran says, 'we can probably upload it from there. I mean, the moment it's online, we're untouchable, right?'

'Why didn't you think of this before?' Anna says. 'I have wi-fi at home.'

'I dunno – before it didn't feel like this was all happening. Now it feels real.'

'Real to who?' Jamal says. 'It's been real for me the whole time. You didn't watch him die. They'll do anything.'

'Jamal's right,' Anna says. 'I don't think the smart move is going back to one of our flats. They found us all in mine. I mean, they didn't know Hari and Jamal were there, but they knew enough to go to that flat. It's too dangerous to go anywhere we have ties – our flats, our friends' flats, anywhere in the block that's anything to do with us.'

Taran looks at her feet. *No*, she thinks. I *didn't* just watch him die. Part of her won't accept he's dead. Part of her won't let her grieve for him till this is done.

'We need to do *something*,' Taran says, raising her voice.

'Don't you think they'll be watching your flat?' Anna says.

'How many of them are there though?' Hari says. 'There are only three of them, right?'

'That we know of . . .' Anna says, under her breath.

'Yeah, well, they have a lot of ground to cover in this building. And they must be watching the other exits too – they can't just sit and watch the front door. We might get lucky.'

'We can't take that chance,' Anna says. 'We have to stay put.'

'How long for?' Taran says. 'We can't just sit in here for ever, hoping these guys will just go away.'

She is feeling restless. They have been here for too long. The air is dusty but all she can taste is revenge.

She looks at her twin brother. She can feel it in him too.

'We can't go out there,' Anna says.

'Stay here then,' Taran says. She walks to the door. 'Hari, either I'm taking you or your phone. So think quickly about what you want to do.'

Hari follows Taran.

Jamal gets up and takes his phone out of his pocket, cradling it. Anna sighs and follows him to the door.

Taran sticks her head out into the corridor and looks left and right. It's clear. She leads them towards the stairs. They're headed home. For better or for worse, they're headed home.

9.03 p.m.

It's quiet.

Usually, this time of night is buzzing with people going out, people coming home, people cotching in the corridors. *Everyone's in the park enjoying Rage's support act*, Taran thinks. *I should be there. Sim was gonna introduce us.*

The communal lights flicker on and off oppressively. Every squelch the boys' trainers make on the floor is like a deafening alarm. They walk in a row, purposefully, their knuckles grazing each other's, silent. They are side by side, but still, Taran leads them.

Every now and then, it feels like the building's trembling, like the world rests heavy on its shoulders. The space around Taran's nose, eyes and ears is airless. The muffled *dank-dank* of her boots feels like a march of death.

Each doorway she passes feels like it's pulling them towards it. *Tractor beams everywhere, pulling me in*, she raps in her head. *This building can be malevolent*, she thinks.

They walk up a flight of stairs, approaching floor twelve.

9.09 p.m.

Anna's at the back of the pack, about to take the top step, when the fire door on floor twelve erupts and Patterson and Roberts burst out into the stairwell. She loses her balance from the shock and trips, crunching her ankle against the steps.

Roberts grabs Jamal and pulls him into an arm lock. Jamal drops his phone. It clatters on to the floor. Roberts bends down to get it but Jamal kicks it, sending it flying down the middle of the staircase into darkness. Patterson jabs his baton into Hari's chest, forcing him against the wall.

'You!' Taran shouts at Roberts. 'Get your hands off my friend. Now.'

'Well, well, well, there you all are,' Patterson snarls, before Roberts can answer.

There's a lull in which all Anna can hear is the sound of her friends breathing. *We sound like we're scared*, she thinks. *I need to do something.*

There's movement in the stairwell above them.

Blakemore storms down the steps, clutching a walkie-talkie and a mobile phone, angry.

'Why are you doing this?' Taran blurts out, uselessly.

'You little shits gave us quite the chase,' Blakemore says.

'Don't be rude,' says Anna. She's got the gun from her bag, and it's pointing at Patterson. She breathes hard, tries to stop her hand from shaking.

Patterson backs up the stairwell to where Blakemore is standing. Roberts freezes, his free hand outstretched to signal for everyone to calm down, the other still holding Jamal's arm firm.

'Safety,' Taran hisses and Anna pulls the safety off.

The gun is cold and heavy in her hands. It feels clunky, like a tool – a spanner, not a murder weapon.

Taran takes Anna's arm and gently encourages her back down the stairs.

'We're walking away now,' Taran says. 'PC Roberts, please let go of Jamal.'

Roberts looks at Blakemore. Blakemore nods.

Roberts releases Jamal and pushes him forward. Jamal stumbles towards Anna and Taran. Taran grabs his hand and he gives a weak smile.

'And you now, badge number triple zero one,' Taran says to Patterson. He drops his baton arm to his waist. Hari breathes fiercely through his nose and whacks the baton out of the man's hands. It clatters on the floor.

Anna jumps at the sound and, as she momentarily drops her guard, Patterson seizes the opportunity. He grabs Hari's neck and squeezes. As he moves his body in closer to Hari's, Anna panics, continuing to point the gun, but powerless to shoot in case she hits Hari.

'Oh shit,' she mumbles. 'Shit, shit, shit . . .'

Hari pushes away from Patterson with his balled fists. Anna watches as his training takes over. All those evenings in the gym, fighting a bag, wanting something real – now he has it. He drops his chin and tries a jab and then an uppercut.

Patterson dodges the uppercut and keeps his hold on Hari's neck.

Anna feels desperate.

BANG.

Anna remembers what Taran did and shoots the ground. The shot echoes around the stairwell after it bursts from the gun and clips the concrete. She staggers back from the recoil.

Patterson continues to squeeze Hari's neck, grimacing. He squeezes hard. Anna doesn't know what to do. She doesn't want to fire the gun again. The first shot scared her. It was too much power to wield. She lowers the gun.

9.16 p.m.

Taran realises in a split second that she needs to take control. She grabs the gun from Anna and points it at Patterson again.

'Let go of him,' she shouts.

Then Taran notices a switch in her brother's eye. She's seen this clarity before, while watching him sparring in the gym. She asked him about it later. He described it as taking stock of his surroundings, replacing aggression with tactics, choosing power instead of form, balance not chaos. All it takes, he told her then, is a deep breath, so he can slow himself down, till he can see every movement. And she has just watched him do that exact thing.

In slow motion, he shimmies his shoulders back like a cornered boxer, on the ropes, so he can flex his arms. He balls his fists. He drops his chin. He ducks. As he does, Patterson grips harder. Hari raises his forearms above Patterson's elbows. He brings his fists down on to Patterson's outstretched arms, whacking as hard as he can till Patterson releases him. Hari stumbles backwards as Patterson lets go. Recovering quickly, Hari uses both his fists to strike at Patterson's chest, to push him away. Taran smiles with pride.

One-two, jab-cross. He punches at Patterson, who absorbs the blows.

Roberts, panic strewn across his face, reaches for the walkie-talkie on his shoulder and Jamal leaps forward to grab it. They tussle, both pulling at the machine. Jamal pinches his fingers into Roberts's hand, squeezing till his nails dig in. Anna tries to help her boyfriend.

Taran points the gun at Blakemore, to stop him from joining in and helping Patterson. She knows her brother has got this.

Hari stumbles as Patterson reaches out again to grab him. Patterson gets his second wind and pulls at Hari's collar, raising a knee up into his groin. Hari lands an undercut to his chin at the same time. Patterson counters by scratching at Hari's forehead, drawing blood.

They fall, and Hari's knee makes maximum impact on the concrete floor. Patterson lies there, winded.

Taran is rooted to the spot with the gun. Her brother is in pain.

She fires. Upwards this time.

The noise is as loud and deafening as before.

'Enough!' Taran yells.

Jamal pulls the walkie-talkie off Roberts, throwing it down the stairs. He steps away from the policeman, towards Taran.

Hari staggers to his feet, limping across to them. Patterson remains on the floor.

'We're leaving now,' Anna says, defiantly. 'I suggest you don't follow.'

They take one flight of stairs, then another. And as they begin the descent into the third, Taran says, 'Come on. Let's get back to our yard.'

She drops the gun in a communal bin they run past.

'I'm not about that,' she says to herself.

9.22 p.m.

Taran pauses on the landing for floor ten, four flights down from CJ's flat, knowing that there are now three coppers looking for them. Taran notices her friends turn to her, like, *Why are we stopping? We're nearly at the flat.* Taran is uneasy. The block is so unusually quiet. *No one is even home*, she thinks. They're all where she should be right now – at the Rage concert.

'This is a bad idea,' Anna says. 'Going back to yours . . . We should have stayed at Jamal's mum and dad's.'

Taran turns to her.

'What else can we do?' she says. 'We need to go where we know the territory, where we know the parameters, where we know the wi-fi points, where we know the people.'

'We stick to the plan, Anna,' Hari says.

Anna stops dead.

'No,' she says. 'One of us could have died just now. We need to go back to Jamal's old place. They don't know it's his place. *That* should be the plan. I'm going. Jamal, you coming with me?'

The others slow and circle back to Anna.

'Anna, no,' Taran says. 'We're in this together. You have to stay with us.'

Jamal puts his hand on Anna's shoulder. 'Guys, we can't fight, not now.'

'Who you going with, Jamal? Me? Or these guys?'

'We shouldn't split up, Anna. That would be uncool. And more dangerous.'

'This is too much. This is too big,' she says. 'I can't believe you want to split up. You could get killed.'

'Anna, this isn't the time,' Jamal says, tenderly. 'We need to look after each other. These guys are right. We need to be where we know. And we need to stick together.'

Anna is silent. She takes a long, deep breath. Taran can feel her friend's frustration.

'OK,' Anna says. 'We stick together. But it's still the wrong move to go to Hari and Taran's flat. If you want somewhere we know, I have a better idea. We should get to Sim's flat. Before they do.'

Taran tries to swallow her impatience with her friend. 'Why are you saying this now?'

'Look,' Anna says. 'I've agreed to stick together, but if we're gonna put ourselves in danger, we may as well do it for a good reason. Sim said he had evidence. Something that can clear my dad. So we should go to *Sim's* flat right now and find whatever it is. It's on this floor. Floor ten.'

'Is it really the time for that?' Taran says. She doesn't want to go into Sim's flat. She never went into it while he was alive. The last thing she wants to do is visit it now he's gone. 'We just got away from the cops, and anyways, we have a video of—' She stops. She can't think about what's in it. She can't relive it again.

'If it's all linked, we need all the evidence we can find,' Anna continues. 'If we're gonna put that video online, we need to know the whole story.'

'We can't keep chopping and changing the plan,' Hari says. 'We're going to our flat. We're nearly there.'

'And Sim's flat is literally just there,' Anna says.

Taran is confused. She can see the value in Anna's suggestion but there is no way in hell she is emotionally prepared to just go into his flat.

'Someone decide something,' Jamal says. 'It's not like we have loads of time.'

'Guys, it'll take two minutes,' Anna says, stressing every word. 'Sim's flat is right there.'

Taran catches Anna's eyes and glares at her as if to say, *What are you doing to me?*

Anna looks away. For a second, Taran is angry, feeling betrayed.

Taran considers for a minute. Sim does live right there. *If we do this*, she thinks, *it isn't a plan. There isn't time or a space to think any of this through. We can only keep moving.*

'Fine, Anna,' she says. 'I get it. Let's seize the opportunity. Get the extra evidence.'

'Thank you,' Anna says.

'But I ain't going in there,' Taran says quietly. Anna nods as if to say she understands.

9.27 p.m.

The hallways breathe. Slowly. Quietly. Taran feels the pressure. Every step takes her closer to Sim's flat. She tries not to think about it.

They roll past a few old men and women who probably don't have a clue who Rage is, let alone want to go to his concert. The old folks always sit with their doors open so they can call out as people go past – to say hi, to feel connected.

They jog past two little kids running their scooters up and down the corridor, because where else can they play? They walk past discarded Coke cans and chip boxes.

They rush past the doors of people they don't know, but still part of the Firestone House family, part of their world.

Taran had felt sad about moving from where they used to live. She didn't want to leave the corner shop across the road where the owner let her and Hari read all the comic books for free. She didn't want to no longer live a few doors away from her school friends. She didn't want to admit that they were moving because Dad was getting ill.

The day after she and Hari overheard their parents discussing the sudden rise in rent, Taran asked her dad if she could help. He was reading through their tenancy agreement. It said their landlord could raise the rent from month to month if he fancied, and even chuck them out with only a month's notice. The wording used in the agreement was so confusing, it took her and her dad ages to work it out. That evening, Taran emailed their MP. It was unfair, she wrote, that the agreement they had signed was allowed to be legally binding, given how terrible the terms were to the tenants.

Her dad asked her, 'What's the point?'

'Because it's our home,' she said.

The MP never wrote back.

A couple of times after they moved to Firestone, Taran walked past her old house to see who lived there. There was now a 'VOTE GREEN' poster in the window and a door knocker in the shape of a fox. She wondered who these new tenants were. And just how they could afford the ridiculous rent.

Her dad deteriorated rapidly after that, and the cancer came back. He died wearing a T-shirt Hari made him that said 'I BEAT CANCER' in Helvetica capitals, using those iron-on transfers. He was wearing it at the end because it was the only thing anyone could find that was clean and near to hand when he vomited bile on to his pyjamas. Taran held his naked body as she and her brother changed him, while their mother cleaned the clothes in their tiny kitchen. His skin was feathered, weathered, crinkled and weak.

Now when Taran smells coffee, she thinks of their old house, a happier time, her father, standing at the stove, waiting for his coffee to be ready, singing ABBA songs at the top of his voice. And how being forced out sent her father down a certain path, how it weakened him.

No matter where you are, everywhere eventually becomes profitable in a city. Sim loved to talk about how these cycles worked.

Poor people get council housing in the inner city. Then the artists move into the inner city, into the warehouses and the spare rooms of the council flats because it's cheap and doesn't feel mainstream yet. Slowly the artists' work brings people in, for installations, DIY gigs, poetry nights, the cutting-edge cool-as-shit parties, and then once the artists have created the buzz, someone writes about it on a cool blog somewhere, and more people flood in. More and more people come. You start to forget what the community was when it was just yours – for you, by you. And then the worst thing happens – the young rich people, they need somewhere closer to work so they can just roll out of bed and go and earn that money-money, make that money-money. And where are they gonna want to live?

The current cool area. It's a bonus that house prices are still cheap there. Meanwhile, the artists have decided that this place is so over, and they've moved out, to somewhere cooler and more hidden. And you're left with the young rich people with all their money, and what are they gonna want to do? Make the area into something they want it to be, sanitise it, so it resembles something they understand, something unthreatening to them and their lives. Gentrification isn't just about posh coffee shops appearing. Gentrification is about who can pay to live and exist in these spaces.

No one cares about the families who lived here first because it was all they could afford.

Then, suddenly: 'Ramsaroop, I see you . . .' A voice, from behind her. Taran turns to see Inspector Blakemore closing in on them.

'Taking it easy now? No more running? You think we'd go, just leave you to it?' he calls out, laughing. 'We just want to chat. We know you ain't armed any more.'

'Go!' Taran shouts to the gang.

9.42 p.m.

Hari takes two paces before Patterson appears at the opposite end of the corridor. They're trapped.

He notices he's standing in front of Sim's flat. The door is ajar. They must have been there already.

He looks back at Patterson, who is approaching him.

Round two, Hari thinks.

He drops his chin and raises his fists, placing his feet shoulder-width apart, facing ten o'clock. He's a southpaw.

'We don't want to fight you,' Jamal calls down the corridor.

'We're just kids,' Anna adds.

'You can run all you want,' Patterson says with his eyes closed, pinching the bridge of his nose. 'We'll keep coming. We'll keep coming and coming. And you can't stop it. Know why? We're the authority here.'

'You're murderers,' Hari hisses.

'How do you know? *You're just kids*,' Blakemore sneers.

'We saw you kill him!' Jamal shouts. 'We saw you kill Sim Francis!'

'You don't know the half of it, my friend.' Patterson smirks and spits on the floor. 'Whatever you think you know, it's not even half.'

'What are you talking about?' Hari says.

'Why does it matter about Sim Francis? Would it matter if it was someone else?' Patterson spits again. 'What can you even do about it? It's your word against ours.'

'We're going to leak that video,' Hari hears Jamal say under his breath. 'One way or another.'

'Why did you do it?' Hari shouts.

'There are bigger things happening here,' Blakemore says, getting closer.

'Why did you do it?' Hari shouts, louder now.

'Murderers!' Taran screams.

'Look, we need whatever Sim gave you to hold on to, and then we'll call it a day. It's late,' Blakemore says. 'Oh, and your phones. Wouldn't want you ringing anyone . . .'

'Why did you kill him?' Taran asks, near tears.

'Who says we did anything at all?' Blakemore says. 'Who's to say any of what you say is true? I don't think you know what you know. All this running around in the dark. None of you have the answers.'

'Now, your phones please,' Patterson says, approaching them with a hand outstretched. 'He has qualms about knocking you all about, but I don't.'

'The thing is,' Blakemore says, 'Taran Ramsaroop, Hari Ramsaroop, Jamal Ahmed, Anna Johnson, there's nowhere left to run.'

Patterson's nearly upon them. So's Blakemore. Hari feels the others move closer to him, until all their backs touch.

'Phones, now,' Blakemore says. 'That's the last time I'll be polite about any of this.'

'No!' Taran shouts. 'Help!' she screams. 'Help us! Help!'

Blakemore raises his baton, ready to strike her, shut her up.

A nearby door opens.

'What is all this noise?' a voice asks. Out steps Silas, Old Man Patrick's son, wearing Hulk slippers and a robe over a grey tracksuit. 'Officers. What is going on?' he says, rubbing his eyes.

Silas is in his thirties, one of Sim's neighbours. He's a marathon runner and he leads youth sports programmes. He always looks sad.

Being his dad's carer must be tough, Hari thinks.

Taran sags in relief.

'Nothing to see here, sir,' Blakemore says. 'If you could just go back into your flat, that would be wonderful, thank you.'

'Are you bothering these kids?'

'That is none of your concern, sir,' says Blakemore. 'This is a police matter. Please step back inside.'

'Hari, you are bleeding,' Silas says. 'Are these officers bothering you?' Hari nods. They all nod. 'Come inside. Into my flat, quickly. Inspector . . .?'

He pauses.

'Blakemore.'

'Inspector Blakemore, you should know better, sir. Hassling these kids. If you have an official reason to arrest them, you can let me know now. But if you don't, and it's just harassment, then you need to leave them alone. Taran, Hari, Jamal, Anna, come inside. We'll get in touch with your parents, let them know you're all OK.'

Hari leads the others towards Silas's front door, keeping eyes on Patterson and Blakemore.

Sometimes it's a bad thing that everybody knows your name in this place, Hari thinks. *But today, it's definitely good.*

Blakemore steps between the kids and Silas's door. He holds his hand up to stop them.

Silas says, 'You know, my dad plays dominos with the chief superintendent. I wonder if we should give him a call? Wonder if he'll mind being dragged away from the match tonight to chat about his officers harassing a bunch of local yoots. What do you think?'

Blakemore throws his hands up. He takes a cigarette from his pocket and steps back.

'It's a no smoking area,' Taran says as she walks into the flat. 'Don't make me report you to the authorities.'

Silas stares down both of the officers as he closes the door on them.

10.01 p.m.

Taran loves how other people's flats look different when you go inside, but are still the same. You know the layout, but not the lie of the land.

Silas's flat definitely looks like two bachelors live here. There are photos of a woman – Taran guesses Silas's mum – on the mantelpiece and, next to those, a framed Liverpool FC top that's been signed by the players. The television is massive and all the furniture points towards it.

Taran feels at home.

The television is on. Silas's dad, Old Man Patrick, is sitting on the sofa watching the news. He nods at them all as they enter.

'What was that about?' Silas asks.

'It's fine. Police being standard, innit,' Taran says. 'Always giving us trouble.'

'Look, Taran, I don't necessarily need to know what it was about. Unless you're in trouble. Are you in trouble?'

Taran thinks about telling Silas everything. Surely they can trust him?

Anna's phone rings. She takes it out of her pocket.

'It's my mum,' she says.

She steps out of the room to answer it.

'Are you in danger?' Silas asks Taran quietly.

Taran looks over at Hari and Jamal, who have sat down on the sofa. News about a football match is on the TV screen, and while neither care much about football, they're both letting Old Man Patrick give them a rundown of what happened in the game.

Silas follows her gaze and smiles.

Taran decides to keep the information to herself. Not because she doesn't trust Silas or his dad. It's just, what if something happened to them? She doesn't want anyone else involved. They need to keep the circle tight. Because those guys outside are dangerous.

'We're fine,' she tells Silas. 'They're just hassling us cos we're young, innit?'

'You sure that's it?' Silas says.

Taran nods.

'I'll put the kettle on,' Silas says, and heads to the kitchen. 'Anyway, I thought you'd all be at the Rage gig tonight. I hear it's gonna be sick.'

'Yeah, innit,' Taran says. 'We were on our way, actually. But then this.'

Jamal gets up from the sofa and walks over to Taran.

'Did you tell Silas we're in trouble?' he whispers. 'He's cool – we should tell him.'

Taran shakes her head.

'Why not? Old Man Patrick plays dominos with their boss. You heard the man.'

'So what? We *need* that evidence. You heard what Blakemore said. They want whatever evidence Sim had. That's what they're after. That's what we need to find. But we don't know what it is, so we need to know what we're dealing with before we just go blabbing to everyone and their dads about what you two saw.'

'Hari said Sim's flat door was open,' he whispers.

'Right,' Taran says, thinking.

Jamal places a hand on her shoulder. 'We may have to assume the evidence is gone.'

'Dammit, we should have stuck to the plan,' Taran hisses, looking around her.

Jamal nods. He disagrees with her, she can tell, but he smiles and skulks back over to the sofa to pretend to be interested in a football match.

Anna comes back in, holding her phone.

'I have to go,' she says. 'That was Mum. She said she'd heard some stuff about what's going on, and wants me home. She's worried. You know how she is.'

'You ain't going out there yet,' Taran says. 'We're not splitting up, remember?'

Silas walks back into the room with two steaming mugs of tea. 'Yes, Anna. I want you guys to give it a little while, wait for those men to move on.'

'She sounded really worried,' Anna says. 'Look, I'm only a few flights up. They can't touch me with my mum there. I'll be home in two minutes.'

'You're abandoning us,' Taran says, as Silas heads back to the kitchen to get more teas. She sips at the one he has handed to her. It needs sugar but it's still a comfort.

'No, I'm not – Mum called me.'

'Anna, come on,' Taran says. 'You've seen what these men can do. We promised to stick together. We need to find that evidence.' She whispers the last bit.

'Come on, Taran. It's my mum.'

Taran throws up her hands in frustration. 'What about justice for your dad?'

Anna smiles, but it's not a kind smile. 'That's not fair. It's not about him, is it? This is about you avenging your secret boyfriend.'

Taran reels, like her friend's slapped her in the face.

'I loved him,' she whispers.

Anna sighs, rubs her eyes. 'I know you did, T. I'm sorry . . . Look, I want Dad free too. But I'm terrified. And I know that all I have to do is talk to Mum about what's gone on tonight and she will help us. She's an adult. You stay here. And when your mum's home, go back to yours and tell her everything. Please. Now I need to go.'

'I can't believe you're leaving us,' Taran says, coldly. 'That's dark.'

'See you in a bit,' Anna says.

'I know there's no point in trying to change your mind once it's made up,' Jamal says, earwigging from the sofa. 'But at least let me walk you.'

'You also know how Mum feels about me having a boyfriend,' she says. 'No, you know what you need to do. OK? I just need to go.'

Silas looks at everyone. This is not sitting well with him, Taran can see.

'Text me when you get back,' Taran says to Anna. She puts her hands in her pockets. 'Be safe,' she adds, quietly.

Anna nods, hugs Jamal, waves at Hari and heads to the door with Silas.

Taran watches from the front door as Silas walks her friend to the stairs and checks there is no one waiting in the stairwell.

He places a hand on Anna's shoulder and squeezes it. Then she disappears from sight.

Taran is more scared than she has ever been before.

10.10 p.m.

Taran is trying to distract herself from the fact that there hasn't been a text from Anna. She concentrates on the news, trying to avoid checking her phone every minute. She knows that Jamal and Hari are worried too.

None of them say anything.

Even though her eyes are on the screen, her mind is elsewhere. She notes the aerial shots of the crowds at the Rage gig, big enough to make the evening news. *Rage must be coming on by now*, she thinks. *Or maybe he has more than one support act?* Tears prick at her eyes; she should have been there with Sim.

Hari asks her if she's OK and she says she is fine, but she knows that he knows she isn't. He nods. Silas makes another cup of tea for everyone. Taran agrees to another mug even though she hasn't finished the last one he gave her. He seems to want the distraction too. Old Man Patrick tuts at the news. Jamal tuts at the ads. In another universe, it could be a family occasion.

'Is Anna home yet?' Silas asks as he re-enters the room.

'Can I use your landline?' Jamal asks, quietly. Hari looks at him and then at Taran.

'Where's your phone, Jam?' Hari asks.

'Drop-kicked it, remember?' Jamal says. 'In all the chaos, I just didn't have time to get it.'

Taran can see the look in her brother's eyes – fear. There's only one copy of the video left.

Silas points to the phone by the door. Taran goes over to listen as Jamal dials.

'It's gone straight to voicemail,' he whispers to her. 'Something's wrong.'

10.14 p.m.

They try a few more times and each attempt goes straight to voicemail. Taran's trying not to panic.

Anna's mum isn't answering her phone either. Silas has the digits.

'We have to go now,' Taran tells Silas.

Silas stands in front of the door, his arms folded.

'I can't let you go out there. You don't know what's happening,' he says. 'Stay here. We'll wait. I'll head up to Cynthia's flat. We'll see. Please. Wait here.'

'Silas, bruv,' Taran says. 'Thank you for your hospitality. But we're going to head to the Rage gig. Via Anna's house. My mum's waiting for us at the park.'

The lie stings her. Every time she has to use it. That their mum is waiting for them, being a regular mum, not working all hours of the day.

'She'll know what to do about the police,' Taran adds.

Silas holds his mobile up.

'Take down my number,' he says, and Taran and Hari tap the digits into their phones. 'Not that any of you young people ever have any credit.'

As she leaves, Taran notices Silas's school photo on the fridge. There, smiling next to a young Silas, is Anna's dad. They're both wearing a school football kit.

She feels her heart jolt with sadness.

10.17 p.m.

Taran looks back to see Silas watching them head to the stairwell. They walk past Sim's flat. Taran turns to look at it.

The door is ajar. She can't see inside. She feels her heart thud out of rhythm and she nearly collapses to the floor. She wants to run in. But she can feel herself being watched.

Silas only closes his door when they reach the end of the corridor. They huddle inside the stairwell, on alert.

'Where's Anna?' Jamal whispers. He repeats it louder, angrier, more anxious: 'Taran, where's Anna? Why did I let her go?'

Taran puts her arm around Jamal. 'Jamal, she's fine. Probably with her mum.'

Jamal pulls away from Taran.

'How do you know?'

'I just know. She's fine,' Taran says. She's lying and it doesn't work; she can feel Jamal tense.

'No. She always finds a way to text. Always.'

'Jamal, be calm, bruv. It's gonna be OK.'

Jamal shakes his head furiously, his face folding into tears. 'Where is she, Taran?'

Taran doesn't reply.

10.22 p.m.

Taran eyeballs Jamal and Hari. 'We need to get back to ours and make a plan.'

'A plan? We don't know where she is,' Jamal says. 'What are we supposed to do?'

'Do you think she's been arrested?' Hari says.

Or worse, Taran thinks.

'What if Taran phones the station pretending to be Cynthia, and asks if Anna's there?' Jamal suggests. 'See if she's been arrsted?'

'If it'll put your mind at ease . . .' Taran says. She pauses. Thinks. 'OK, this is what we do. When we get back to the flat, I'm going to phone the station and see if they can give us any information on Anna. Then we'll get on the wi-fi, upload the film and let all hell break loose. These arsehole coppers who are chasing us will be called back to the station to answer to the footage. While that's happening, we can actually get into Sim's and look for this evidence. Just in case they didn't find it. OK?'

'Why didn't we just go into Sim's flat now and do that?' Hari asks.

'Silas was watching,' she says. She's secretly glad. Even though it's a necessary part of the plan, she wants to put it off as much as she can. She doesn't want to know that side of him now he's gone.

'None of us got any credit; how we supposed to phone the station?' Hari asks.

'I think I have like eighty-three pence left or something,' Taran says. 'Enough for a call. Not for data.'

She takes her phone out. There's a text waiting for her.

Jamal grabs her phone. 'Is it Anna?'

Taran snatches it back. She knows it's from Sim, from earlier in the day. She'd been too busy to check it, and then . . . Then this all happened and now she can't bring herself to look.

'Nah,' she says, slowly. 'It's from . . . it's from Sim, all right. No big deal.'

'Why is Sim texting you?' Hari asks. 'When did he send it?'

'Like, hours ago. I haven't had time.'

'What does it say?' Jamal asks, exasperated.

Taran tucks in a breath. She has to control herself. She opens the message.

UR BRO IS SICK. AND HIS BOY JAMAL. BIG LOVE> Sx

The time stamp for the text is around the time Jamal and Hari were running to the underpass to set themselves up as Sim's documentary crew. Taran can't stop the tear that is now rolling down her cheek.

Hari wipes it from her face.

'T,' he says. 'Why is he texting you though?'

Taran doesn't answer.

She looks at the ground, the brim of her cap covering her eyes, shielding her from the questions in Hari's stare. She watches as another droplet falls from her chin to the floor.

RIP beloved, she thinks.

10.30 p.m.

The run back to their flat is surprisingly clear.

Maybe the police have left the building, Taran thinks, hopefully. *And most people are at the Rage concert. Which was supposed to start at 10 p.m. But you know these rappers and their timekeeping.*

They enter the corridor that leads to their yard.

'Working man.'

Hari, Jamal and Taran all look down the hall to see CJ standing there, by himself, hovering in front of Taran and Hari's front door.

'I knew you'd be stupid enough to come back here,' CJ says, calmly. 'Come, let me into your yard. I would like to hear all about my brother.'

He holds one hand in the cupped palm of the other and stands tall.

Taran freezes and looks back the other way.

'Oh, I have it on good authority that the police are that way, and you can't really get through me, so I suggest you invite me into your flat for a cup of tea.'

Hari looks like he has had enough. He steps forward and pulls himself into a boxing stance.

'Come on, working man,' CJ says. 'Be real. My caffeine levels are dangerously low. I need a cup of tea.'

Taran steps between them.

'OK,' she says. 'You can come in, but you have to drop any weapons on the floor now and slide them over to us.'

'I don't think you understand, darling,' CJ says. 'None of you have the power in this situation. None of you. So come on now – open the door, stick the kettle on, ya get me? I come in peace and all that.'

Taran walks to her door, Hari right beside her. CJ stands behind. She can feel the man breathing on her neck as Hari reaches into his bottoms to retrieve the keys.

'You cool?' she asks him, which is twin-code for: *You sure you want to let this guy into our house? We drew a gun on him and we're never entirely sure whose side he's on, plus, I heard he can be a vengeful psycho.*

'Yeah, man,' he whispers.

'Look at these guys pissing in their pants like the bunch of snitches they are!' CJ shouts to the empty corridor. 'Bringing the cops into my yard, telling me damn lies about my brother. Look at you trembling, working man. Come on.'

Hari fumbles with the lock and drops his keys. He and CJ

both bend down to pick them up. As they do, CJ grabs Hari by his shirt and presses him into his own door.

Taran pulls at CJ's arm, but CJ pushes her away.

'Stay back,' he says, pushing his face closer into Hari's. 'This is for pulling that stunt in my yard earlier.'

CJ presses in tight for two seconds. Hari gasps in pain and CJ lets go, letting Hari fall to the floor, his back sliding down against his door. Hari's fingers close around his keys as he tries to catch his breath, his chest heaving in and out violently.

'You OK?' Taran asks.

Hari nods. CJ offers a hand to Hari. Hari hesitates but CJ pulls him to his feet.

'We're even now, bruv. The air is cleared.'

'Yeah,' Hari says. 'Yeah, sure. I didn't even pull any stunt in your yard.'

'And yet,' CJ says, grinning, 'you were just the person I wanted to take it out on.'

Hari spits on the ground next to their doorstep and puts his key in the lock. Except the door's already open.

Hari barges in, confused. The others follow.

10.42 p.m.

It takes Taran a second to realise their flat has been ransacked. Hari's framed GTA poster has been ripped off the wall, the same for Taran's Tupac collage she and Anna made in Art class. They're on the floor. Torn. Ruined.

Taran stares at the fruit bowl that's been up-ended on to the counter. It seems unnecessary, as if to prove a point.

'Either you youngers live in filth or . . .' CJ says.

'It wasn't us,' Taran says. She's a neat freak, and proud to share that quality with her twin.

'You guys get robbed?' CJ asks.

'We got nothing worth taking,' Hari sighs, picking up his limited edition signed Akira print, sighing at the smudged boot print on the edge. 'Except the TV and this . . .' He holds up the print.

'Good taste, bro,' CJ says. 'Now, I know you're being hunted by the police and whatnot.'

He pauses and lets out a heavy sigh. Taran catches him looking at her and he immediately looks away.

'Oh man,' Jamal says. Everyone turns to him. 'Your wi-fi hub's been smashed up properly, you know.' He points at the detritus on the floor.

'I've been trying to reach Sim since you left,' CJ tells them. 'For a while, his phone just rang and rang. And now it doesn't even ring – straight to voicemail. I'm worried. I didn't believe you earlier. But now I don't know what to believe. Tell me where my brother is. Now.'

'We'll tell you whatever you need to know,' Jamal says, then looks at Taran to see if he shouldn't be saying what he's about to say. She just nods and looks at the ground, feeling tired.

CJ turns to Jamal and shakes his head. 'Not you,' he says. 'I want to hear it from the working man. Working man,' he says, turning slowly back to Hari, 'where is my brother?'

'In the underpass, man,' Hari says, quietly. 'He's lying in the underpass. Dead.'

'What? You just left him there? That's your sister's man,' CJ says.

CJ places a palm on Hari's chest and pushes him back against the wall. The back of Hari's head snaps against a framed photo of their dad and it falls to the floor, smashing.

'Hari, I don't like being lied to, bruv,' CJ says, calmly. 'Is he really dead?'

Hari looks at Taran, but she just turns to the sofa and sits down. She feels bleak. She has lost everything. The love of her life. The place where she lives. She picks her mum's shawl off the floor and folds it.

'We have a video,' Jamal says.

Hari takes out his phone and holds it up. CJ snatches it from him.

'What's your passcode?' CJ asks, pressing buttons and swiping away at the blank, cracked screen. 'Also, you got like ten per cent battery left, bruv.'

'One two one two,' Hari says.

CJ taps it in, and hits the video app. There's only one. He watches it.

SMACK.

SMACK.

SMACK.

Taran sees Hari flinch when the sound of those body blows come again. CJ drops the phone on the floor, and stumbles backwards. He shakes his head, puts his hand to his mouth, wipes at the corner of his lips.

Hari swipes his phone from the floor, pocketing it. Taran, nodding at him, grabs a charger from the kitchen counter.

CJ picks up a chair from the small table set the twins found on the street when they moved in. He holds it up, hesitating. He puts it down again. He looks around at everyone wildly. His eyes are burning, wide in his skull. He stamps his feet on the ground, one after the other. His breathing gets less controlled. It's like he is hyperventilating.

'Why didn't you stop it?' he says, shrill, between breaths. 'Why did you both just sit there?'

'He told us not to move,' Jamal says. 'His words – "Whatever happens, just stay there, like documentarians." '

CJ stops. Suddenly still. A tiny smile. 'He said that? Documentarians . . . damn.'

Taran can see CJ struggling at whatever memory this has triggered in him. Then the sadness creeps in. She can see it on his face.

He smashes the wall next to him with a fist. They all flinch. The plasterboard cracks.

'Man, listen,' Hari says. 'It's not . . . it's like . . . not . . .'

Taran takes control. 'Look, CJ, I know all this is a lot of information for you right now, but the same men who killed Sim, they took our friend Anna.'

'What do you mean *they* took her? Who took her?' CJ says, turning to face Taran, his fist still raised.

'The police.'

He places his open palm on the wall and leaves it to rest there as he closes his eyes.

Taran wants to put an arm around him and say she is hurting as well. So they can share the pain. So that he doesn't feel alone in this moment. So that she can finally take a second to stop running, and just grieve.

She holds back.

CJ stands up and walks out of the front door.

10.57 p.m.

They sit in silence.

Hari cradles his phone and wills it to charge quickly. Jamal tidies around him.

'Jamal, leave it, bro,' Taran says.

'I don't like seeing your place like this,' Jamal says. 'Don't worry. It's fine.'

'You OK, Hari?' Taran asks.

'Cool, sis. Cool,' Hari says, but he knows she can tell his mind is elsewhere.

CJ walks back into the flat.

'You all need to come with me to my place,' he says. 'We'll get you on my wi-fi, upload that video, take this shit down.'

'Take what down?' Taran asks.

'These people who did this to my brother,' CJ says. 'Who are they?'

'Inspector Patterson and Inspector Blakemore,' Jamal says.

'Yup. Two police officers,' Taran adds. 'Also, PC Roberts is mixed up in all this somehow too.'

'Roberts? He's OK,' CJ says. 'I know Blakemore as well. He's a nasty piece of work. I don't know any Patterson though.'

'He's worse than both of them,' Hari says, without looking up from his phone.

'So if it's police who are after you, police who killed him,' CJ says, 'we need to get this footage online.'

Taran takes a deep breath. *No point holding back now*, she thinks. 'Look, CJ,' Taran says. 'There's more to tell you. It's . . .' She stops, unsure how to even begin explaining what they have discovered. What they *think* they have discovered.

'He knew something was up, you know,' CJ says, almost to himself. 'He came to me today, gave me something to hold on to.'

Hari looks up from his phone at this. 'Sim gave you something?' he says to CJ. 'What was it?'

'I don't know,' CJ says. 'It was in an envelope. I didn't pry. He said to ask no questions, I just had to hold on to it. PC Roberts gave it him or something. From school. Sim said he'd sent him this thing and it was important, and I had to keep it safe.'

'Roberts . . .' Taran looked at Hari. 'He said he was on our side . . . Weird though. He *asked* for Sim. He didn't know he was dead. And he helped Blakemore and Patterson when they tried to stop us earlier.'

'Didn't he say anything about what was in the envelope?' Jamal asks CJ.

'Nah. Only something about some next gen or something.'

'Shit! NextGen Properties?' Taran asks.

'Yeah, probably that,' CJ says. 'I didn't ask much more. His business is his business, and this morning, before any of this happened, I weren't that bothered.'

Taran's on her feet, pacing now.

'NextGen have got their fingers all over this,' she exclaims. 'Everywhere we look, it's them.'

'We need that envelope,' Hari says. 'That's the key. We can prove the police killed Sim, and why, and also expose everything else. NextGen, Mr Johnson . . . Come on, let's go.'

'Wait. Now I have to ask, what are *you* talking about? Mr Johnson? What's he got to do with any of this? And what were you going to tell me, Taran?' CJ says.

'We'll explain it all, but we can't upload that video yet,' Taran says. 'We need to know what evidence Sim had. Especially if you have it. Once you uncover something, it uncovers you.'

'Innit,' CJ says.

'CJ,' Taran says, hearing the desperation in her own voice. 'We need to know what's in that envelope. That's the only way we can get proper justice for Sim.'

CJ thinks for a minute, then grins. A flash of gold tooth. 'All right then,' he says. 'Time to take the power back.'

11.12 p.m.

Taran is the first to spot it. CJ's front door has been bashed in. It hangs off its hinges.

CJ stares at the door incredulously.

Taran pushes past him and peers inside, listening. She feels sick to her stomach.

CJ nudges her out of the way and strides into his flat.

'They came here too,' CJ says.

'Yeah, man,' Taran says. 'Sorry. They're probably after the same thing we are. Whatever Sim gave you.'

The flat is as it was earlier – anonymous, no discernible signs that anyone is living here. But now there are turned-over chairs, a bashed-up table, bits of the wall gouged out in places.

CJ checks out the other rooms.

'So as well as looking for us, they've come here for whatever Sim had,' Hari says. 'Damn.'

'Let's hope they didn't find it,' Taran says.

'Guys, we *need* to get Anna back,' Jamal pipes up. 'I've been patient, but I'm not waiting any more. I need to know she is OK.'

'Yes,' CJ says, walking back into the room. 'We need to get your missus back. But first, this.'

11.15 p.m.

Jamal wants to shout at the top of his voice for them to stop ignoring him. He wants to run to find Anna, but he knows he has to stay put. No more splitting up.

CJ holds up an envelope. He tips the contents into Jamal's lap. A USB stick falls out.

'What's that?' CJ asks.

Hari shoots Taran a look as if to say, *Seriously?*

'It's a USB stick,' Jamal says, gently.

'Make it work,' CJ says.

'You got a laptop?' Jamal asks.

CJ disappears briefly. Returns with a laptop. 'Make it work,' he repeats.

Jamal opens up the laptop and switches it on. It whirrs into life, like it has been asleep for a long time. Jamal wonders how often CJ uses it.

Eventually the desktop loads up and CJ sits on the sofa next to Jamal. Taran and Hari hover within sight of the screen, shoulder to shoulder, letting Jamal do his work.

The wallpaper shows a couple. Jamal looks quizzically at CJ, who shrugs. It's two white people, one with brown hair and a suit and the other blonde and wearing a party dress – they look like they're at someone's wedding.

Maybe CJ bought it off eBay and didn't know how to rebuild it, Jamal thinks, trying to put the obvious out of his head.

Jamal turns back to the screen, plugs the USB into the laptop and waits for it to load up.

CJ watches him with the amazement of someone who doesn't use computers that much, but who also expects it to work faster, like in the movies.

Jamal clicks on the folder and it opens up.

There are two videos in there. One pdf.

Jamal clicks on one of the videos. It takes him a second to work out what it is.

The view is from a ledge, looking into an office. Anna's dad is sitting at a desk. Anna's dad, in the one grey suit he always wore. Anna's dad, with his balding head, the horseshoe of hair you'd only ever see as he hunched over his Bible, tracing each line of scripture with his index finger.

'That's Patterson,' Taran says, pointing. 'He was wearing that same shitty suit today.'

Patterson walks up and down before stopping in front of Mr Johnson and placing his hands on the desk.

Anna's dad: I do not like your methods here. You want me to be complicit in helping you to evacuate a building? So it can be turned into luxury housing? What about the current residents? Where do you expect them to go?

Patterson: I'm sure they will be rehoused appropriately. But that's really not my concern.

Anna's dad: *I'm* a resident. If you want my help, I think you need to make it your concern. You're asking me to make myself, and hundreds of people, homeless.

Patterson: Look, it's going to happen anyway. The building is decaying. It's going to cost money the government doesn't have to do all the necessary upkeep to make it safe and habitable. Which it isn't at the moment. There are empty homes in Gloucester, in Bridgwater, in Swindon. I don't know. People will be rehoused *somewhere*. All we're asking is that, as a pillar of this community, you help us make the transition seamless.

Anna's dad: As I said, there is no reason for me to help you. Or NextGen. You're asking me to do your dirty work, the government's dirty work, the council's dirty work, NextGen Properties' dirty work. And for my trouble, I lose my home and have to move somewhere I have no roots, no community?

Patterson: So what you're saying is, you don't want to help us clean up this area?

Anna's dad: Hold on a second there. You're asking me two different things. *Cleaning up this area* is looking at the crime, the opportunities, the safety and the wellbeing of the current residents, improving the infrastructure, making everyone's lives happier. The other, what I think you're saying, is moving the residents from this social housing block, so that homes for rich people can be built instead. That's not cleaning up an area, it's gentrifying it!

Patterson: I'm asking you to help us make the area a better place. One that people actually want to move to.

Anna's dad: But people already live here. Communities are already established here.

Patterson: It's going to happen anyway. We'd rather you worked with us, Mr Johnson.

Anna's dad: I really don't like what you're asking.

Patterson: I'm not asking. I'm telling. You can either help us, and be handsomely compensated for your efforts. Or you can be the man who stood in the way of the council's plans to improve this city, the mayor's efforts in trying to change things for the better.

Anna's dad: Mayor Ross is involved in this?

Patterson: Let's just say she really wants change in the city. And we are willing to offer her that change.

Anna's dad: What you're asking me to do is impossible. Who are you anyway? I've had the NextGen development and transition team visit the youth club, and I have a feeling you're not a developer nor an architect. Who are you?

Patterson: Where you're concerned . . . I'm God.

The video cuts out, leaving a hiss of silence that chills Taran. Hari and Jamal are silent.

Jamal looks at CJ. He nods at Jamal to proceed.

Jamal clicks on the next video.

It's the same office.

There's a crash and something is thrown into shot. It's Anna's dad. Patterson appears, picks up Mr Johnson by his tie, and pulls at it till the half Windsor knot chokes him. Blakemore walks into shot and leans against a bookshelf, smoking a vape pen.

Anna's dad: Inspector Blakemore . . . please . . . why are you letting him do this?

Blakemore: I'm just following orders, pal.

Anna's dad: I will not betray my community.

There's a swift bash to Mr Johnson's face and he falls out of shot, limp.

Jamal flinches.

Patterson: Is he unconscious?

Blakemore: Yeah.

Patterson: Wake him up. He's not getting off that lightly.

Blakemore: Come on, mate, you already knocked him around pretty good. It's pub time.

Patterson: He wasn't giving me the right answers.

Blakemore: Look, whatever. I was never here.

Patterson [laughing]: There's never an officer around when you need him.

Blakemore: What do we do now? He ain't gonna budge.

Patterson: There are other ways of getting rid of blockages like him.

You can hear the sound of Anna's dad's distressed wheezing off camera.

The video cuts out abruptly.

No one knows what to say.

Jamal clicks on the pdf. It's a scan of a bank statement belonging to Patterson. It shows some large withdrawals and deposits. Jamal notices he goes from being two thousand pounds overdrawn to having a six-figure amount.

Just like that. From living in debt to living large. With one transfer.

Jamal scans through the document, trying to piece together the important information.

'Look at the reference,' Taran says.

'NGP?'

'NextGen Properties,' she says.

CJ looks at it.

Taran looks at Jamal.

'Jam . . .' Taran says. 'Anna's dad. They were paid to get rid of Anna's dad, get him out of the way.'

'That's why they killed Sim,' Jamal says. 'He was going to prove Anna's dad's innocence. That they're trying to get this building emptied so they can flip it.'

'It doesn't even sound like Patterson's a copper,' Taran says. 'Jesus.'

'What?' Hari says.

'So, we've been running away from him this whole time, shook that he was the law. Blakemore's superior or something. But he ain't no law man. He's just some thug employed by NextGen to make sure they get the building emptied in a timely fashion. Why are actual police running around with him? Badge number triple zero one, for god's sake,' Taran says, punching the wall lightly in frustration.

CJ laughs. They all look at him.

'Seriously though,' he says. 'If he's a private citizen then why are you running away from him? You should be running towards him. With fists. This the guy who killed my brother?'

Hari nods.

'Blakemore's still police,' Taran adds.

'Who can we go to then?' Jamal asks. 'Even the mayor's involved. I remember Anna's dad saying he went to school with Susan Ross. Anna's mum works for her. Mayor Ross sat in on every single day at his trial, on his side of the court. Anna thought she was so supportive. Damn.'

'The people,' CJ says suddenly. 'We go to the people! How do we get this online?'

'What's your wi-fi?' Jamal asks.

'The network's FrancisFi. Password, CJisdope.'

'Network's not listed,' Jamal says.

'Hang on,' CJ says, and starts rummaging around the room. 'I'll reset it.'

'Any luck?' Jamal asks.

'Shit. Look,' CJ says.

He's holding up the broadband router. It looks like it's been stamped on. Hari drops it to the floor.

Jamal checks through the other wi-fi options but they're all locked off, password protected.

'We can't get online,' he says. 'CJ, you got a mobile we can tether to?'

'Nah, mate, they can track your every movement. You know my line of work. I have wi-fi for Netflix and that's it.'

CJ punches the arm of the sofa.

'OK, OK. Listen up,' Taran says. 'We have evidence of a conspiracy; we have evidence of a murder. Both involving a policeman, and a man working for some corrupt company. They name our mayor. Fam, we are sitting on some dangerous shit. And we've been running around this building for six hours now. I suggest we go back to our original plan – we head to Mum's work, tell her everything and take it from there. Jamal, I know you're worried about Anna, we all are, but she'll be fine. They won't have harmed her, cos they want the evidence, and while they don't have it, she's a hostage, right? We need to go.'

Jamal starts to protest. 'How can you be so . . .?' But he stops himself.

Hari turns to his sister and reaches out for a hug. He clutches the back of her head and pulls her to him. His forehead knocks the peak of her snapback and it falls off her head.

Taran grabs her scalp in horror and spins round to pick up the hat.

'Where's your hair?' Hari asks, aggressively.

Taran's hair is grade one all over – a buzz cut, like she's a marine. No step, no fade, no big mass of unkempt hair no one ever sees, just a single number one all over, though some places are messier than others where she hasn't been as thorough as she could have been. *But it's a distinguished buzz cut*, Jamal thinks.

Taran mutters some panicked vowels and stutters out a series of beginnings to sentences.

'What?' she says, puffing out her chest to Hari. 'You got something to say, little brother?'

Hari reaches up with his left hand and he rubs at Taran's hair. He strokes against the grain and when he reaches the back of her head he rubs down to her neck, underneath the skull, in the little ridge, up and down furiously. Then he does one sweep up and over the top of her dome and finishes with his middle fingers lightly brushing against her forehead and the line it rubs up with.

'You look like Dad,' he says.

'I know,' she replies. 'I know.'

'Remember that grade one we gave him . . . the week before—' He stops the sentence before the thought can complete but Jamal knows where he was going with it.

'I remember, bro,' Taran says softly. 'I was scrolling through my phone and I saw this photo of him and me and I was just . . . I just wanted to see if I looked like him. I don't know. I wasn't thinking. I saw your clippers on the side of the sink, and I just did it.'

'Yeah. You look like your dad,' Jamal says.

'Your edging is terrible, sister,' Hari says, laughing, pulling Taran to him for another hug.

'Hate to break this up, but I don't like your plan,' CJ snarls. 'How's your mum going to help us get justice for Sim?'

'Hey,' Hari says. 'What do you know about our mum?'

'What did you say to me?' CJ launches himself at Hari.

He pins Hari to the wall and stares at him, nose to nose. Hari holds himself. This time, he doesn't crack.

'You're OK, CJ. You're OK. You're OK,' Hari says calmly, again and again.

Then, in one movement, CJ slips a hand into Hari's hoodie, pulls out Hari's phone and runs for the door. He stops and swivels round.

'You're slowing me down, working man,' he says, shrugging. 'I ain't got time for this. I need justice for my brother.'

'CJ, no—' Jamal shouts, but CJ has already gone, his boots clattering down the corridor.

'My phone,' Hari says. 'The video.'

He punches the air with the side of his fist.

'We need to go,' Taran says. 'We still have the USB. Let's go. We've been here too long.'

11.40 p.m.

A van screeches to a halt in the courtyard way below. The sound makes Taran head to the front balcony, Hari and Jamal close behind her. Taran peers over the edge, but leans too far and her snapback, not properly back on, falls. It lands not far from the van, just as Roberts gets out. He looks up. Taran swears and ducks down behind the concrete balcony, pulling Hari and Jamal down with her.

Taran turns to them, panic in her eyes. 'We're not gonna make it out.'

A door slams, somewhere down the corridor.

'OK, thinking out loud here . . .' says Jamal. 'Roberts is watching the exit, and Patterson and Blakemore are god knows where, but we need to get out the building. So how can we do that without being seen?'

Hari shrugs. Taran too.

'In a crowd, bruv!' Jamal looks pleased with himself.

'But people are only just starting to get back from the gig,' Taran says. 'And with the amount of people there to see Rage, it's gonna take them some time to get home . . .'

'Yeah, but not *everyone* from the block's there, right?' Jamal replies. 'Some people here are old, or have little kids. Silas was home.'

'True . . .' Taran says, unsure where Jamal is going with this.

'And what is at the top of every flight of stairs opposite the fire door?'

'A fire alarm,' Hari replies.

'And where does that fire alarm sound?'

'In every flat,' Taran finishes, grinning now.

11.59 p.m.

Hari opens the fire door to the stairwell. A rush of breeze comes up the stairs towards them.

It's refreshing out here, Taran thinks. She lets Jamal and Hari step in front of her and then places the back of her bald head against the pane of glass in the fire door. She breathes slowly as the cool sends a pleasing shiver up and down her spine.

She realises how hot her body is from running for the last few hours.

Jamal lifts up the plastic flap for the fire alarm. It requires a simple, decisive pull downwards. Jamal isn't decisive.

Taran and Hari both take in a breath.

They wait.

Jamal bares his teeth.

Taran feels a bead of sweat roll down the back of her head. She rubs at it.

'Come on, Jam,' Taran says.

'Yeah, come on, man,' Hari adds, croakily.

'OK,' Jamal says, calmly. 'Give me a second. I just need a second. One second. That's all.'

He grips the lever, the plastic flap, caked with grime, snapping back against his knuckles. He closes his eyes and he breathes slowly, in through his nose and out through his mouth.

He yanks the lever down.

They wait.

Nothing happens.

It's an anticlimax of space and lost particles. A pit of quiet and carefree silence.

Then, like the start of a song that begins all muffled and bassy until the treble is turned up, a dull thud syncopates into a triumph and a pulsing noise surges its way up through the building.

It reaches the floor they're on – floor fourteen, the top floor.

They all cover their ears.

DAY 2

12.06 a.m.

The din of the fire alarm is incredible.

Taran looks into the stairwell, right down to the silver grey sheen of the bottom floor. And then back to her brother and Jamal. Jamal smiles at her. She returns the smile nervously.

The alarm operates across all octaves, it spills into every register, it is simultaneously high and low and present in the middle.

It is a crashing of cymbals, a windy cavern, a thunderous round of applause as it buzzes with no regard for anyone. It is like there is nothing else in the world that exists.

Taran feels strangely calm. *My whole world has been taken away from me*, she thinks. *But in this moment I get to take the power back.*

12.09 a.m.

Jamal is still holding on to the alarm, feeling its power vibrate through him.

He lets go and he stands back. He looks at the little lever with the plastic flap and he smiles, raising his outstretched hands to his waist level, absorbing the power around him, of the entire building screaming.

Hari is looking down the stairwell, waiting for someone, anyone, to appear – someone for them to run out with. Taran props the fire door ajar, scanning the corridor of floor fourteen, waiting for people to emerge.

No one does.

'Why is no one coming?' Hari shouts. 'There's nothing happening. Everyone can't be out!'

'No one here neither,' Taran shouts back.

'What do we do?' Hari yells at her.

'What?' she shouts back.

'What do we do?' he shouts.

She shrugs.

'I don't know,' she says, not even bothering to shout now.

Hari walks over and takes her hand. 'It'll be OK, sis,' he says.

Jamal catches this moment of solidarity between the twins and an outpouring of love for them both swells his heart. When he first met Hari and Taran he spent the whole day asking them questions about weird twin stuff. Did they ever feel the same thing? Did they ever say the same thing at the same time? Did they know what the other was thinking? How long had they been apart at the longest time? Who was more this and who was more that?

He asked them questions separately, like what number they were thinking of and what colour they were visualising and what the other one was thinking about, and both of them got the answers in sync. It blew Jamal's brain out that they both thought of the number seven (the number of their new flat), they both thought of the colour black (what else did you wear round here?), and they both thought Jamal was really weird (he kind of was).

They laughed at his goofiness. But they also told him later they loved his ability to make anyone in the room feel comfortable. Especially outsiders like they were, on their first day at school in a new area where everyone already knew each other and they knew precisely no one.

Jamal quickly felt like they'd been friends for years – they all felt comfortable together, knew each other's ways, how to be with each other – and that was a comfort for him when he felt untethered by his family situation.

'Jamal,' Taran said to him once, as he sat on her bed next to Hari, their backs against her Tupac-postered wall and their bare feet dangling over the edge, 'you're the kind of person I'd normally only pretend to tolerate but, really, you're at the heart of everything.'

Jamal had laughed at her bluntness. Admired her for it.

'I like your girlfriend too,' Taran went on. 'She cares too much what people think, but she seems solid, you know?'

'It's a good sign,' Hari said. 'Maybe round here's all right, you know.'

A few stray shouts pull Jamal back from his memories. People are appearing in the corridor and stairwell. The residents start to descend the stairs at speed.

A man and a woman holding a baby girl run through the fire door and into the stairwell. The woman sees the three of them and says, 'What's going on?'

Jamal shrugs.

'Did you do this?' she asks again.

They all shake their heads.

A few beats later, more people start appearing in the stairwell. As this new group arrives, Jamal pulls Taran away from the fire door and joins the crowd in their climb down the stairs, Hari following.

'Do you know what's going on?' Jamal shouts to the people – youngish, tattooed, in tracksuit bottoms and band T-shirts. 'What's set the alarm off? Are we safe?'

'Dunno,' a girl says, shaking her head.

She looks half asleep. Or waved. It's hard to tell.

Jamal pushes past the girl and Hari and Taran follow. They peel down the stairs, purposefully, but not too bait as to make it look like they're more panicked than everyone around them. They run into people from other floors as they go. No one knows what's going on. No one is happy. No one is moving particularly fast. They don't seem worried though, like it's an actual emergency or anything.

'Probably just kids being kids,' Taran hears a man say.

'Bloody kids,' his wife agrees. 'We need to move somewhere else.'

Jamal sighs – kids, blame kids for everything. They are responsible for all problems everywhere. Kids, feral kids, lawless kids, smartphone kids, grime kids, estate kids, ends kids, feckless kids, ya-get-me kids, kids who don't give a shit, kids with no rules, unruly kids, kids kids kids – if people want to blame anyone for these areas being ruined, it's always the kids.

'Stop blaming kids,' Taran shouts, at no one in particular. A few heads turn but people walk on regardless.

Hari turns to her and glares at her, as if to say, *Shut up – we don't want to draw any attention to us!* But Jamal knows that Taran would never just let that sort of comment lie. He smiles to himself.

They go down several flights of stairs to floor nine, where

they come to a halt in a bottleneck of people as everyone makes their way down to the main doors at the bottom.

Jamal listens to the people around him talk.

'Something's not right,' someone says.

'What do you mean?' a woman replies.

'That fire alarm hasn't gone off in the entire time I've lived here. With that Rage down the road, there's probably some sort of trouble following him. There is definitely something up.'

'I remember when Rage was a little yoot running around these corridors,' a man interjects. 'What a lovely boy. I won't hear a bad word said against him.'

'Maybe they're finally cleaning up the place,' another woman says. 'The sooner NextGen come and redevelop, the better.'

'Nope,' someone beside her says. 'The sooner that bloody NextGen stop trying to change this area and leave it as it is, the better, as far as I'm concerned. I've lived here my whole life, same as my mum and her mum, and you'll not find a closer-knit community than the residents of this building. Even if we don't all know each other's business, we have each other's backs.'

Jamal smiles. She's right, that woman. Everyone in this building is part of a community that looks out for each other. It's something Anna's dad used to say.

I need everyone out of my way, he thinks.

12.13 a.m.

When the queue to get out bottlenecks for a second time, around floor six, Jamal gets frustrated and starts to push his way to the front. Taran notices a second too late to be able to get to him, hold him back, calm him down.

People don't like his aggressiveness and tell him so, instructing him to wait his turn, be slow, hang back with his friends, let older people and people with young children out first. Stop being selfish. Jamal looks back at Hari and Taran, sheepishly, and slows to the pace prescribed by the people around him. He's not got far at all.

Taran and Hari talk tactics over the din of chatter and shouts of complaint.

'I have no idea what CJ's going to do with that video,' Hari says. 'I hope he doesn't do anything stupid – like, what if he releases it, and, like, no one sees it? We need it to have impact. He barely knows how to work a laptop, let alone a major social media blam.'

'If we could just coordinate with him, include the videos of Anna's dad too, that would be game over,' Taran says.

'But what game do we play after that?'

'What do you mean?

'If it's game over once we've brought down these two men, what game comes after? How do we bring down NextGen?'

'One step at a time, bro,' Taran reassures him.

Jamal looks back at them then, and turns to walk against the flow. When the thickness of the people behind him stops any progress forward, he moves sideways into the path of the fire door for floor six, where more people are streaming into the stairwell from the corridor. Where everyone meets on the staircase of floor six becomes a standstill. No one can come up or down. No one can leave floor six. No one already on the staircase can move forward or back. Jamal stamps his feet. A surge of frustration. He nods at Taran to come with him. Hari follows.

He pushes through the bodies with all his might. Hari and Taran follow closely so as not to lose him.

Trying to get through the fire door in the opposite direction to everyone else, they push past a group of old women. Jamal, being Jamal, apologises.

They stumble into the corridor. There are three or four people left on the sixth floor, waiting to go out into the stairwell.

Jamal leads them away from the stairs.

'What's wrong?' Hari asks, loudly. 'Why aren't we getting out?'

'How can we move in that bottleneck? No one's going anywhere,' Jamal shouts over the fire alarm.

'Let some of them leave,' Jamal says. 'Otherwise we're just gonna be caught up in that.'

'The whole point was to leave in the thick of them, undetected,' Taran says.

'Yeah,' he replies. 'But this is a standstill; I can't bear it. I feel like I'm gonna lose my shit on a staircase because people can't move in an orderly fashion.'

The alarm suddenly stops.

There's a cheer from the staircase.

'What now?' Hari asks.

'It must have been turned off by the fire brigade,' Jamal says.

'People will be going back into their flats now, no?' Taran asks.

'Nah, come on, a building-wide fire alarm? They'll wanna check it out before letting people back in. My guess is, people will still be leaving.'

'And if I were Patterson or Blakemore,' Taran adds, 'I'd want everyone to be outside cos it makes it easier to go into flats and look for us.'

'Yeah, so if they're in here, that leaves us free to look for Anna outside.'

'Innit,' Jamal says.

Taran looks at Jamal. 'Roberts will be outside. I saw him in the van.'

'So where are Blakemore and Patterson then? It could be a trap,' Jamal says.

'It can't be a trap – *we* tripped the alarm. You tripped the alarm. That means you set it off. That means that you're probably in trouble,' Hari says.

'Look,' Jamal says, 'if they've switched the alarm off, that means they're on to us – they know what our plan is and they're probably covering all the exits. We need to find a new way out. If they switched off the alarm, they'll be monitoring the exits somehow.'

'Well,' Taran says, pointing at an apartment door, ajar, 'if we're not going to risk hiding in the crowd, we could hide out here for now? Charge all our stuff. Eat something. Maybe we'll get lucky with the wi-fi and we can call CJ, or try to get in touch with Anna, or even Anna's mum . . .'

'You got Cynthia's digits?' Hari asks Jamal, who shakes his head. 'We're not getting in touch with her mum then,' Hari says flatly. 'She hates us anyway. Always has. Always thought we were a bad influence on Anna.'

'Has she rung any of us, to check on where Anna is?' Taran asks, looking at her phone. 'Well, just me, actually. Jamal's phone's broken, and yours is with CJ, Hari.'

'Not that she would anyways – she never acknowledges my existence,' Jamal says, sadly.

Taran strides up to the door and pushes it open.

'Hello?' she calls into the darkness. 'Anyone home? We heard the fire alarm. Just making sure you're OK in there.'

Silence.

Taran walks into the flat. Hari follows, making a beeline for the kitchen.

'I'm hungry,' he says, to no one in particular.

'Charge your phone, T,' Jamal says. 'Check what the wi-fi situation is.'

'Yeah. I'm just gonna flop here for a bit. I am so tired,' Taran says, falling on to the sofa, covering her eyes with her hands. 'This sofa is tight,' she murmurs. 'It's so comfortable. It's like lying on a cloud made out of Mum's hair.'

'Mum's hair?' Hari says.

'Yeah, dude . . .' Taran says, rubbing her eyeballs.

'Check this out,' Hari says, peering into the fridge. 'Everything is the super expensive Waitrose stuff. Like gourmet olives . . .'

'Chuck me some . . .' Jamal says.

'Seven types of cheese,' Hari continues, sliding the olives across the counter. 'Guys, this all looks nice, you know.'

'Eat some fruit,' Taran murmurs.

Jamal and Hari look at each other and shake their heads.

Hari grabs everything he can carry from the fridge and dumps it on to the worktop, picking through it all and shoving food into his mouth.

'I know this is wrong, nicking someone's food, but I'm starving.'

'Look at the flat,' Jamal says. 'Packing boxes. I bet they just moved in.'

'Lots of people moving to the area,' Taran says. 'We did.'

'You didn't move here cos you thought it was cool though,' Jamal replies.

'No, but so what, right?' Taran says.

'I just don't like that these buildings, which are supposed to be social housing for people who need them, now have all these rich people who've moved into the area. They're the ones who end up living in these NextGen developments.'

'How do you know they're rich, Jamal?' Taran asks. 'Cos they have seven types of cheese in the fridge? Bruv, come on, there's more to it than that.'

'Look at all the posh art on the wall.'

'I have art on the wall,' Hari says.

'What, that picture you drew of Tupac, that *bad* picture you drew of Tupac . . .?'

'Art is subjective,' Hari says, biting off a chunk of chorizo and smiling. 'This munch, man, I am hungry.'

'Although,' Jamal says, 'having posh art on your wall ain't saying anything. My uncle has a print of those sunflowers on the back of the door of the toilet. I'm just saying, Firestone House, it's a community. I dunno. I'm tired. I'm frustrated. I don't really know my point.'

'Allow it and eat some cheese, Jamal,' Hari says.

They laugh. It's the last thing Taran hears as she closes her eyes and allows herself to drift off into sleep.

She is standing on top of their tower block, with Sim. He's watching her. She's facing the ledge, looking east over the city, seeing the point at which it falls away from concrete and ring roads and suburbs, into countryside. Sim watches as she spits. She rhymes with ferocity. She rhymes with clarity. She rhymes with so much diction you can hear each syllable hit home, each syllable counts, each syllable makes you stand up and *be* counted. Sim's hands are in the pocket of his long puffa coat. She's just rapping. And he's stumbled on her. This is the first time they've ever met. And now she's pulling back and watching it with a CCTV mind's eye so she can get some distance from it.

Now, all she is rapping, over and over again, is: 'Sim, where are you? Sim, where are you?'

Sim says, 'You are a queen, you know it.'

It's the first time she's met him, yet Taran isn't surprised to see him. She looks him up and down and sucks her teeth. 'You ruined my flow.'

'It's a good flow. You recorded anything?'

'What the hell do you think?' Taran pulls out her left tracksuit bottom pocket and does the same on the right side, then each side of her hoodie and each side of her coat. Sim looks at her, bemused. 'Oh sorry,' she says. 'I thought I'd left my multi-million-pound record deal and high-tech studio with one hundred and twenty-eight channels and eight producers with the hottest beats in town in one of these pockets. Nah, I must've left them all in my flat. What do you think? Studio. Idiot, man.'

She pauses, then continues, 'Sim, where are you?'

'Want to get in the studio?' Sim asks.

'You go round asking a lot of girls if they wanna come to your studio, man? Because I've heard about those kinds of guys, those sorta liars, and I don't watch that, you get me. I'm fine.'

'You know there's a studio on the fifth floor? We put all this money into it. We were like, it's a good resource for all the young people to come and learn. All the young talent can sound hot and rep their ends, and we get to do something useful with our money.'

'Look at you, Mr Philanthropist Money Bags,' Taran says, clapping.

'It's up to you.'

'It's always up to me,' Taran says.

Sim smiles.

'Taran,' her brother hisses in her ear. 'Taran . . . T, wake up.'

Taran opens her eyes, ready to complain about being woken. Hari places a hand on her cheek and presses a shush finger to his lips.

Taran mouths, 'What's happening?'

Jamal is standing with his back to the front door, sweating, completely still.

In the corridor, she hears it – the far-off thump of boots, the shouts of 'Clear!' and the *bang-bang-bang* 'Open up it's the police.'

The shouts gets closer. The voice is unmistakeable. It's Patterson.

Taran's face falls. She and the boys need to hide. She slides off the sofa. The laminate flooring cracks and squeaks under her Tims and Hari shushes her. She turns to him and shakes her head. They're getting closer all the time, she can hear it. Are they going right into the flats too, to check inside?

With a flick of his wrist, Jamal summons Taran and Hari into the bedroom. It's messy, with glittery tops and suits strewn on the floor – not like there's been a robbery, but like these guys are sloppy. Jamal pulls out some drawers from under the bed and beckons for them both to get in. Taran stares at the drawer. Jamal pulls out the quilt that's filling it and spreads it on the bed.

'Get in,' he mouths.

Taran shakes her head, feeling the claustrophobia itch all over her skin. Hari starts to get in, on auto-pilot.

'And you?' Taran asks, quietly.

'I need to push the drawers back in,' Jamal says, and demonstrates with Hari's. She can hear rustling for a few seconds as Hari gets comfortable.

She stands in the other drawer and crouches down to a kneeling position, then she lowers herself gently on to her front. She nods. Jamal pushes the drawer underneath the bed. She can feel Hari shifting nervously next to her. She can empathise. She is uncomfortable. She wishes she hadn't chosen to lie on her front. She wants to kick and thrash violently. The laminated plastic of the drawers feels cool against her bald head. She can feel where her cap has pulled at the bristles of her scalp and rubs at the side of her head, above her ears. She breathes slowly to calm herself, suddenly feeling enclosed. She breathes in through her nose, as much air as she can, and then slowly releases the breath through her mouth.

'You OK, man?' she asks Hari, feeling the bed get smaller and smaller, closer to the ground.

Then she hears the little airy puppy breaths of a sleeping Hari and closes her eyes, willing her subconscious to take her back to her happy place, where she was a few minutes ago.

She waits.

12.30 a.m.

Jamal struggles to find anywhere to hide himself. He tries to fight the rising panic. *Quick, Jam, make a decision*, he urges himself. But nowhere looks right.

He looks behind curtains, in wardrobes, and finally finds a cupboard in the en-suite bathroom that doesn't look like a cupboard. There's an ironing board in front of it. He moves the board and holds it upright with one hand as he slips into the cupboard, wedging himself between the door and the wall until he can fit his wiry body into the small space. Before he shuts himself in fully he edges the ironing board towards him and lets go, so it falls back against the closed door.

He stands in the dark, feeling that there is a stack of towels to his left and a miscellaneous collection of buckets and sponges to his right. He tries to sit on the towels, but falls, and feels the bucket bang to the floor as it tips on its side. He jumps at the sound and shoves an elbow out, jerkily hitting the door, which releases the precariously replaced ironing board. It falls forward, banging against the shower cubicle.

'Shush!' he says to himself.

He wipes sweat off his forehead. He stays still, half sitting, half squatting. He feels his legs crumbling, his muscles jellying, his strength depleting, and all he wants to do is move. And scratch. And throw his arms about in search of space.

Concentrate! he tells himself sternly. *Think of Anna.*

It's a mixture of memory and fantasy and he's concentrating so damn hard he can't tell which is which.

The first time he meets Anna, she's just dropped all her shopping out of a split carrier bag as she's walking through the estate. The yoghurt spills all over the pavement.

Except that's not how they actually met.

Now he's in a classroom, watching Anna take notes, hoping she'll look at him. She does, when he makes a loud scraping noise with his chair. She turns to him . . .

Except that's not it either.

They're both sitting in a circle. They're seven years old and both their hands are touching a pass the parcel when the music (Boney M) stops. They argue about who has rights to open it. Eventually they agree that Anna should because it's not technically his until he has sole ownership of it.

Except that's not it. They didn't even know each other when they were seven.

They're both running through the recreation grounds that link the school to the estate. The grounds that you don't really go through because all the white kids hang around on the swings and you ain't welcome. They are running as fast as they can. They're not being chased. They're not in danger. They are both feeling gleeful. The sun is pounding down on their heads. And as they near the exit of the park, to the road – where home awaits across it – she trips and takes him down with her.

No, wait, he's remembering it wrong. That's not it.

He's trying so hard to take himself out of his situation, Jamal's brain is conjuring up scenarios from his life where Anna has definitely not been – Christmas, family meals, church, football – yet she is there every time. There is no escaping her. She is standing over his shoulder as he brushes his teeth. She is standing over his head as he sleeps. She is tying one shoelace while he ties the other. She is holding his pen as he takes notes in class. She is sitting next to him as he watches films. She is everywhere. She becomes the face on the Laughing Cow triangles in the fridge, every face on every album cover. That A Tribe Called Quest poster on his uncle's wall – every face is her. And he starts to feel his chest inflate with warm air, expanding till it is ready to burst into a sauna of anxiety – and not just because he is stuck in a tiny bathroom cupboard.

Now he's there in the underpass, filming Sim, watching Hari – who is also Anna – film Sim too. And Anna is helping him to steady his phone. And Anna is wearing Sim's coat, it looks like, on the screen, so Jamal looks at the scene, and the three police officers – those pigs, those filth. They are surrounding Anna, in Sim's coat that trails on the floor underneath her feet, and they each take out a gun and shoot her in the face, standing over her and firing repeatedly, the back blast of flame giving their sour faces a milky glow, glinting off their sallow yellow teeth as they stand over her, grimacing with delight. And then it's Jamal being fired at – he's on the floor and each bullet is entering his body at a furious speed, as he jolts with the impact of each one severing his bones—

BANG!

His eyes snap open.

12.40 a.m.

They all hear it, even Hari, who wakes up with a start, banging his head against the bed and whimpering as Taran clamps her hand over his mouth. She wills him with everything in her to be quiet.

The door bursts open in the next-door room.

'Clear!' someone shouts.

Blakemore? Taran's not sure. Whoever he is, he sounds mad.

There are stomps, furious clatters and the shuffle of boots stepping around the bed, in and out of the room. In the silence, every noise feels like it's being played through the speakers at that club, Motion.

Taran breathes slowly but feels the panic rise again. She can hear every aching muscle screaming. She can hear every inch of her body crying for release.

Boots clatter into the bedroom.

'On my way!' the voice shouts.

She breathes as quietly as she can. She feels like she's going to burst.

The boots clatter on into the en-suite bathroom.

There is no sound.

Drip, drip from the tap.

A pause.

Drip. Drip. Drip drip drip.

A door slams shut. Maybe the bedroom door?

Taran blows out a sigh of relief, as slowly and as silently as she can. She waits.

There is a continuing shuffle of bodies and murmuring in the next room that she can't quite make out. She rubs at Hari's hair, massaging the back of his neck like their mum used to, when she'd pour coconut oil into her palm and slowly rub, with force, oozing the oil down the roots and into the pores.

Hari lifts his hand up and covers Taran's as she massages him. She smiles, feeling tears just behind her eyes. The tenderness in Hari's touch makes her think of Sim.

'Sim,' she says softly.

Oh god, he's gone, he's really gone. Sim is not coming back. He's dead. And there was so much they needed to say to each other. So much that she felt she needed to learn from him and give to him. She never told him she loved him, apart from that first time, but not properly, even though she knew she did, and even though he said it to her, a handful of times. Even though it was true, she never said the words properly. She didn't want to retract them or try to write over them if they stopped being true. Or if he disappointed her, as men do, she needed to protect herself. Keep herself emotionally insulated. Like Hari, who was leaving the city for London as soon as school was done; like her dad, who was no longer here.

And just like Sim.

Sim was a kind-hearted person, trying everything in his power, good and bad, legal and illegal, to make his community a better place for the people who lived there. He had other people's needs at the forefront of his mind at all times. *Sim was Batman*, she thinks.

Sim loved Batman.

The hovering tears ooze closer to the front of her eyeballs.

Then the drawer is jerked out into the air.

She gasps at the cool breeze on her head.

Taran squints up at the twilight silhouette of Jamal.

'Shhhhh,' he breathes. 'The door's still open.'

Taran nods and stands up as quietly as she can. Her body aches from the confined space but the cool night air fills her nostrils with clarity and purpose.

Jamal pulls out Hari's drawer and offers him a hand. Hari sluggishly pulls himself up and turns to Taran. He puts his hands on her shoulders and smiles.

'You and me, T,' he says. 'It's only you and me. Family. You know that right?'

Taran can see, despite the dark, that Hari has been crying. She holds him.

'What about me?' Jamal says.

'You're like a third cousin twice removed,' Taran says.

'Yeah, the family doesn't like to talk about it too much in case people know we're related, but everyone's super embarrassed by you,' Hari adds.

'I'm still family though, right?'

'Obvs,' Taran says.

She brings him into the group hug and Jamal buries his head in the crook of Taran's neck.

'Family, listen. We're currently down a member and we need to go get her back. They've murdered my boyfriend—'

'Wait, what?' Hari says. 'Sim *was* your boyfriend? I thought CJ was just chatting shit earlier. What the hell, Taran?'

'We don't have time for this now,' Taran says, turning towards the door. 'We'll chat later.'

'No,' Hari says, grabbing her bicep and pulling her back. Taran spins round, prepared to fight, hands up ready to throw at him. 'No, you don't get to drop a bombshell and leave. He was your *what*? Him? Sim Francis? He was your boyfriend? I can't believe you didn't tell me. We don't keep secrets, you and me.'

'Screw you, Hari,' Taran says. 'This isn't your place to judge. We have a job to do.'

'Sim? Really? That man was up to all sorts of shady business. I know he didn't deserve to be murdered, but why was he running with them feds anyway?'

'You don't get to talk about him like that,' Taran says, shaking her arm to release it from Hari's tight grip. 'He was a good man. And he . . . look, we don't have time for this.'

'We don't keep secrets,' Hari says, shaking his head. 'How am I supposed to trust you?'

'Because I'm still your sister. And I don't need to explain myself to you in order for you to show respect for my choices.'

'What do you think about all this, Jamal?' Hari says. 'You're being quiet.'

'I just wanna get Anna back.'

'Come on then,' Taran says and walks out of the bedroom.

Jamal follows her.

Hari starts to complain, but stops when Taran gives him a look like, *Leave it, bruv, now's not the time.* She tuts as he then jerks it out of his body, filing it for later.

'Did Anna know?' Jamal asks Taran.

'Yeah, she did,' Taran replies, turning back to Jamal. 'She knew. She was happy for us. She didn't give me any shit about it. That's why only she knew. I know what my brother thinks of him.' She shoots a look at Hari who is walking behind them solemnly, blank faced, staring into nothingness like a zombie. '*Thought* of him . . . Shit. I—'

The butt of a baton comes down hard on to Taran's shoulder. She drops to the floor, exclaiming breathlessly in pain, falling immediately where she stands.

Jamal yells and holds a hand out to Hari as everything moves into slow motion.

An officer, wearing a balaclava and wielding a baton, bursts into the flat.

Jamal rushes at him. Hari, standing behind Jamal, drops to the floor, hoping to find a weapon. Jamal collides with the officer, but the man is sturdy, knocking the wind out of Jamal and sending him flying backwards on to the sofa.

'I don't want any trouble,' the officer says, holding up his hands and dropping the baton on the ground. 'Sorry, Jamal, Taran – you caught me by surprise.'

Taran recognises the voice, but not in time to stop Hari, who, not finding a weapon, throws up his fists, jumps towards the officer and punches him in the face.

The officer reels backwards and Hari grabs his fist, wincing in pain.

'Stop,' Taran says.

Jamal ignores her and, picking himself up from the sofa, runs at the stunned officer. They both crash to the floor.

Squatting over the man, Jamal raises a fist. Hari grabs a rolling pin from the counter.

'Stop!' Taran hisses. 'Just stop. I know that voice.'

She bends down over the officer and pulls off his balaclava.

It's PC Roberts.

He looks terrified.

'Don't hurt me,' he says. 'Please don't hurt me. I need your help.'

10.07 p.m.

Anna is pushed down the stairs by Patterson. She ran from Silas's place up the first flight of stairs and was met by a grinning Patterson, who grabbed her and pulled her straight back down with him.

Her feet are heavy and she feels stupid for leaving her friends. Not that she would admit it. But it was stupid. And now here she is.

When she reaches the next floor, Blakemore is waiting. He holds up a pair of handcuffs and places them on her, roughly, silently. Her arms ache. She can feel her pulse from where her wrist touches the cold metal of the cuffs. She can feel Blakemore looking at her chest. *Piss off*, she thinks.

'I need to update Mr Digby,' Patterson says, before running down the stairs, clutching his phone.

Blakemore smiles and turns her around to face the stairs. He pushes her down the first step. She walks reluctantly, dragging her feet.

She tries to slow her heart rate. It is pounding so fast, she fears it might burst out of her chest on to the floor. She tries to breathe calmly but her body is telling her to run. She can feel the cuffs around her wrists, digging into her, weighing her down. She knows what it is to be free. And now she knows what it is to be trapped.

At the next floor, she realises Blakemore is standing really close to her. She quickens her pace. She is wondering if she can run back to Silas's flat. It's not too far. If she can make Blakemore trip, maybe. If she can make him stumble, she might have a chance. It's just him and her. Patterson's off making his phone call. She just needs to get to Silas's front door and scream the corridor down.

She breathes quickly. *I don't know if I can do this*, she thinks. It might make it worse.

Then she remembers what Taran said to her: 'We need to stick together.' She should have stayed. Idiot.

She decides to go for it.

When she takes her next step down, she feels him brush up behind her again. She swivels to one side, pulls her body away from him and, when Blakemore reaches out to her, he loses his footing and falls down a few steps. She turns and takes off back up the stairs.

Running up stairs with both hands in cuffs isn't easy and Blakemore soon catches up with her. He grabs her from behind. She recoils from him, but he is strong, and turns her to face him.

Blakemore grabs her throat with an outstretched hand, lifts her off the ground, using his grip on her windpipe for leverage, and swings her against the wall so that the railing is cutting into her back.

'You'd better not try anything like that again, or next time I won't be quite so forgiving,' he snarls, his stale breath all over her face.

He lets go, and Anna falls to the floor. Because she can't reach out with her hands to stop herself, she slides down the hard concrete stairs to the next level.

Dammit, she thinks. *I shouldn't have done that. What was I thinking?*

She won't let him see how frightened she is, but she knows it's written across her face. She is terrified. So terrified she can barely move. She wants to call for her mum. Really, she wants to call for Taran. But that is a bad idea.

Blakemore pulls her upright. She finds her footing and continues walking in front of him as they head down towards the exit to the building. They do three flights of stairs in silence before he asks if she's OK.

'Why do you care?' she asks.

'I don't,' he says. 'But I need to hand you back to your mum roughly how she left you this morning, don't I?'

He laughs, to himself, some private joke in his head, and she doesn't know what's funny about it.

'Am I under arrest?' she asks. She has worked so hard to not be seen since her dad's arrest. Now she is visible, and in danger.

'Does that even matter right now?' he murmurs. He pauses. 'Do you know what's funny?' She stops and turns to him and shakes her head. 'Your friends are currently trying to outrun us in this block. The joke is, they have nowhere to run. We know every inch of this place. We've been studying it for months. So they can run, they can hide, they can try to beat on us and play silly buggers. But we will always find them, and we will win.'

Patterson runs up the stairs towards them and pulls Blakemore aside. Blakemore shoots a look back at her as if to say, *Don't try anything.* He holds a baton at his waist, pointing in Anna's direction.

'Mr Digby is not pleased,' Patterson says quietly.

Anna watches his face. It's pale. He's clearly scared of whoever this Mr Digby is.

'What are we supposed to do now?' Blakemore says. 'The other kids are with that guy. We wait them out?'

'No,' Patterson says, standing up taller. 'We're on a timeline to find what that youth was hiding. Besides,' he says, cutting his eye at Anna, who immediately looks at the ground, 'now we have a bargaining chip.' He pauses. 'Get Roberts to sit with her in the van. We've got some other jobs to do.'

'Like what?'

'Well, there can be no trails leading back to Mr Digby. Or anyone else. OK? We need to tie up any loose ends. Or else the deal's off.'

'OK,' Blakemore says, gulping.

Patterson pats him on the shoulder.

'It'll be fine. You're just doing your job. Now, go and drop her off with Roberts. Meet me at floor ten. Sim Francis's flat. OK? We'll search that first. Then we'll hit his brother's. If it's not in one, then it'll be in the other.'

'All this running up and down,' Blakemore says, heavily. 'It's no good for my heart. Someone should fix that lift.'

'You need the exercise,' Patterson says as a parting shot as he heads upstairs.

There is silence. Blakemore ushers Anna to carry on walking.

Anna shoots an eyebrow at Blakemore. 'What are you looking for in Sim's flat?'

'That is definitely not something you need to be worried about right now. You're in a lot of trouble. Now, you could take the fall for your friends. Or you *could* tell me exactly what I need to know.'

'*I don't know* what you need to know,' Anna mocks, imitating him. 'Why don't you tell me what you think I know?'

Blakemore moves closer to her, placing two hands on her shoulders, and pushes her down with all his might. She falls to her knees, banging them on the sharp edge of the concrete steps, and cries out, scared and in pain.

'I don't know anything, I don't,' Anna says, bursting into tears.

She suddenly feels like she can't breathe, like the floor is hurtling towards her. She reaches out to steady herself but grabs at Blakemore by accident.

He must think it's an attack because he bats her hands away.

Blakemore's smile drops, for a second, into the snarl she saw earlier. Anna tries to bend over to breathe through the tears.

'Don't worry, darling,' he says, angrily. 'It'll all be over soon. You'll soon be with your family. But first, tell me where your friends are.'

10.28 p.m.

Anna is leaning against the wall, her breathing now normal. She can feel her tongue dry. She's desperate to not babble. *Don't say anything*, she wills herself. *Shut up. Do. Not. Babble*.

'I promised your mum . . .' Blakemore says. 'I . . . Come on.'

He rubs at her arm.

Instinctively, feeling sick, she swats it off her.

'Don't touch me,' she seethes.

She puts her hands across her chest, defensively. Patterson has rejoined Blakemore. They stand next to each other, ushering her to hurry up.

'What do you mean you promised my mum? How do you know my mum? Why are you even *talking* to my mum?' she asks, fiercely.

Blakemore pushes her round and down the stairs.

'Walk,' he says. 'Till we reach the outside, you walk.'

Patterson moves down the stairs and Anna reluctantly follows, with Blakemore by her side.

'God, you're slow, Martin.' Patterson laughs. 'Here – I need your keys.'

Blakemore tuts and hands Patterson some keys from his jacket pocket.

'What about my mum?' Anna asks again. *Do they have Mum hostage as well? Are they gonna hurt her? Is that why she phoned?*

There's a ring and Patterson gets his phone out. He holds it up and stares at the screen. Anna looks over his shoulder. The screen says 'DIGBY'.

He answers.

'Hello. Yes. I'll hold. Hello again, Mr Digby,' he says, meekly. 'No, no update here. We're trying, sir. We have made every effort. Sir, I . . . Sorry. Sir, I have to assure you. Sure, yes. I appreciate that. No, Sir, NextGen are nowhere near this. No one suspects . . . Sir, I appreciate your concern . . . I am sorry.'

The call ends.

Patterson shoves the phone in his pocket. He pushes at Anna to move. 'We're running out of time.'

'Don't worry,' Blakemore says, in a sing-songy way. 'NextGen will get what they paid for soon enough.'

He flashes a look at Anna.

So this is *about NextGen?* she thinks. She decides not to say anything, not to let on she knows – to play innocent and continue to glean information from them both. She bows her head and keeps walking.

'This is taking too long,' Patterson says suddenly. 'We need to check those fucking flats.'

Patterson rushes at Anna and picks her up into a fireman's lift, throwing her over his shoulder and running down the stairs. They're on floor four when a couple of young people appear, giggling as they make their way up the stairs.

They stop and look quizzically at Anna, and then at Patterson. Anna wants to ask them for help but can't find her voice. Then one of them bursts out laughing and Patterson carries on. Blakemore said he needs to return Anna to her mum in one piece. *Mum will know what to do*, she thinks. She stays quiet.

She remembers the chorus of one of Taran's songs. It flashes through her mind and the jolting, bumping movement of Patterson's steps starts to melt away . . .

We don't fight, we defend

To the end, my friend, to the end.

She whispers it to herself, trying to keep the fatigue from taking over her body. She is tired and as much as she needs to stay awake, something within her stops fighting sleep.

10.56 p.m.

Anna wakes slowly. She is so exhausted that she can't open her eyes. It would require a monumental effort. Her eyelids are heavy. Her eyeballs sting. She can feel her arms lying heavy in front of her. She thinks she is slumped in a seat but she can't be sure.

Open, eyes. Come on, eyes, open up.

She can't. She tries to keep her breathing consistent.

She can hear Patterson talking.

'Sorry, sir, I was with the policeman earlier,' he says, quietly. 'Mr Digby, I'm sorry this is taking so long . . . I know the contract needs to be signed by the morning . . . I know how much you stand to make from the deal . . . I know how much you stand to lose. I understand that. I know it's a lot of money . . . I still can't understand why the council has to spend the money by the end of the month. What happens if they don't? They just have to give it back to central government? That's ridiculous. Who would work in the public sector, eh? Sorry, sir, yes. I understand . . . It's not funny. Sorry . . . It's nearly done. No need to involve the mayor. For now . . . Everyone is still at that concert . . . Worst comes to worst, I can just light a fire. These buildings wouldn't survive . . . Yes. I didn't realise that . . . About an inquest . . . You're right. It could take years . . . OK, plan A. Sorry. Thank you. Bye.'

Anna keeps her eyes closed.

11.15 p.m.

Anna finally manages to open her eyes.

This time she feels alone. She can't see anything; everything is so dark around her. She is so tired. Everything this evening has sapped all of her energy from her. She can keep sleeping. There's nothing she can do for her friends from here . . . *Is that bad?* She's going back to sleep.

Her body can't help it.

Her eyes close; she falls into a fitful doze.

11.56 p.m.

Anna wakes again with a start. A physical jolt, right through her body.

She's not alone.

It's still dark, but now there is an intense hum, disrupted by the occasional electronic beeping noise. There is something buzzing around her brain.

She lifts her hands and remembers: she's still cuffed.

Her muscles kick into action and she shifts into a stiff seated position. She looks around, focusing as quickly as she can in the dimness.

The beeping is a radio.

The hum is from electronic equipment.

There are flickering lights coming from the equipment.

She's in the back of a police van.

This is it, she thinks. *I'm done.*

PC Roberts sits to her right, tapping a pen against his bottom lip, scrubbing backwards and forwards between various CCTV feeds on a laptop. Her heart stops as she sees three familiar figures on his screen. She wills them on, silently.

Every time he finds her friends running about or entering a flat, he writes something down. The time and location, maybe? But why? Is he establishing some sort of a timeline? Is he looking through old footage to build up a narrative of where they are?

The black and white rendered images display a familiar surrounding. Anna realises he is looking at every floor of her block. And she knows exactly what he is looking for.

Every floor. Every corner. Every nook. Every cranny.

There is nowhere to hide. There is nowhere to run. There is nothing her friends can do to shield themselves from the view. She realises that every fire door has a camera above it. She has never noticed them before. She didn't know that in all the communal areas they were always being watched. Taran and Hari must not have known either. Otherwise, they'd have realised – running around the block like they are – it's all a complete waste of time.

Roberts flips on to a new screen. Then he goes back. Back one screen.

Anna sees why. Hari and Taran and Jamal are entering CJ's flat. With CJ. Roberts makes a note. They're being toyed with. Roberts texts something and shoots a look back to Anna. Anna glares at him.

On another screen, she sees Patterson standing outside CJ's flat and looking at something in his hand. His mobile? He's clearly frustrated, because he turns and kicks at the door violently. Eventually, it caves in. She sees a smirk on Roberts's face.

They want Hari and Jamal badly. So badly. *Come on guys*, she thinks. *Get out of there.*

Jamal, Anna thinks, *poor Jamal. He doesn't have the stomach for any of this.* Jamal's biggest fear at any given time is that someone around him might be unhappy. He will work in overdrive to ensure everyone is happy, contented, feeling comfortable, feeling listened to, wanted, liked, whatever, everything. *He's such a good boy*, she thinks. And then laughs. Because Taran always says Anna treats Jamal like he's a puppy dog and she's his owner.

Jamal always laughed at her dad's jokes. And Dad would make more of them, just to make Jamal laugh harder.

'You good?'

'Superman does good, I do well.'

This was her dad's favourite, always followed by a bottomless guffaw. Anna and her mum would roll their eyes at each other from across whatever room they were in, and slowly edge away from the conversation, but Jamal always laughed with him. Even though Anna could tell he didn't find it funny either. The one time Anna scolded Jamal for laughing at her dad's unfunny jokes, her loving, wonderful boyfriend simply reminded her that 'those jokes are a part of who he is, and that needs to be acknowledged'.

She may have sighed to Jamal's face whenever he defended her dad, but secretly she knew, this boy was loyal to the end.

Right now, she thinks, *he'll be plotting how to get me back. He'll be obsessing because he knows I need to get out of here, he knows I'm in danger . . . he knows.*

Jamal, she says, wordlessly. *You are my everything.*

She stares at the CCTV. PC Roberts takes an endless drink of water, his eyes on her, like he's flaunting hydration in her face. Suddenly, Anna's throat feels like sandpaper.

He stands up and gets off the bench. He walks to the back of the van, opens the door and jumps out.

'You grew up here,' she says after him. He turns back to face her. 'Why are you doing this?'

'I'm on your side,' he says. 'I promise. I'm working with Sim Francis. I'm going to help you and your friends get out of here. OK?'

He closes the door.

Anna is alone again.

12.04 a.m.

Anna waits for Roberts to come back. *He's on our side*, she thinks. Earlier, she's sure Taran said he was on their side too. She doesn't know if she's remembering it right. Everything feels fuzzy now. *He can get me to my mum.* Roberts doesn't immediately come back and she has no concept of how much time is elapsing. She starts to feel very alone. She scans through her memories to think of something. Anything other than what is happening around her. Something happy. A happy memory. Anything to take her out of this van.

She thinks about becoming friends with Hari and Taran, after showing them around her dad's youth centre that day. In the weeks after they moved here, her dad and their dad became firm friends, pub buddies, always drinking whiskey and watching cricket together.

Those were good times.

She remembers Roberts – when he was younger, he used to hang around the youth club. What happened to him?

She hopes he will come back soon. The van feels cavernous with just her in it.

How does the story end? she thinks, as the warmth of the van, the numbness in her arms, the tiredness crash over her all at once.

12.21 a.m.

The door to the van opens. Anna's woken up by the sound. A sliver of drool has run down her face.

Roberts climbs back in. He crouches in front of Anna.

'Do you know where Sim's USB stick is? It's the only evidence we have. Tell me you know where it is . . . I need it. I won't say anything to Inspector Blakemore. You can tell me,' he says, smiling. 'I'm on your side, remember? It'll be our secret.'

Anna is confused. What USB stick?

She shakes her head to say she doesn't know. It's the rule around here – never ever trust a policeman.

'I don't know what USB stick you're talking about,' she says quietly.

She looks him straight in the eye. *He seems different from the others*, she thinks. *Less angry, more desperate.*

'I honestly don't know what you're talking about,' she repeats.

'We just need to find it,' he says, looking to the door. 'We don't have much time. All I need to know is that it hasn't fallen into the wrong hands. Your dad. It can help him if you get it to the authorities. Please help me. I can get you out of this, but I need you to help me.'

Anna stares at him, silent. *It's the evidence. Must be.*

'Look, I'm a friend of Sim's. I don't know where he is either . . . His phone is off. No one has seen him in hours. I'm worried something's happened to him,' he says.

Anna raises her eyebrows in surprise.

'You don't know?' Anna replies. *If he doesn't know this, then maybe he is telling the truth?*

'Know what?' Roberts says.

'Sim's dead,' Anna says, her pupils burning with tears.

Roberts pauses, processing the information. Then he grabs Anna's handcuffed hands from her lap. She wrenches them away from him.

'Don't touch me,' she says.

Roberts withdraws, clearly embarrassed. 'Listen, my fellow officers have had enough tonight and they're using this random fire alarm to their advantage. Everyone is evacuating the building while they wait for the all-clear, so they're using me and CCTV to quicken up the search, and track your friends on to floors, and into flats. So, if one of your friends has Sim's USB stick, we need to get them to hide it till later. Anna, please. Help me ensure it doesn't fall into the wrong hands.'

'You keep saying you're one of us,' Anna says. 'But you're still wearing the same uniform as them.'

'What do you mean?' Roberts asks.

'You grew up here. You used to come to Dad's youth club. I remember you setting up the book club. I wanted to join but you said I was too young and everyone laughed at me, so you made everyone read *We're Going on a Bear Hunt* so I would feel included. I remember.'

The van door suddenly opens.

Roberts swivels on to the bench opposite Anna. He grabs at his iPad and swipes at the screen.

Blakemore gets in. Followed by Patterson. They both sit on the bench either side of Anna. Neither of them look at her. Anna stares at Blakemore, who has his head in his hands, and then Patterson. Patterson holds his phone and taps his heel vigorously.

'You've had loads of time to review the footage,' Blakemore barks at Roberts. 'Get out and go pick them up. Now.'

Roberts focuses on his iPad and swipes.

'I'm still looking,' he says, without glancing up from the screen.

Patterson reaches over to Roberts and pulls at his jacket.

'He said, *get out*,' Patterson hisses, up in Roberts's face. 'You can look for them on the go. My lord, is this how you train officers?' Patterson says to Blakemore. 'To be slow and insubordinate?'

'I only reply to my superior officer,' Roberts says, squaring up to Patterson.

'Just go,' Blakemore says. 'Please, PC Roberts.'

Roberts scratches at his face, looks at Anna and leaves the van.

The quiet that he leaves behind is deafening.

Patterson holds out his hands in front of Anna, fists clenched. He turns one fist and opens up his fingers so the palm is stretched out. Anna looks at it. There's a silver key sitting there. Small. Small enough to open her handcuffs.

Anna looks up at Patterson. He smiles. He throws the key up into the air. He catches it in his hand. He pulls at his belt and drops the key into his pants. He swallows. Looking at Anna the entire time.

'Looks like you're stuck here,' he says. 'Oh, shame.'

'Shame, shame, shame,' Blakemore says.

'Now,' Patterson says, over him. 'Which one of your idiot friends has the USB stick? Your idiot boyfriend or your idiot friend's idiot twin?'

'What USB stick?' Anna says, meekly. 'I don't know about any USB stick.'

Patterson kicks at her ankle violently. She flies forward, slipping off the bench and on to the floor.

Blakemore pulls her back up by her hair and places both of his hands gently on her cheeks. Anna tries to struggle but he holds her head tighter. Patterson lights up a cigarette. The confined space quickly reeks of smoke and old rotten tobacco, like an old man's coat.

'Who has the USB stick?' Blakemore says. 'Because I'm done waiting and I'm done chasing and quite frankly, I'm done being nice.' He looks up at Patterson. 'Yes, that's right. We've been nice up until now. Imagine us *not* nice.'

'I thought you weren't going to hurt me,' Anna says, scared.

Blakemore wrenches at her hair again. 'I only said I needed to return you to your mum like I found you. Who's to say how I found you . . .? Now,' he says, making his grip even tighter. 'Where is the USB stick?'

Anna can feel her ankle throbbing. Her scalp stings where her hair has been pulled.

'*What* USB stick?! I've told you, I don't know anything about a USB!' Anna hisses, her mouth dry.

'The one Sim gave them. We know they have it.'

'Why did you do it?'

'Do what?' Patterson says, the cigarette drooling from his lips.

'Why did you kill Sim?'

'Who says I did anything of the sort?' Patterson says. 'Come on, Blakemore. The clock is ticking. As I keep reminding you. Do what you need to. Let's get on with it.'

The air is acrid with smoke.

'OK now,' Blakemore says. 'I'm going to ask you a question. You're going to tell me the correct answer. And if you don't . . .'

Anna smiles and spits on the floor, channelling Taran. What would Taran do? Make a statement about her space?

'You'll beat up on a teenager?'

'You think I care how old you are?' Patterson says. 'This is so much bigger than you, than all of us.'

'Just give us a second, mate, will you?' Blakemore asks Patterson. Patterson takes a long drag on his cigarette then gets out of the van. He slams the door behind him.

Blakemore leans against the bench and takes out his own cigarette, lighting it and sucking it dry. He looks at Anna as he smokes. She stifles a cough. Because to cough would be to let him know that she is bothered. She feels a tickling burn at the base of her tongue.

She hears a familiar voice.

Mum?

She can hear arguing, protesting, out-of-breath sounds, high pitched but muffled through the van door. The voice is getting nearer. Anna doesn't look at the door, she keeps looking at Blakemore. He can see her trying not to panic. She can see him smirk. He knows she knows what's coming.

The door flings open and Anna's mum falls into a weeping heap in the van, her bangles clanging against the metal floor.

'Mum!' Anna calls, her face falling.

A grin creeps across the whole of Blakemore's face.

'Mum, you OK?' Anna asks.

'Anna?' her mum says, lifting her head in shock. She picks herself up to crouching, so she's resting on a bench. 'Why are you in cuffs? Oh, Anna, what have you done?'

'Mum, you OK?' Blakemore imitates.

'Mum,' Anna hisses. 'Mum, help me. I haven't done anything. Help me.'

'Right,' Patterson says as he jumps up into the van again, slamming the door shut behind him. 'Let's play a little game, shall we?'

He pulls out a gun.

Anna and her mother both recoil.

Patterson points the gun at Anna's mum. She flinches. He bangs the gun on the side of the van. *BANG*. The noise shudders through the tight space. Anna's mum jumps and loses her balance, falling to the floor and banging her head on the bench.

'You're a little bit jumpy, aren't you?' Patterson says, standing over Anna's mum and pressing the gun, hard, into her neck.

'No!' Anna screams. 'Stop it!'

'I'm going to ask you one more time,' Blakemore snarls at Anna, his spit splattering all over her face. 'Where is the USB stick? The one with the videos of your dad. Who has it?'

'What? Videos of my dad?' Anna says, caught off guard.

Her mum catches her eye and gives the tiniest shake of her head. Anna looks back at Patterson, panicking as she sees him push the gun further into her mum's face.

'Three . . .' Patterson counts. 'Two . . .'

'Wait! Stop, stop – I'll tell you everything, please,' Anna shouts, her face flooding with tears. 'I'll tell you everything you want to know.'

12.43 a.m.

Jamal stands up off Roberts's chest. Taran drops his balaclava on to the floor.

'So what?' Hari says, rolling pin raised. 'Are we just trusting anyone here? Just cos he says he needs our help . . .'

'Not yet,' Taran says.

Jamal pulls Roberts to his feet, slowly, with Taran and Hari standing guard over him.

Taran steps into Roberts's space so that he has to edge backwards. He trips and falls back on to a sofa. Jamal runs to the kitchen and rifles through drawers till he finds some string.

He runs back to the sofa and loops it around Roberts's wrists and his ankles.

Roberts is compliant. Smiling, even.

'What's so funny?' Taran snaps.

'Nothing,' he says. 'You're right not to trust me.'

'Where is Anna?' Jamal asks.

'Anna is fine,' Roberts says. 'She is fine. For the moment. But the more time ticks away, the more desperate these guys are getting. And I honestly don't know what they'll do when they become really desperate. They are not good people.'

'How did you find us?'

'Because I could hear you breathing, Jamal. In the bathroom. Patterson got a phone call and ran off to answer it so I came back in.'

'Is he gone?' Taran says.

'Yeah, I heard him run down the stairs.'

'You heard me, huh?' Jamal says.

'You sounded like you were breathing through a megaphone.'

Taran and Hari flash Jamal a look.

'Anyway, whatever, man, none of that matters. Where is Anna?' Taran asks.

'They're keeping her in a van. In front of the building. And they want that USB. Where is it?'

'How do you know about it?' Hari asks.

The question hangs as Taran fishes it out from her hoodie and holds it up.

'I have it. And I'm holding on to it.'

'OK, good. Listen, there is evidence on there that can release Anna's dad. And also prove what's happening here in the building. We need to leak it to the press. Or find some authorities who aren't corrupt. Make sure the mayor doesn't give NextGen that contract. Maybe this building can stay how it is. Maybe we can make a case for getting things like the lift fixed and better heating and all the things the building needs. Sim wanted to go the legal route. And I was happy to leave him to it so I wasn't exposed. But now? Goddamn it, let's bring it all down.'

'Why do you care so much?' Taran asks.

'Cos this is still my home.'

Taran nods and turns away. She can't breathe in this room.

She walks into the bathroom and stares at herself in the mirror.

She looks down at the toothbrushes, lined up neatly. The smallest is a Spider-Man one. Next to it is a framed photograph of a family. She recognises the kid. Definitely she's seen the kid before. She studies the photo and then goes back at herself in the mirror.

She is standing in front of the building, rapping away to anyone who will listen. Hari and Jamal and Anna are with her, forming a circle. Another rapper, MZ, is waiting for her turn, and Tek-Nique, MZ's friend, just spat and he is now nodding along appreciatively to Taran's bars. She is rapping about the election and how the politicians make decisions about people like her but would never come down and meet her and sit and have a cuppa and chat about the things that affect her.

A family is walking past, carrying shopping bags from the supermarket. They all stop to listen to her. She has not seen them before. The kid is wearing a Spider-Man costume and clutching something in her hand. She's smiling at Taran. Her mum tries to usher her to the door, but the kid protests. Taran keeps rapping, trying not to skip a beat or lose her place in the cypher or give any hint to MZ and Tek-Nique that she can fuck up occasionally.

The child is still resisting her mum's attempts to get her inside. In the struggle, the kid drops whatever she's holding on to the floor as she is pulled away.

It's her teddy.

Taran reaches down, without skipping a beat, picks the teddy up and returns it to the child, who beams at her.

'Thank you,' she says.

'No problem,' Taran says, ending her verse right there and throwing to MZ, who picks up the last bar.

'Problem, problem . . . we got bare problems,' MZ raps.

Taran waves at the kid as the family enter the building.

Taran picks up the photograph and smiles at the memory. She puts it back on the sink. She lets cold water out of the tap and cups her hand under it. She wipes the cold water against the back of her head.

She closes her eyes.

There's a knock on the door.

She hears her twin brother's voice.

'Sis, you OK in there?' Hari asks through the door.

'Yeah, cool,' she says.

'I'm sorry about Sim,' he says. 'I didn't know him. It was unfair of me to treat him like someone I knew when I clearly didn't.'

'Thanks, bro,' she says.

'I am sorry.'

She feels a tear fall quickly down her cheek. She doesn't want to do this, but in the moment, she realises that it is what she has needed to do all along.

She gives in to her tears and lets herself cry.

12.48 a.m.

Taran walks back into the room, drying her eyes. She stands taller.

'Tell us everything,' she says to Roberts. 'You grew up round here. So why have you turned against your community?'

'I haven't,' Roberts says. 'Believe it or not, I want to help. I don't like what's happening and I am trying. But you need to let me go so I can do what I'm doing.'

'What is that exactly?'

'I don't know all the details. It's complicated. There are a lot of different plates being spun here.'

'What do you mean "it's complicated"?' Jamal asks.

'I haven't been in all the discussions,' Roberts says. 'But I know that there is a serious time limit on getting this building emptied. Something to do with contracts and key performance indicators. NextGen Properties want to start getting the building ready to be knocked down. Very soon. Because of funding and city budgets. These city councils have their budgets for a short time and if they're not used, they get taken away. Everyone is operating at a loss. There are cuts everywhere. If the government can find ways to save money, it's gonna take that opportunity. And councils make decisions based on housing. Housing is everywhere. It makes jobs for people to build flats, creates wealth for the city when they're sold. Brings businesses into the area. Brings a new type of resident, with more money to spend on other things. Housing fuels everything. So, if a big housing company wants to buy some social housing that actually cost the council money, all the council has to do is sell the building, rehouse the residents elsewhere – preferably out of their district – and, boom, the city gets richer.'

'What about the people who live here?' Jamal asks.

'What about us?' Roberts replies. 'We don't count.'

'Empty Firestone House? Good luck with that, bruv. This place is always packed out,' Hari says.

'They don't need it empty tonight,' Roberts says. 'They just need the contracts signed and assurance that nothing, like Sim's evidence, is gonna backfire on them. Although, it being empty kinda helps.'

'All those residents who they're planning on rehousing, how do they expect to do that without a backlash?' Taran asks.

'Bit of community cohesion, some arts projects, maybe a nice free concert from a local celebrity done good and then moved out maybe?' Roberts says.

'Shiiiiit,' Jamal breathes.

'Rage. Everyone was there,' Taran says.

'So, the Rage concert?' Hari picks up the point. 'That on purpose?'

'Yes, I'm sure of it,' Roberts says. 'It's not on any of the posters, but it's been sponsored by NextGen Properties. They're a big property company. Run by some guy called Digby. His son's a low-ranking Conservative MP. They've built lots of complexes in London. Now they're here. This area is the focus for redevelopment. And the free concert

– that's just their PR to make this all look like a lovely thing for the benefit of the community, make the area look unified, right before it's torn apart.'

'Why are they on a time limit?' asks Taran.

'It's to do with contracts and funding. I think it's something like if the money isn't spent in time, the government thinks the council doesn't need it. Meanwhile, this is big business for NextGen. Redeveloping a large area in a city and flipping it into something luxury so they can sell off individual flats for a lot of money? They stand to make billions. Listen, right now, we need to get you out of here. The longer it takes to find you three, the more chance we have of saving the building. Cos I imagine NextGen won't like any loose ends. You all are loose ends that stop those contracts being signed. And I need to get back to Blakemore. Find out what I can.'

Taran rubs at her head. 'This is too much,' she says. 'I don't really know what to think. What are we supposed to do when we get out of here?'

'There's a hashtag, for the concert: "RageIsBack". Flood it. With the video from the USB.'

'We also have a video of Blakemore and Patterson killing Sim,' Jamal says. Hari hits him, but he continues, 'On Hari's phone. Which we no longer have.'

Roberts turns to Jamal.

'What?' Roberts says.

Taran can see the blood draining from his face. He looks shocked. He stares into the distance.

'There's a video as well?'

'Yeah,' Taran says quietly.

'This whole thing is beyond messed up. I . . . I'm so sorry, I . . .' Roberts's voice tails off.

'I don't want your apology,' Taran says. 'It's hard to not see you as one of them. I'm trying, but still.'

Roberts sighs. 'I'm still from here. I was born here. On floor seven. My mum still lives there. But they always have to come to see me. Because apparently I'm a sellout for joining the force. Imagine. I can't come to my childhood home to visit. I'm only allowed to come on official police business and people shout 'bacon' or whatever at me. I fell down the same stairs as everyone else here, ran with the same people, carried shopping bags up the same flights of stairs cos the lift wasn't working, did everything you lot all do. I thought I was doing a good thing joining the force.'

'Well, look at how well that's working out,' Hari says. 'How can we even trust you? How do we know you're on our side?'

'I gave Sim those files. I know where Anna is. And I can help you get to her.'

12.53 a.m.

Taran picks up a bread knife from the kitchen counter and walks over to Roberts. She saws at the string around his wrists until he is free.

Hari protests.

Taran flashes her twin a look that says, *This is happening. Let it.*

Roberts stands up and shakes out his limbs.

Taran senses her twin tense, ready, just in case.

'So,' Taran says. 'We've shown you trust. Now your turn. We need some detail. You gave Sim the USB stick that got him killed. How did you come to have it in the first place? Why did you give it to Sim?'

'And why didn't Mr Johnson use those videos at the time of the trial?' Jamal says. 'Surely it would have proved he was being intimidated?'

'We need answers, *PC Roberts*,' Taran says.

Roberts nods and silently walks over to the sink. He pours himself some water, and sips it slowly.

'Come on, dude,' Taran says. 'We're running for our lives. A bit of urgency, yeah?'

'OK, sure,' Roberts says. 'But as I said, I'm still figuring some of this out myself. Still piecing it all together. But I will tell you what I do know . . .'

Footsteps stomp down the corridor and Jamal flinches. Taran steps towards Roberts to block him.

The footsteps carry on past the front door.

Roberts sits on the sofa. Jamal flops down next to him, folding his arms and looking at the police officer.

'It's a long, strange story . . .' Roberts says. 'Where to start? OK. You know I used to use that youth club? I've been going there since I was kid, man. Mr Johnson's door was always open. Always. For whatever you needed help with. Me, I really wanted to get into the army. That's all I ever wanted to do. He helped me find out all the things you needed to get in. And you know what, when it said on the list that asthma could disqualify you, he kept being, like, *could*. Could. That was Mr Johnson all over – always encouraging you not to give up hope. But I didn't listen. The army seemed too hard for me, so I went into the police force instead. Anyway, I spent a lot of my time at the youth club. When I found out he was trying to organise a CAT, I thought I'd help him. I had some money left over from when my dad died and all the equipment at the youth club just looked dead. So I bought five iPads that he could use to get young people to roll through. Play Candy Crush, watch YouTube – whatever. That youth club needed to stay open. It was such a part of the community. Silas, Sim and CJ . . . we all went there over the years, to name just a few. So yeah, anyway, Sim and I set up those iPads with my iCloud settings so that no one could be scamming the password off Mr Johnson and downloading bare apps. One day, Blakemore approaches me at work and asks if I grew up in Firestone House. And I'm like, "Yeah, I did." He says, "Good. I want you to start placing yourself there. We've got news of big dealers doing business out there and there are major investors in the area wanting to know if it's safe and crime-free. All we need you to do is observe. Don't make any arrests. Monitor. Gather information. Don't ruin any other ongoing investigations by causing trouble. It's potentially primed for redevelopment, but it's already described in the press as a no-go zone. Maybe it could be turned into something residential." I'm like, "It's a city, what do they expect?" He's like, "Do not question me. This request is coming from up high." I'm like, "Bruv, I grew up round there and I'm now a copper – how do you expect them to treat me?" He didn't care.'

'Get to the point, man. What's this got to do with Sim and Mr Johnson?' Hari asks.

Taran shoots him a look as if to say, *Allow it*.

'So one day, when I'm just watching the courtyard, showing my face and whatnot, Sim approaches me and asks for a chat,' Roberts continues.

'What did he want?' Jamal says, leaning forward.

'He asks about a man called Michael Patterson, who's claiming to be a tenant, and has joined the resident management board that Mr Johnson sits on. He's upselling this place called NextGen Properties to them. Hardly anyone here owns their flat. But Patterson is talking about transforming the area and how the residents can benefit from the regeneration. Also, he keeps blocking the board signing off on Mr Johnson's CAT request. And the thing is . . .'

'Michael Patterson ain't no resident.'

'Nope,' says Roberts. 'So here's where it gets interesting. Mr Johnson follows Patterson from a residents' meeting one day – an occasion when he's been particularly difficult. And guess where he's heading?'

'If the answer isn't NextGen Properties HQ, somewhere fancy, then bloody hell you're stringing this one out,' Hari says.

'Exactly,' Roberts says. 'Mr Johnson follows him to the offices of NextGen Properties. Sim gets in touch with me and asks if I'd heard of NextGen. I look into it and they seem just like any other property developer around. He also asks me about this Patterson guy but I haven't come across him. So Sim, being Sim, wants to prove Patterson works for NextGen, rather than him being a concerned tenant. He sets up a fake Hotmail address for Patterson and phones NextGen HR to ask them to forward him the receipt of the bank transfer for the last job he did, to his new email address. Those idiots are completely taken in by it. And he gets this pdf of a bank statement. So Sim has this evidence that Patterson is taking money from NextGen. But that's not enough for anything just yet. So he sits on it and waits.'

Taran feels the warmth of pride in Sim wash over her.

'What about the videos? Why was Mr Johnson filming these conversations?' she asks.

'I don't know for sure, but he clearly had suspicions about Patterson, as he followed him from that meeting. Whatever the reason, I'm glad he did. Because he used one of the iPads. And it saved to my iCloud. And months after the trial, guess what I find when I run out of storage space for my photos? Two videos I don't remember making. And guess what they are?'

'The ones of Patterson and Blakemore threatening Mr Johnson,' Jamal says.

'Innit,' Roberts says. 'Along with the bank statement, there are two videos that show a corrupt police officer working with the employee of a housing developer to threaten a resident to move out. If Mr Johnson had got the CAT and had taken over ownership of that youth club, then that would have been it, they wouldn't have been able to raze Firestone House to the ground, even if the council had granted them the contract. So they stitched him up and got him sent to prison. To clear the way.'

'This USB could properly expose Patterson, and Blakemore,' Taran says, clasping her palms together.

'Yes,' Roberts replies. 'They're probably terrified NextGen will make them take the fall if you make this USB public. Even without your other video, it's enough evidence to stop NextGen Properties getting the contract. They stand to lose billions.'

Jamal holds his hand up. 'Hold on a minute,' he says. 'If the videos are in your iCloud, then we have them without needing the files on the USB.'

'I took the videos off my iCloud,' Roberts says. 'I didn't want any of this leading back to me. That way, I could stay the man on the inside without compromising myself. I gave them to Sim because he'd know what to do with them. If I knew he'd die for them . . .' He tails off and holds a fist to his mouth. He stammers. 'L-listen, I didn't want to compromise myself further. I . . .'

He steadies himself.

'Look, bruv . . .' Taran starts to say, but then she feels emotion well up in her too.

A crackle comes through on Roberts's radio. It snaps Taran out of it.

'Roberts, where are you?' Taran recognises the voice immediately. Blakemore. 'Any sign? If not, come back here – we need to have a word.'

Roberts stands up.

'I'm on my way,' he says into the radio.

Taran folds her arms. 'So, what – you're gonna go hang out with your work colleagues?' she says.

'Yes,' he replies. 'To check that Anna is OK.'

Jamal stands up at the mention of Anna's name. 'Take me with you,' he begs. 'Say you found me separated from these guys. Please.'

'Jamal, what are you saying?' Hari says. 'We can't keep splitting up. We are stronger together.'

'Hari's right,' Taran says. 'Let Inspector Dibble over here go and check in on our girl.'

'You three stay here. OK?' Roberts says. 'No one knows you're here except me. You stay and let me handle things. Now, Taran, can I have the USB stick please? I'll take it from here.'

'No fucking way,' Taran says, stepping to Roberts. 'You didn't want to compromise yourself so you gave it to Sim to sort out. You didn't want to do it back then. What? So now his death has made you a man of action? No way. You check on our girl. You make sure no one else gets hurt. OK? The love of my life died for this evidence and I am not letting it out of my sight.'

'OK,' Roberts says. 'I know Sim's death is on me . . .'

He pauses.

'Whatever you do, however you start it, make sure it's loud,' he says. Taran wants to smile at him using her lyric without even realising it. 'The hashtag, for the concert: "RageIsBack". Flood it. With the videos on the USB. And, Taran . . . I'm sorry for your loss.'

He leaves.

1.07 a.m.

Taran is flicking through a poetry book by Kate Tempest she found on the coffee table, while Hari and Jamal search the flat for a router, hoping the wi-fi password is on it. Taran likes the title – *Hold Your Own*. It sounds like something she would say. Taran's struck by a particular bit in one of the poems:

> *Foul smell of the things that we do to escape*
> *There is no glamour in this. No rock and roll.*
> *This is just endings. This is just grief.*

When Dad died, Taran thought the feeling of loss would completely overwhelm her every second of the day. And when that didn't happen, she ended up wracked with guilt. Sometimes she forgot. Sometimes she moved on. Sometimes she was left rigid with sadness. Sometimes she thought about him and remembered something nice. Each time, she beat herself up for not thinking about him the way she felt she should. 'Foul smell of the things that we do to escape' indeed.

She thinks about phoning her mum.

Everything recently has been about making sure her mum doesn't need to worry about her or Hari. They have an agreement to fly under the radar as much as possible. Not missing too much college, doing all their coursework and assignments on time, helping each other where needed, all so that there isn't anything worrying Mum.

But money is also a concern. So Hari works two jobs, sometimes three, to save up cash for his move to London. He figures that all the proper jobs are there. He can send money home; maybe Mum won't have to work so hard then. And Taran knows the only thing she's really good at is rapping. She has every confidence that when her mixtape drops, that'll be it. Extra funds to help them all.

Their poor mum.

Taran was mad at her for so long. She thought that Mum throwing herself into her work, taking herself away from her kids, was a shoddy move. But slowly, she came to realise that you do what you need to do to get by. And all the anger she had towards her mum was because she had never seen her cry. But why would you allow yourself the space to do that when you were too worried about providing for two kids? And if you have to shove aside your grief so that you can make ends meet, you do it.

She misses her mum as much as she misses her dad.

Taran looks over at Hari, who is punching in a password from the router. He groans as it doesn't work. Jamal tries it. Hari tries again. They both stamp their feet in frustration.

'They must have changed it,' Jamal says to Taran who nods.

Taran is still too lost in thought to register what Jamal says.

Mum did what she did for her family. Out of love.

Mr Johnson did what he did for this community. Out of love.

Sim did what he did for the residents who needed him. Out of love.

She raps about her new community and the people who need each other. Out of love.

Anna. We need to rescue Anna. Out of love.

'Guys,' she says. Hari stops punching. He and Jamal face her. 'Allow Roberts. Let's get Anna back. If we can't get online, we're just useless here anyway.'

'About bloody time,' Jamal says, punching one-two at the air.

1.11 a.m.

There's a key in the lock.

Panicking, Taran grabs Hari and Jamal and they run into one of the bedrooms.

Hari protests. 'There's no way out of here . . .'

Taran can't think. This is a survival moment. Her chest beats, sweat plummeting down her back like she's a kid on a waterslide.

'Shush,' she says.

They're in a child's bedroom. There are Spider-Man posters all over the walls. Avengers bedsheet. Spidey pillowcase. Jamal trips over a toy on the floor.

'Ouch,' he says, but is shushed again by Taran.

She listens.

Woman: You didn't lock the door! Ollie, you have to lock the door . . . You can't just leave it open.

Man: Babe, I grew up in this flat. It's fine. Everyone knows me.

Woman: That's not really a comfort. Anyway, what a waste of time. What was all that about?

Man: Dunno.

Child: Mummy, I'm sleepy.

Woman: I know, darling. Let's get you back to be— Ollie, has someone been in here?

Man: What? No. Everyone's still outside.

Woman: What's that string on the floor? Also, is that a half-eaten banana?

Taran looks at Jamal, who ate half of the banana and left it on the counter. She edges back from the door, steps on something on the ground – maybe a Lego house – and it makes a crunching sound.

Woman: Ollie, did you hear that?

Man [whispering]: Shhh.

Woman: Ollie, is there someone in the flat?

Man: Beth, take Gem outside. Let me have a look.

Taran hears the metal *plink* of a knife being taken slowly and quietly out of a drawer. It's got to be a knife. You wouldn't attack someone with a spoon.

Hari tenses but Taran waves at him to calm down. They are stuck. There is nowhere for them to go. And they can't have these guys call the police. They can't risk Blakemore being alerted to where they are.

Woman: I'm calling the police.

Taran whispers, 'No, no, no—'

Jamal rushes to the door. He nudges it open with a toe, gently, carefully. He holds his hands up and steps out into the main bit of the flat.

Taran follows on his heels. If Jamal's restrained, next thing that'll happen is the police will come busting through the door.

Hari is rooted to the spot, terrified.

'My name is Jamal Ahmed,' Jamal says, slowly. 'We mean you no harm. We were hiding from someone. We didn't take anything. Well, a banana. Maybe some cheese. Sorry. Please. We'll go. Sorry.'

The man yelps in shock.

'Hello, I need the police.' It's the woman on the phone. 'There's someone in my flat.'

'Please hang up,' Jamal says. 'We're in danger.'

Jamal jumps back as the man wails in terror, his eyebrows pursed, and stabs at the air between them with a sharp kitchen knife.

Jamal collides into Taran, who puts her arms around his chest from behind and pulls him back into the bedroom. The man, trying another wild stab, slashes at Jamal's torso and cuts into his arm.

Jamal cries out in pain.

'Please, stop,' Taran says. 'Please, we're not robbing you.'

'Mummy, singing lady. Singing lady,' the kid says. 'It's her. No problem. No problem. Mummy, it's her. She's nice.'

Jamal is shaking.

Taran looks at the kid and smiles.

'Mummy, mummy,' the kid says. 'It's her. She's nice. She's nice.'

'I know you,' Beth says, hanging up the phone. 'Ollie, put down the knife.'

He starts to lower the knife but Hari chooses the wrong moment to appear in the doorway.

Ollie raises his weapon again.

'Daddy!' whimpers the kid. Her mum scoops her up.

'Sir,' Taran says, swivelling Jamal away from the knife. 'Please, sir . . . stop, please. We are in your space. I get it. We're hiding from some bad people and we dashed in here.'

All Taran can hear is the deep breathing of all of them. The floorboards creak behind her.

'Ollie,' his wife says.

Hari steps out into the room and flexes his knuckles. Ollie hesitates, looks at Hari and then at Jamal and the trail of blood down his arm.

'I did that,' he says. 'Oh my god. I did that. Are you OK?'

He turns to his wife, momentarily confused. Taran uses the opportunity to ease Jamal to the floor. He drips blood on to the lino. She crouches next to him and eases off his tracksuit top to see where he's been cut. Luckily, it's a slice across the fleshy bit of the arm, near the shoulder. It bleeds enough to look awful but isn't serious. Hari passes her the bandana tied to his wrist.

She is about to wrap it around Jamal's arm when Beth clears her throat.

'Do you want something clean?' she asks.

She is holding a tea towel. She passes it to Ollie, who hands it to Taran.

Taran ties the tea towel around Jamal's arm, tight. He cries out in pain.

'I'm really sorry,' Ollie says. 'Like, really, really sorry. Oh my god, I've never . . .'

'It's fine,' Taran says. 'I'm sorry we violated your space. You OK, sis?' Taran says to the kid, who puts her hands over her eyes and squirms.

She buries her face in her mum's shirt.

'Singing lady,' she whispers loudly.

Hari walks over to Ollie and gestures to his hand. Ollie looks down at it. He's still holding the knife. Hari smiles.

'I'll wash it for you,' he says. It still has Jamal's blood on it.

Ollie drops the knife into Hari's hand. Hari takes the knife to the sink.

Taran watches as he washes the blood away. She turns back to Jamal.

'You cool?' she asks.

'I've been slashed, what do you think?' Jamal moans.

'Technically, you've been a little bit cut, not slashed,' Hari says.

Jamal snorts a laugh.

'Sorry,' Ollie says. 'I thought—'

'Don't apologise,' Jamal interrupts. 'I get it. You were protecting your family.'

Taran squeezes Jamal's non-injured shoulder and stands up. She watches as Hari dries the knife and places it back in the cutlery drawer.

Beth stands directly behind Ollie, still holding the kid. 'Are you OK?' she asks. 'You said people are chasing you? Some bad people?'

'Yeah,' Taran says. 'Some bad people. We saw them do something they shouldn't have done and now they're chasing us. How come you guys aren't outside? Didn't you hear the fire alarm?'

Ollie nods.

'Yes,' he says. 'It took us ages to get down – nearly an hour, because of the slow moving on the stairs. And then Gem lost her teddy so we had to find it and then when we did get to the bottom, the alarm had stopped and we thought everything was fine. And it was late, so we just came back up. Naughty, I know. What are you going to do? Can we help? We can phone the police. Are you in trouble?'

Taran feels a rush of warmth. Beth and Ollie started off terrified, ready to call the police. But as soon as they recognised Taran, knew she came from the block and realised she and her friends were in trouble, it changed to concern. *Community*, Taran thinks. *In the end, you'll always want to help one of your own.*

'We'll be OK,' Taran says. 'The less you know, the better. The less involved you are. I'm just sorry that we came into your space. The door was unlocked and we needed a place to check ourselves for a bit. Jamal will be OK. It isn't a deep cut. It's all love.'

She reaches down and helps Jamal get up.

'Please don't tell anyone you saw us,' Jamal says. 'Especially the police.'

'Seriously,' Hari echoes.

'Are the police the bad people?' the kid asks.

'Sometimes,' Taran says.

She, Hari and Jamal head towards the door.

1.17 a.m.

Outside the flat, the air is cool and the building feels empty. Taran isn't sure how she can tell that there isn't much life around her, with all the doors shut, but she can. It just feels dead, flat.

All she knows is, they need to get to that van, and to Anna.

They head towards the sixth floor stairwell.

Hari helps her with Jamal, who insists he is OK, but he's holding his hand over where he's been cut.

He needs to have it seen to, Taran thinks.

She yawns. Hari catches it.

Her bed feels so far away. Her flat feels like somewhere she can never go home to. And even if she could, she would not be the same person who woke up there this morning. So much has happened. So much has changed. She has to try to envisage a life without Sim.

'Yo, Taran,' she hears, and she stops moving.

She recognises the voice, but it's not her brother, or Jamal. It's more snarly.

It's CJ. He emerges from above, a black hoodie over his head. She flinches.

'They've locked everyone who went down for the fire alarm out of the building. Put police tape up. Those two dickhead policemen,' he says. 'We're all trapped now. In here. The second any of us walk out that door, they'll see us.'

He sighs and lights up a cigarette. The stairwell is filled with the smoke.

'People must be screwing,' Taran says.

'Yep,' says CJ. 'My man on the outside says there are a lot of pissed off people. It's a hot night, it's late . . . I can't see this going well.'

'What do we do then?' Jamal asks.

'OK,' CJ says. 'I called a few people. We have options, depending on where we get out from, but whatever, they're going to get us far away from Firestone House. You with me?'

'No,' Taran says. 'We need to get Anna back.'

'I know,' CJ says. 'That's part of my plan. Why do you think I have this?'

He pulls out a gun from his hoodie and hands it to Jamal, who panics and passes it to Hari.

'Why do you have it?' Jamal asks.

'You gonna go and shoot up a bunch of police?' Taran asks. 'You're an idiot.'

'What did you say?' CJ says, squaring up to her. 'I ain't a killer. Or an idiot. But it's a good intimidation tool. These cops ain't got guns, have they? Just batons and notepads and shit.'

Taran looks at Hari holding the gun. She can see the moment of hesitation in her brother's eye. Hari looks almost comfortable with it.

'Easy, bro,' she says, calmly.

'It feels different to Call of Duty,' says Hari.

Hari looks at the gun, then he points it at the air and aims, squinting, closing one eye. He has never held a gun before, Taran knows. She has. It's heavy. It's cold. It's all the clichés. It looks so robust. So powerful. She can see it in Hari. He's thinking, *I don't want to like this but I do. It's good.* Then he seems to remember himself and hands the gun back to CJ.

'What made you come back?' Taran asks CJ softly.

'I was nearly clear and something kept hitting me in the skull. My brother's gone, and he was always the kinder one. What would he do? Where are his responsibilities, you know? And I was like, I can't leave those young ones up there by themselves, being chased by police. No way. I came back to get you out with me.'

CJ offers the gun back to Hari.

'That's my spare,' he says.

'Nope. I'm not taking that, man,' Hari says, shaking his head, nervously.

Taran nods at him, thinking, *Hold it down, bruv*.

'Why not? We need to get out of here. By any means.'

'And there's no other way?'

'Have you seen what's happening in these corridors? We're being hunted, man.'

Hari shakes his head.

'Whatever happens tonight, I have to be true to my own code,' he says. 'No guns.'

CJ laughs. 'Ain't you seventeen? Who has a code at seventeen?'

'What about me?' Taran says. 'You not offering me one because I'm a girl?'

CJ grimaces with frustration.

'No, cos you're stood behind me. Come on. Here you go.' He thrusts the returned gun at her, shaking it furiously.

'No, I'm good,' Taran says. 'Hari's right. We've had enough of guns today.'

'Fine, fine, whatever. I guess I'll be the one protecting you lot then.'

'We don't need your protection,' Taran hisses. 'Thank you for coming back for us. But once we get out of this place, we're going to get Anna.'

CJ puts the gun deep in his hoodie. 'You said we were stronger together, earlier,' CJ says. 'I like that.'

He looks at the gang of youngers before him.

'Justice for Sim,' he says.

12.54 a.m.

Anna can hear the roar of a crowd outside, confused and angry. But her focus is on her mum. Patterson is holding a gun to her mum's head. Anna can't think.

'We believe Sim Francis passed your friends illegally obtained videos showing your father and me having a disagreement,' Patterson says. 'Now, stripped of its context, it looks like that disagreement places me in a bad light. I would like access to the videos, to put them back into their proper context. So, where are they, and where is the USB stick?'

'Honestly, this is the first time I've heard about the videos, and the USB stick,' Anna says.

Patterson tuts and leans into Anna's mum.

Mrs Johnson whimpers with fear. 'You do know about them, darling, you do. Sim came round this morning. He said he has evidence. Does Taran have it? Where is she?'

'How do you know this?' Anna says.

Anna is confused. Why would Mum tell the police anything? Mum is asking her questions; these policemen are asking her questions; there's a gun. It's a lot. She puts her fingers to her temples.

'Where is the goddamn USB stick?' Patterson asks again.

'I can't think,' Anna suddenly shouts. 'Give me a second.'

'You don't have a second,' Patterson says. 'We're closing in on your friends. And when we find them, they're gonna pay for making us run around all night chasing them.'

Mrs Johnson's eyes widen. 'What are you going to do?' she asks.

Anna watches as Blakemore's body language changes, becoming fidgety. He leans into Patterson.

'Let's take a break,' Blakemore says. 'I need a fag. You.' He points at Anna's mum. 'Convince your daughter.' He taps his finger against his temple. 'Because I'm about to run out of threats.'

Patterson puts the gun back in his belt, tuts and follows Blakemore out of the van.

In the silence, Anna tries to control her breathing. She feels like she could burst into tears at any second.

'Mum, what are you doing here?' she asks.

Mrs Johnson leans in to her daughter.

'Darling,' she says. 'We don't have much time. Sim told us he had evidence that Dad's innocent. We need to find him, and we need to get that evidence to the proper authorities. They'll know what to do. They can do whatever they need to do for your father but they can't do anything if your friends are playing hide and seek with it. They need to bring it to us. Imagine what it could mean for your father.'

'Mum,' Anna says. 'Sim . . . he's—'

'Sim was so sure about this evidence,' Mrs Johnson interrupts. 'I know Sim's reputation wasn't good in the block, his or his brother's, but he's changed. He's always willing to help out, do good things for people in need. And when he helped your dad with the CAT, I knew he was worth believing in.'

'Mum,' Anna says. 'Stop—'

'We *need* to find Sim,' Mrs Johnson says. 'He has the evidence. Once he hands that over to these men, that's it. We can both go home. Let's just give them what they want. They can use it to help your father. They're the law.'

'Mum,' Anna says again. 'Sim . . .'

'Yes,' Mrs Johnson says, breathlessly. 'Where is he? These people, Blakemore and Patterson, they're aggressive. They're dangerous. Nothing like the police we usually have round here. Like PC Roberts – he grew up around here, I went to school with him. Two or three years below. He may have moved away from Firestone, but he never really left.'

'Sim is dead!' Anna shouts, surprising herself. 'Mum. Listen. He's dead. These men, they . . .'

Mrs Johnson freezes. Something changes in her eyes. She swallows, then continues as if she's heard nothing. 'When this is over, we're leaving . . . I have cousins in Birmingham. And we have some money saved. We'll start again in Birmingham. You know what they have there? A Harvey Nichols—'

'Mum!' Anna sighs. 'Are you for real? Are you even listening to me? These men killed Sim! He's *dead*.'

'You can't bring up children around here,' Mrs Johnson continues. 'Discarded chicken bones and empty cans everywhere. I can't bear to watch the neighbourhood disintegrate. So we're going to relocate when Dad gets out. What is keeping us here? Certainly no family or friends. You can finish your schooling in Birmingham. And the uni. Lord above, now that's a university. Eh, Anna?'

'Chicken bones?' Anna sobs. 'Sim died so you don't have to step on chicken bones?'

Anna is crying. Her face stings as tears stream down it. She can't wipe them so they collect as a moustache on her top lip. She licks them away.

'Darling,' Mrs Johnson says.

'Mum, please,' Anna cries.

They fall into silence.

Mrs Johnson looks at her daughter. 'I'm sorry,' she says, eventually breaking the stillness.

Then she says it again, louder.

'For what?' Anna says.

'Yes, for what?' Blakemore says, jumping back into the van. 'Oh, does she not know?'

'Know what?' Anna says.

'Oh, Cynthia,' Blakemore says. 'Your own daughter. Tut-tut. Anyway, your time is now up, Anna Johnson. Where are your friends? Where is the USB stick?'

1.24 a.m.

As they walk down the stairs, Taran tries to stay as far away from CJ as she can. The USB is sitting, sweaty, in the palm of her hand just in case he tries to grab it, like he did with Hari's phone.

'Why do you do it, CJ?' Jamal breaks the silence.

'Do what?' CJ asks.

'What you do . . . the job you do. Why do you do it? Why

don't you work in a shop or as an accountant or something? Why are you doing what you do?'

'That's a stupid question. I'm my own boss – I choose my own hours and I make money. And I'm in an industry that ain't ever going away. So, you know what? Why not? Beats the other option.'

Taran knows that CJ did very well at school and even did a semester studying law at university before dropping out because he was worried about being able to pay the fees. Sim had told her his brother was adamant he wouldn't run up debt. He also said that when CJ had enough money to pay for that degree, that's what he planned to do.

'So, I been thinking about all this NextGen shit,' CJ says. 'And it reminded me of Wasim.'

'Wasim from . . .' Taran doesn't finish. She knows who Wasim is.

CJ pauses.

'Yeah, that Wasim, from Waterbridge House. He asked to meet. It's not like me and Wasim have ever had beef, but that's because we've respected all our boundaries and geographies. My brother and I went to school with him. And we would beat on him and his boys all the time in Year Seven. Back then, the rivalry meant something else; it was about standing your ground rather than keeping it. But we're cool now. It's just weird he wanted to meet.'

'So what happened?' Taran asks.

'Come on,' Hari says. 'We have to go. Now.'

'One sec, bruv,' Taran says back.

She gestures to CJ to carry on.

'Wasim texted me. I'm not even sure how he got this number. Who knows. Anyway, he asked if he could roll through the manor and see me for a few minutes. He was willing to come to me,' CJ says. 'And I thought, that has to mean something. He must want my help.'

'And?'

'He's all, "Bruv, can we talk?" *Screw it*, I think. *Let's see what this man has to say.* So I get in his car and he's all like, "Bruv, I'm not here for any other reason than to give you a warning shot, OK. Don't say I ain't looking out for my bredrens. Read this." And Wasim thrusts a letter over to me. It's an eviction notice. The building Wasim lives in, Waterbridge House, has been condemned because it has failed some fire safety tests and the estate is being sold off to a private building company, NextGen Properties. They plan to renovate the area into the next dream place to be for upwardly mobile young professionals.'

'So they're doing it there too?'

'Yeah.'

'But it's messier here,' Taran says. 'Cos there's a video of some illegal strong-arming they did.'

'Yeah, it's not for nothing Mr Johnson is in jail, you know?' CJ replies.

'Taran, come on!' Jamal says this time, as he walks on ahead of her.

'Wasim said current residents have first dibs on the new flats when they're built in two years' time, and they get to pay whatever the going market rate is then.' CJ shakes his head. 'And they get that privilege for *one week*, bruv. A one week head start on the rest of their lives. Imagine.'

'So, wait, where they moving Wasim to in the meantime?' Taran asks. 'They have to move them, right? They have to give them somewhere else to live.'

'Into UKIP country – maybe that's how they'll convince us

to go back to where we came from, ya get me. Maybe that's been the plan all along. Get us comfortable. Let us set up communities. Pull the rug from underneath us.'

'Yeah, it's messed up,' Taran agrees. 'All of this floor, it's probably gonna be a heated swimming pool for some dickhead who earns millions. You're on the spot where they'll put the radiators to keep his towels warm. Firestone House is next. The move is happening now. It's just a lot more violent this time.'

'You should have seen the brochure Wasim had,' CJ says. 'The buildings. Damn. Seeing what they think this place could look like. It was like a scene from *Blade Runner*, all futuristic and clean and perfect looking. Everything was this cold blue. This is what those people think is the best possible version of us. All these people eating fish dinners on the balcony, laughing into their glasses of white wine. The models are all white people too.'

'Standard.'

'I can't see myself in that picture,' he says.

1.43 a.m.

Jamal waits beside Hari as Taran and CJ approach them. Jamal can tell they've been having some serious conversation. Who'd have thought any of them would ever say more than two words to CJ?

'Waterbridge House is going down too,' Taran says. 'Damn.'

'NextGen,' CJ says.

'NextGen,' Jamal echoes.

CJ and Jamal lead the charge down the stairs. Hari and Taran are close behind.

They make it down to floor two, where CJ stops and turns to everyone. 'All we have to do is get out the door and some people will meet us and help get you guys into cars. Get us out of here, innit. Then we can work out how to leak the stuff, and how to get your girl back, Jamal.'

'What if we're seen?' Jamal says. 'We need to be smart. People are milling about in their pyjamas and coats.'

'So what?' CJ says. 'It's people.'

'So, we need to blend into that crowd,' Jamal replies. 'We need to look like we've been woken up in the middle of the night, innit.'

'How do you propose we blend in?' CJ says.

Jamal turns to the nearest flat door and tests the lock. It's shut. He moves up the corridor, testing out the doors. The third flat down, he finds an open door. He runs in and runs out, coming back with two raincoats, a long cotton mac and a leather jacket. He gives a raincoat to Taran.

'OK, so we're incognito,' Jamal asks. 'Now we pretend we've woken up.'

'So we stride down there and pretend we're evacuees?'

'Yeah, man, they're looking for four hoodies – you think they're checking faces? They're checking street uniforms. Allow the hoodies. Let's wear these posh people's coats, blend in, and then once we're in the courtyard, we can go find Anna. No one's going to be beating on us in public, in plain view of all the residents, right?'

'Worth a try,' Hari says.

Taran nods her approval.

CJ shrugs. 'Better than nothing, I guess,' he says, putting on the mac and hiding his guns in the pockets.

Taran, putting on her raincoat, looks at him and laughs.

'So,' she says. 'When we get to the bottom, we should split into two – me and Hari, and you two – and we go get Anna out of the van. We avoid Blakemore, we avoid Patterson, we avoid all po-po. We don't start anything.'

'I know that you want to go about this in this way,' CJ hisses, 'but I have a hunger for revenge for my brother right now.'

Taran stares him down.

'What you do once we get Anna back is your business. But this is the plan. The game-over situation isn't killing these guys, it's making them pay. We have a video of them committing a murder, remember?'

CJ nods.

They move.

1.34 a.m.

Anna is confused. She flicks her eyes between her mum and their captors. Her stomach is churning. There's a discordant white hiss in her head that's making it impossible for her to think. She can't focus.

'Mum, what does he mean?'

Mrs Johnson leans forward on her bench, trying to grab her daughter's hands. Anna stiffens and moves back.

'Oh, darling,' Mrs Johnson says, dismissively. 'He's just being silly. Don't worry about it. Be quiet.'

Anna hates it, always being told to be quiet, to not worry, to stop thinking. Her mum is on a mission to make her feel anxious about every thought she has.

'Babes, you gonna tell her?' Blakemore says.

Cynthia and Anna both look up at him. Anna can feel sweat on the back of her neck. *Babes?*

'Martin,' Cynthia says, softly. 'Give us a moment please.'

'I'll give you a moment,' Blakemore says, jumping out of the van and lighting a cigarette while he closes the door a little. 'Cynthia, please find out what we need to know. Quickly.'

Anna's mum waits until Blakemore is out of earshot.

'Darling,' she says. 'You need to get out of here. You need to get that USB stick, give it to me and I'll take care of the rest. I didn't know Sim was . . . Otherwise we don't—' She stops. 'Anna, I'm so sorry. This has escalated beyond my control and I'm scared for your friends. You, I can save. But the others. While they have the USB stick, we're in danger. They're in danger.'

Cynthia hands her phone to Anna.

'Mum,' Anna says. 'What is going on? Why did that man call you babes?'

'Phone Taran,' Cynthia says, ignoring her daughter's questions. She pronounces it properly, Anna notices, something she never does. A slight 'th' on the first T and 'ahhhh' as in 'bar' not 'aaaa' as in 'arrogant'. 'Phone her. Tell her to bring it here. And it'll be OK.'

Anna shakes her head at her mum and starts inching down the bench to the doors of the van.

'Mum,' she says. 'What have you done?'

Cynthia puts her hand on Anna's knee. 'Phone Taran,' she says, firmer this time.

'Mum, tell me what's going on?' Anna says, as a tear streams down her face.

'Please, darling, where is the USB stick?'

'I don't know,' Anna says.

'This is for our future. A fresh start, that's what this family needs. Right? Come on, Anna, darling,' Cynthia says.

Anna blurts, through tears, 'Why are you doing this, Mum?'

'For us,' Cynthia replies, calmly.

'Mum . . .' Anna says. 'Did you know Dad was innocent?'

Cynthia thinks for a second and is about to say something when the van door opens. Anna jumps, turning to see Blakemore.

'Cynthia,' he says, 'I hope you have the information we need.'

Blakemore takes Cynthia's hand in his.

'Now's not the time, Martin,' she hisses.

Anna's heart stops. Her brain can't compute what she's seeing.

Blakemore bends down to kiss Cynthia but she pushes him away.

'What are you doing, Martin?' she hisses.

'Does she not know about Birmingham?' he says, holding on to Cynthia's hand even though she is trying to pull it away.

Anna feels physically sick. She doesn't know what's happening.

She feels the tension in her legs, the restlessness telling her to get out of here. She feels itchiness in her hands, willing her to just go. There is no one at the back of the van. Patterson is nowhere to be seen.

'Martin, STOP,' Cynthia says, then turns to Anna. 'Darling, let me explain. I love your dad very much, but—'

'Are you two together?' Anna says. 'You don't want Dad released, do you?'

Blakemore smiles. He holds his hands out to Anna.

He laughs.

'Just call me Dad,' he says.

Anna throws up all over his shoes.

1.40 a.m.

Anna looks up at her mum. Cynthia has pulled herself away from Blakemore. She reaches out to Anna, wiping the corner of Anna's mouth. Anna spits out some bile on to the floor.

'Mum, you betrayed our family,' Anna says.

Blakemore swears as he dabs at his shoes with tissue.

'Babes,' he says. 'Can you give me a hand?'

'You promised,' Cynthia says, suddenly angry. 'You promised to let me tell Anna in my own time. What have you done? You've ruined everything.'

Blakemore shrugs. 'She had to find out sooner or later. She's a big girl.'

'She's my daughter,' Cynthia says. 'How dare you?'

Blakemore moves to hug her.

Mum looks angry, Anna thinks. *I've not seen her mad like this in a while.*

Cynthia slaps Blakemore across the face. Blakemore laughs.

She slaps him again, then turns to Anna.

'Go,' her mum says. 'I've made a mistake, letting you find out like this. Go, find your friends. Go, now.'

Cynthia goes to slap Blakemore a third time but he grabs her hand.

'No one is going anywhere,' he says. 'Especially Anna.'

Cynthia shoves Blakemore, sending him crashing into the wall of the van. She moves towards him, her arms outstretched. She scratches at his eyes.

'You ruined everything,' Cynthia shouts. 'You were supposed to be my ticket out of this dump.'

Blakemore grabs her hand with his meaty fists and pulls her towards him roughly. She winces in pain.

He drags her close, saying he's sorry, whispering things into her hair. He keeps calling her babes and saying it's going to be OK. Cynthia whimpers.

Anna, realising she has a clear run to the door, stands up and gets ready to move. She hesitates. She is confused. Her mum has betrayed her, and her dad. But now Mum is protecting her. Anna doesn't know how to feel. There isn't enough time to work it out.

Blakemore has his hands around her mum's throat. She is squealing and choking and batting at his hands as hard as she can. Then Cynthia looks at her daughter, and her fingers scrabble for something on the bench. She grabs whatever it is.

'Go!' Cynthia rasps. Then she sinks a biro into Blakemore's leg.

The police officer yells and releases her, clamping his hands around his punctured thigh.

'Run!' Cynthia says. 'Run!' And she jumps on Blakemore, pushing him into the side of the van.

Anna doesn't think about it – she moves quickly, pushing open the van door and stepping out on to the ground. It feels funny beneath her feet. The door swings shut behind her. Survival takes over.

She runs.

As she gets further away from the van, she realises she is surrounded by police in riot gear. Where did they come from? What is going on? She feels the acrid burn of vomit at the back of her throat.

Riot police. Twelve of them. Batons aloft.

And people. In their bed clothes. All milling around. Anna's confused. *What time is it? What's everyone doing outside? Why is everyone standing around in the middle of the night?* She is surrounded by so much noise. Chatter everywhere.

She is ten steps away from the van when she hears a scuffle behind her.

THUD.

A scream and a yelp, distinctly her mum. And another noise, clanging against the side of the van. *BANG.* No more sounds from Mum.

A shiver cascades down Anna's spine and she stops running. She is still.

But all she can hear is the blood thumping in her ears.

Do I stay? Do I go? She doesn't know the best move to make. Anna turns to the van and prepares to run back, to get her mum, to rescue her, but her feet are rooted to the floor. She's still frozen when the door bursts open and Blakemore scrambles out of the back. Blood is streaming down his face.

'Patterson,' he screams. He scans the crowd. 'Where the fuck are you?'

Then Blakemore spots Anna and runs in her direction. 'Anna!' he shouts. 'I just wanna talk. Come back.'

He is desperate. She can hear it in his voice.

Anna runs.

She heads towards a crowd of people waiting to go back into the building, tired from the day, from summer, from the evacuation.

'Anna Johnson.' She hears his voice behind her, getting closer. 'I don't want to have to arrest you. Anna, it's all gonna be fine. I just want to talk.'

She hears gasps from people around her, turning their attention to the chase. No one intervenes.

She approaches a group of students with blue rinse hair, smoking roll-ups and watching the proceedings with ennui. They are documenting everything that is happening around them on their phones. One of the smoking students notices Anna and raises her eyebrows as if to ask if she's OK.

Anna mouths, 'Help.'

They look at her and breathe smoke through their noses, then they edge backwards, like they want no part of this frantic teenager running towards them. All they need is the video.

'Help me please,' Anna breathes as she runs towards them.

One of the girls filming proceedings trains her phone on to Anna.

Anna, growling in frustration at their need to film but not intervene, looks around and carries on running past them.

She spots Silas with Old Man Patrick. Finally someone she can feel safe with. He took them in earlier. She stops in front of him. She pants.

Silas is still dressed as he was then. Still wearing his Hulk slippers and robe.

Silas lets go of his dad's hand and reaches out to Anna. He pulls her into his arms and gives her a cuddle. Old Man Patrick coughs. There's shouting behind her but she can't hear anything clearly through Silas's hoodie. He spins her around to shield her.

'Where is Taran? The others?' Silas asks.

'I don't know,' Anna shouts, angry at herself from splitting up from them. A coward's move.

Blakemore's voice rings out.

'You,' he says at Silas.

'Leave her alone,' Silas says, firmly.

'Step aside, now. I don't have time for this,' Blakemore says. He looks worried. 'Anna, you are under arrest.'

Anna turns to face Blakemore. He is sweating, wiping his brow in frustration. This evening has got away from him, she can tell. She wants to laugh. Be defiant. *No, I am not under arrest, you murderer.*

More people in the crowd start to take an interest. Over two hundred people here, and along with the blue-haired students, a few more are beginning to look at them.

'Why she under arrest?' Old Man Patrick says. 'You still harassing these kids? Have you got an arrest warrant now?'

Blakemore hisses at Old Man Patrick, 'You stay out of this, old man.'

'Why you taking it there?' Old Man Patrick says, coughing and reaching down to his oxygen tank, tapping it like it's going to suddenly give him the O2 he needs. 'I'm not too old to box you around the ears.'

'Answer my dad. Why are you still harassing these kids?' Silas demands.

'What's that to you? You're not her legal guardian,' Blakemore says. 'Anna, you're coming with me, one way or the other.'

Silas releases Anna and faces up to Blakemore. Anna breathes deeply, her entire body shaking.

'Sir,' he says, as politely as he can, 'if she's not under arrest then I'm afraid she's going to stay here. Unless you want to explain to me *why* she is under arrest. Or why you are chasing her through her ends. Or why arresting a teenager is a high priority right now. Look at us – we've all been made to leave our flats in the middle of the night, for reasons still unexplained. We're standing out here in the middle of the night like lemons. We'd like answers. And when we get those answers, maybe we can then see about whether Anna Johnson here is under arrest.'

Blakemore shrugs and throws a punch at Silas. The blow lands on his chin and Silas falls backwards.

Anna reaches for Silas, tumbling with him, feeling her body tense up ready for the impact of the floor.

Old Man Patrick cries out, but the wheelchair stops him from rushing to his son's aid.

Blakemore pulls at Anna's shoe and wrenches her backwards until she is free of Silas.

'Where is the USB stick?' he hisses.

As Blakemore bends down to pick Anna up by her armpits, Silas springs up and pushes his way into the space between Anna and Blakemore.

'Leave her alone,' he says.

Blakemore pulls out his baton, twirling it menacingly. Silas crouches, lowering his centre of gravity, on the defensive.

Anna steps backwards until she is standing next to Old Man Patrick. She grabs for his hand. She scans back to the van. Is her mum OK?

Her mum and Blakemore.

That sick feeling returns.

Anna looks back as Blakemore strikes Silas with his baton. Silas falls to the ground. He blocks Blakemore's next strike but the force of the following blow is too much and

Silas's head snaps back on to the pavement. Blakemore strikes at the side of his head with his baton.

Silas is still.

1.57 a.m.

As CJ rushes ahead of them, Taran leads her gang out into the courtyard. She's surprised at how easy it is. There are no police officers guarding these doors. There's not even any annoyed people who've been evacuated from their flats. As she and the guys head out of the exit in the southernmost corner of the block, she breathes in the air.

It feels fresher out here, quieter, less claustrophobic. She feels more alive being outside, like everything in her mind has been held captive by the block. For a second, she doesn't know where she has been or where she's going to. It's like there is a moment of disconnect between her and her surroundings and she doesn't know who she is any more.

She remembers it's summer. She rubs at her itching scalp. The breeze cools the back of her head.

She is pulled out of her trance by Hari tapping her on the shoulder.

'T,' he whispers. 'You OK?'

Her surroundings snap back into focus and she suddenly hears noise again. She's no longer caught in the silence of her own head. They are not alone. It is not quiet. There is noise and sound everywhere. The yells and hubbub of a concerned crowd, chanting, chatter, and official-sounding voices telling people to be calm. There is a gap between the entrance to the building and a line of riot police, all holding up shields and keeping residents from entering, who are all up in arms and arguing with the police. But this riot line is thick and there is no way they can breach it. The arguing is so intense, no one seems to notice the three teens and their hooded companion in the shadow of the southern exit.

'What the hell is going on?' Jamal asks.

This has escalated, Taran thinks.

'Let's go,' CJ says, walking away from the commotion, towards the railway track. He turns back and shouts, more urgently, 'Come on. While they haven't spotted us.'

Jamal shakes his head. 'Anna,' he says, quietly.

CJ runs back to him. 'Come on, let's go,' he urges.

'You guys go,' Jamal says. 'I'm gonna look around, see if I can find Anna. I need to know she's OK.'

'We can do that later,' CJ says. 'We need to stick together.'

Jamal smiles and looks at the crowd. 'I need to find Anna. I'm sorry.'

'OK then. You go get your girl. I'll come back,' CJ says. 'I got some people doing some bits. I'll be back, I promise. You coming, Taran?'

Jamal looks at Taran.

'I need to find Anna,' he repeats.

Hari and Taran reach their hands out to Jamal. He grabs both.

'She's family,' Taran says. She looks at CJ. 'We have to stay with Jamal and look for her. You go. Do what you have to do.'

'You sure about that?' CJ says. 'It's chaotic around here right now, and none of us knows how this will play out. We'll do a better job by going to find my people.'

'I hear you,' Taran says, keeping hold of Jamal's hand. 'But we need to find Anna.'

'I understand,' CJ says. 'I understand. Look, I've lost a brother tonight. You shouldn't lose your sister as well. Can I keep the video at least?'

Jamal lets go of Taran's hand and runs off. She lets him go and turns back to CJ.

CJ looks at Hari and stretches out his hand. He has Hari's phone.

Hari seems confused.

'I'm asking your permission this time, working man,' CJ says, breaking into a grin. 'I know what to do with it to get justice for my brother.'

'You keep it, CJ,' Hari says, closing CJ's hand around the phone tentatively. 'Just . . . give it back to me tomorrow. So I know what shifts I have at Shah's . . .'

'Working man,' CJ says, laughing. He daps Hari's hand.

CJ smiles and pulls the hood of the mac up, glancing towards the chaos. He puts his hands in his pockets, and he turns. As Taran watches, he runs down the hill to the train tracks. He runs like he hasn't been running all night. He runs with the fresh legs of freedom, of someone unencumbered. He is gone.

Taran looks at her brother. 'You did the right thing in trusting him.'

'He better not let me down.'

They walk in the opposite direction to CJ, vaguely following Jamal, towards the commotion, into the crowd, to see what's causing the noise. Taran is rushing, ever so slightly ahead of her brother.

'Where are you going, Ramsaroop?' Taran hears, and stops.

Hari is standing very still, looking worried.

Taran sees, behind him.

Patterson has a gun to Hari's side. Taran watches as Patterson pushes Hari towards her and points to the building.

'Inside, both of you,' he says. 'Now.'

Taran grips at the USB stick in her hoodie as she stomps back towards the entrance door.

1.47 a.m.

Silas is suffocating.

Blakemore has him in a chokehold. Anna watches in horror as Silas wakes up to find himself being choked. Everything in her is saying, *Go and help him*. But she is terrified, rooted to the spot, squeezing Old Man Patrick's hand as hard as she can, trying to comfort him.

Blakemore is on Silas's back, pushing into his body with his knee, his hands clutching at Silas's arms, pulling them backwards in their sockets till they nearly snap.

'Stop,' Anna shouts, uselessly. Blakemore doesn't notice her.

The students, dropping their cigarettes, film the encounter as subtly as they can on their phones. One of them, George, is a YouTube vlogger – this is exactly the material he needs to keep his channel alive. Anna has seen his InstaStories. He is a master at pretending to text or tweet, while really he's letting his camera roll, unimpeded. She hopes it goes viral.

Old Man Patrick tugs his hand out of Anna's grip and moves his wheelchair as close to his son's body as he can. 'He can't breathe,' he rasps at Blakemore, again and again, as loudly as he can. But Blakemore just applies the baton in a choke hold to Silas's throat, pulling it upwards against his trachea, while his forearm presses down from the other side.

'You're hurting him. Leave him alone,' Old Man Patrick wheezes. 'Stop!'

Anna, emboldened by more people gathering, follows Old Man Patrick and screams in the police officer's face. Blakemore laughs, dollops of sweat dripping from his forehead on to his hands, and aims a powerful kick into Anna's side. It winds her, sending her down to the floor.

Blakemore's phone rings. He drops Silas, who goes limp. He is still breathing but is unconscious.

Blakemore takes his phone out of his pocket. Without thinking, Anna hauls herself up from the ground, ignoring the pain in her side, grabs the phone from his hands and runs off. She looks down at the display which reads: 'NextGen HQ'.

Blakemore shouts after her.

'Leave her alone,' someone yells back and Anna glances behind her to see Blakemore standing frozen and staring at her in panic.

She hits the accept icon, opens the call and grunts.

'I can't reach Michael. Inspector Blakemore, where is Michael? What is going on down there? You're all over the news. Why is it not done?' a voice barks at her.

2.05 a.m.

Jamal runs through the crowd, looking for Anna.

He can't find her. He keeps calling her name. But no one pays him any heed. People seem angry.

Where is she?

2.05 a.m.

Taran and Hari grip each other's hands as tightly as they can as Patterson leads them back to the building. As they walk, Taran catches sight of her neighbours.

She pleads with her eyes at Muhammed and Tara, his wife, who both nod at her. Muhammed even looks at Patterson and salaams him, confused.

'Listen,' Hari whispers to Taran. 'You need to go.' He turns to Patterson. 'Let my sister go. I was the witness. Not her. I saw it happen. I was the one who saw you beat Sim to death. You do what you want with me, but let her go.'

'Hari, what are you doing, man?' Taran says.

'Shut up,' Patterson hisses. 'You've both caused me enough trouble tonight.'

'Let her go,' Hari repeats. He stops walking and spins round to face Patterson. 'Take me. Not her. Just me.'

'You both need to give me what I want. What we're looking for,' Patterson says. 'I will get that USB stick back.'

'Why did you do that to Mr Johnson? Send an innocent man to jail?' Hari says. 'You're evil.'

'You're a murderer too,' Taran says.

'Because he stood in our way. Simple. Everything that is happening is bigger than you, me, Mr Johnson, Sim, this building. We are all cogs in the wheel of progress.' Patterson stops talking. He thinks, then adds, 'You think I don't have a conscience, do you? Who can afford to have a conscience?'

'Is murder well paid?' Hari asks.

Patterson laughs. He drops his gun to his waist.

'I like money,' he says. 'Why does it ever have to be more complicated than that?'

Hari balls his fists. He launches himself at Patterson, screaming for Taran to run.

She does.

BANG!

She hears Hari screaming, 'Just GO!'

She keeps running.

2.06 a.m.

Jamal pushes past Kamala and her son – they're in mourning after the death of Kamala's dad. When Taran and Hari's dad died, Kamala's family gave them dishes of this rice pudding that Kamala said her mum used to make her as comfort food. She hoped maybe it would offer them some comfort too.

Jamal pushes past this girl he goes to school with, Katia. She once shared his earphones at the bus stop cos she liked the sound of the tune he was bumping.

He pushes past the students who live a few floors above them. They have loud parties every Thursday and Friday. The remnants of their video pranks are often on the stairways, stuff like burst water balloons, whipped cream, flyers for sex workers – whatever they're up to that week for their vlogs.

Everyone is here. The people have been absent from the block for the whole evening. But here they all are. Home.

Jamal pushes past his uncle, Terry, who is too drunk some days to remember his nephew even exists.

He pushes past so many people in the block whose lives intersect with his own, who live above, below, next door, and in the pockets of everyone else in the building.

His friends, they complain all the time about where they live, but are the quickest to defend it if anyone from outside says anything similar. Constantly love-hating this place. *We don't even appreciate how connected we are*, Jamal thinks. *We're residents of a block, existing side by side like it's not a strange thing that we're all shoved into this space together.*

Jamal thinks he sees Anna. He pushes on.

1.54 a.m.

Anna clutches the phone, letting the person on the other end speak as she breaks into a run.

'Sorry, who is this?' she says.

'It's Digby, from NextGen. Is that you, Cynthia? Is Susan with you? Where is Michael? I can't get him on the phone. He promised that you were both taking care of everything. That's why we've invested heavily in this concert. Have you secured the evidence? There is a lot at stake here.'

Susan? The mayor? Mum's boss? *And why does the man from NextGen know Mum by name . . .?*

Anna coughs.

'Who is this?' Digby says.

'It's Colin Johnson's daughter,' she tells him. 'And I am going to take you down.'

She hears the caller hang up.

She keeps running.

Seconds later, she is thrown to the ground as something heavy collides with her.

It is Blakemore.

She shouts out in pain.

Blakemore rips the phone from her hand and, pulling at her hoodie, yanks her up to standing.

'Darling,' he says. 'This is not the best start to our new family.'

'Fuck you,' Anna says and punches him in the mouth.

His tooth tears the skin off her knuckle, which bleeds. Her hand aches from the impact and she shakes it in pain, as Blakemore recoils from the punch.

'Anna,' he says. 'I prefer this version of you to the mouse I thought you were.'

'Step away from her,' she hears to her side.

Roberts approaches, his hands out in front of him.

'Martin,' Roberts says. Blakemore looks at him. 'Leave her alone.'

Blakemore turns to Roberts. He shakes his head. He wipes at his forehead. Anna wonders if she can use this distraction to run away.

Her hand hurts; she is alone; she's not sure she's able to run.

'Martin,' Roberts says. 'We've caused enough chaos tonight. Let's let these people return to their homes and we'll head back to the station and talk about this.'

'Roberts, step back – we don't need you any more. You are relieved. We have this under control,' Blakemore snarls. 'You can go.'

'Martin, look around you. It's bedlam. People are stuck outside in the middle of the night. You're hitting teenagers. What are you doing?'

Blakemore waits till Roberts steps close to him before he grabs his outstretched hand and pulls Roberts close into his body.

'Martin, don't do this,' Roberts says.

'I don't want to,' Blakemore says, as he clutches him by the collar and body-slams him into the ground, hard. Roberts is still. 'But I have to.'

He lets go of Roberts and stands up, wiping his mouth. He looks around. Anna can hear his heavy breathing against a backdrop of restless voices. She feels frozen to the spot suddenly. The briefest hesitation.

Blakemore turns to Anna. The expression on his face turns her blood to ice. He looks like he has nothing left to lose.

2.06 a.m.

Anna hears Jamal's voice, calling for her. She turns to see him running towards her, watching his expression change from joy to horror as he spots Blakemore.

People are shouting Silas's name. Anna looks past Jamal to see the students giving Silas first aid.

The calls of Silas's name get louder.

A missile flies from the crowd.

It's a plastic sports drink bottle. Anna watches its trajectory as it flies through the air, spinning frantically like it's in orbit, and strikes Blakemore in the face. The way Blakemore reacts – belching and yucking his face as the liquid explodes out of the bottle – it's obvious to Anna it's not sports drink. It's piss.

Jamal boulders into Blakemore, his hands outstretched to push him. Blakemore falls to the floor. Jamal trips on Blakemore's feet and lands on him.

He doesn't have any fighting technique, Anna thinks. *All he can do is knock people off their balance.*

Anna takes this as her cue and she snatches Blakemore's blood-flecked baton from the ground where he dropped it, then throws it in the police officer's direction. Despite the cuffs, she manages to get it on target, but Blakemore sees the baton flying towards his face and has time to duck.

Both men clamber to their feet and Jamal grapples with Blakemore. Anna can almost hear him talking her through the moves like he does during the fights he makes her watch with him on YouTube. Years of online UFC and MMA matches have taught him well. She can almost hear his commentary: *Let his body come close to your body. Control his strike areas. Give hard body blows to specific places that will cause limbs to flail*. And now she watches Jamal stand up for himself, at long last.

He throws three punches, right-left-right to Blakemore's middle.

Blakemore absorbs the punches and tries to grab at Jamal's collar to get control of his body, but Jamal drives the closeness by moving into Blakemore with every step the officer takes back, ensuring that every time there's no chance for respite.

Jamal throws more punches, right-left-right – this time connecting with Blakemore's stomach, his kidney.

Jamal steps into the space between Blakemore's feet, immobilising his legs, causing him to stumble backwards, off balance. His arms are useless, with nowhere to strike, no space to strike at.

Anna, spying Roberts stirring on the ground, runs over and crouches beside him.

'You OK?' she asks. 'This is getting crazy.'

'Where is Blakemore?' Roberts asks.

'We need to get you to a hospital.'

'I'll . . . I'll be fine,' Roberts splutters.

'What do we do now?'

Anna looks over at Jamal and Blakemore and sees she hasn't got much time. Blakemore is pushing himself up, shrugging off Jamal's hold.

'Is my mum all right?' she asks.

'I don't know,' Roberts says. He tries to stand up but he falls back to the floor.

Blakemore gets the upper hand. He grabs Jamal, wrenches his arms behind him and puts cuffs on, roughly, before pushing him face first on to the floor.

'What do we do?' Anna repeats.

'What can we do?' Roberts says. 'They've got almost everyone out of the building now. That's what they wanted.'

2.11 a.m.

Taran heads for the underpass. It's the only place she can think of that might be safe. Also, she wants to know where Sim's body is. She won't let him rot there.

When she enters the underpass, the stench of grime is thick. Once more she pulls her hoodie over her face and tightens the strings. She knows that Patterson won't be too far behind but she can lose him in the darkness. She reaches for her phone to use the torch function, but it isn't in her pocket. Shit. She must have dropped it somewhere along the way.

Cars pass loudly overhead; sirens wail in the background; the ambient noise of things moving, rusting, rotting all around her create a thick white noise.

She hears footsteps approach and then slow down behind her.

She creeps towards the middle of the underpass, where the abandoned car sits.

She tries to be as quiet as possible but she finds herself kicking metal, tripping on miscellaneous rubbish. She is terrified. She looks around her but there is no light other than what filters down from cracks and gaps in the road above. There should be lights down here. In a perfect NextGen world this would be a car park.

Soon none of this will be here, she thinks.

'Taran,' she hears. It's distinctly Patterson. 'Come out, come out, wherever you are.'

For a second, it dawns on her that she could die next to Sim. It's messed up, sure, but it could be seen as romantic. *Sim*, she thinks. *I love you. I need justice.*

This would be the perfect time to go after Patterson. He's alone, he's in the dark and she is what he is after. She could take him. He has a gun. But she has the element of surprise. Would he shoot her? She's a minor . . . So she's about to turn eighteen, but this is a situation where she is definitely happy to be seen as a kid. Her mind flashes through every single iteration.

She can feel her heart thudding against her chest. She can feel the hot stale stench of her breath trapped in her hoodie. She can feel the dampness of sweat in her socks and in her bra. She sees a light, probably from a phone, dart about some distance away and she keeps her body as still as possible. When she feels safe, she ducks into the passenger seat of the abandoned car. It stinks. She can feel her boots tight around her little toes. She is so tired. Sitting here, in this stinking rotting car, in the dark and quiet, she could go to sleep.

She closes her eyes. They shut for slightly too long, like another beat and she would be asleep, so she sits up in the front seat. The way she suddenly straightens her body makes a screeching noise against the old pleather of the seat.

There are a few tense seconds where she is rooted to the spot, unsure where she is. But then, it hits her. *Move. You have a clear run to the exit. Move!*

She slides herself out of the car, holding on to the door hanging off its hinges, and she stands up as quietly as she can. When she is confident she can't be seen, she runs to the exit, just as a car passes above, enough to jolt her as the tiny sliver of light she has disappears and plunges the entire space into darkness.

In that second, she hesitates and in that second, she hears a click. It could be the sound of the safety of a gun coming off. She doesn't want to test it. She slips on something and falls to the ground, breaking her fall with her hands.

Confused, she scrabbles around in the muck and mud, scrambling to stand up and move. She is about to get her footing when a light, blinding, shines in her eyes. She holds her hand up to the light and tries to cover it, squinting in pain.

Then, as her eyes focus, she sees the gun.

Then the teeth – grimacing, ever so slightly smiling.

'Taran,' Patterson says. 'Enough is enough now. Hand it over.'

'Fuck you, man,' Taran says.

BANG. She hears the gun go off. She feels a jolt next to her. Patterson has fired it to the side. It is loud and her ears ring. She keeps still. She won't move for him. The gun glints. She is hypnotised by it. She cannot move. She feels her heart thumping loudly with fear and adrenaline.

BANG. The second shot tests her resolve.

'I won't miss next time,' he says.

'Shoot me then, boss,' she says, hearing the terror in her voice despite her defiant words. 'I'm obviously cornered. Why don't you shoot me and then rummage around my dead body to find this USB stick you think I have? Would that give you a cheap thrill? Shooting then fondling a minor? That is exactly the kind of cheap thrill you'd like, isn't it?'

Patterson lowers the gun for a second.

'You don't get it, do you?' he says. 'This is my life.'

'What do you think this is for me? A Christmas dinner?' Taran hisses.

'Give me the USB stick,' he shouts, this time raising the gun and stepping forward, just enough that Taran sees his foot within reach of hers.

She kicks at his ankle with her heavy boot and hears his heel crunch on the bone. She kicks out twice more and Patterson falls to his knees, grunting with surprise. She hears the gun drop and sees the light of the phone falling. She kicks out with her feet until she feels the gun and then she kicks it again. She's about to stamp her other foot down on the phone to kill the light so she can run, but she feels Patterson set upon her roughly and grab her by the throat.

She tries to swat him off but he slams her body into the ground. She feels the wind go out from her and she gasps loudly, trying to breathe. She feels him pinch at the pockets of her trackie bottoms. Then he pats at her hoodie pocket till he feels it.

He has one hand inside her hoodie, one squeezing her neck. She tries to knee him but he keeps clasping at her neck until she cannot breathe and she is gulping at the air.

He lets go. She gasps and gasps air back into her lungs. She sees the light rise as he picks up his phone. He shines it on the USB stick. Taran thinks about grabbing at it and running but she is too slow, too weak. He crashes his boot down on to it, repeatedly.

Smash.

Smash.

Smash.

Taran feels like the ground is emptying under her with each brutal stamp.

He shines the light on his face.

'Well,' he says. 'That's that then. It's over.'

Taran sees him take another phone out of his pocket and dial.

'Mr Digby? It's Patterson. It's done,' he says into the phone before hanging up.

Taran feels tears start to come.

Patterson flings the shattered remains of the USB into the darkness. He smiles down at Taran, his evil face bright in the phone light. He shines the light on the ground until he finds his gun. He picks it up.

'Now, young Taran,' he snarls. 'What are we going to do with you?'

2.11 a.m.

Anna walks in cuffs beside her boyfriend, as Blakemore hauls him to the van. She will not leave Jamal's side again.

Silas has regained consciousness. He sits up, breathing deeply, watching as they pass. Anna sees him flinch, like he wants to get up and protect her, but his face creases in pain and he falls backwards on to his elbows.

'This could have all been avoided. I was going to buy you a car, a gift from stepdad to daughter,' Blakemore says.

'You're delusional.'

'Your mum and I, we want to get married,' Blakemore says. 'One day you'll be able to look at me like a dad. We have a lot of healing to do together.'

'We tried our best,' Anna whispers to Jamal. 'We lost.'

Jamal looks at her and, in that second, Anna feels a tinge of hope. He mouths, 'It's gonna be OK,' to her. It's exactly what she needs to hear. Jamal, the happy-go-lucky guy she fell in love with because he had the ability to see the best in everyone. He hasn't lost his faith in her. She allows herself a smile.

She spies Blakemore noting her smile so she spits at the ground in front of him.

'Where are the others?' she whispers, but Jamal looks straight ahead as they approach the van.

'Not now,' he says. 'Stay focused. In the moment.'

Blakemore opens the back doors of the van. Anna flinches, unsure what she'll see. Will her mum be alive?

Cynthia is lying on the floor, handcuffed. She looks up and around her frantically, like she has been asleep.

'Honey, I'm home,' Blakemore calls out.

'Martin,' Cynthia says. 'Let me go.'

'Look,' Blakemore says, pushing Anna into the van, 'it's all happy families. Me, you, the kid and the kid's boyfriend. I suppose we should have a chat with the boyfriend, eh? So, Jamal, what are your intentions towards my stepdaughter to be?'

Jamal looks at Anna and then Cynthia, confused.

'This guy? Really?' he says. 'And you think *I'm* a bad influence.'

'Martin,' Cynthia says. 'What are you doing?'

'Playing happy families, Cynthia, like you always wanted to. Remember? When we'd meet at my flat or for coffees in town, or when we got that hotel, and all you talked about was us moving away together. About taking the money we're getting from this deal and getting out of here. Look at us, all crammed into a van like we're off on a summer holiday. Happy families. Now.' Blakemore turns back to Jamal, this time brandishing his baton. 'You didn't answer my question. What are your intentions towards my stepdaughter to be?'

'You have a lot of anger in you, man,' Jamal says.

Blakemore heaves the baton with all his might and brings it down hard on Jamal's shoulder. He yells out in pain and falls to the ground.

'Mum,' Anna screams. 'Stop him!'

Cynthia bursts into tears as Blakemore throws the baton at her. It narrowly misses her head and clatters into the middle of the van.

'Darling,' she says, sobbing. 'I'm so sorry. I was trying to make our life better. Your father didn't want our life to be better. He just wanted to stay here, where he grew up. He was trying to build a community that had no interest in him.

He should have been thinking about us first, not this community. Us. We're his family. Not them. I'm so sorry. Listen, it's going to be OK. We're protected. The mayor has our back. She asked me to be the go-between with NextGen. When this deal goes through tomorrow, we are going to be so rich. Darling, do you understand? Where is the USB stick? Please just give it to him.'

'Yes,' Blakemore says. 'Yes, darling. Do you understand?'

'Don't,' Cynthia snaps at him. 'Martin, it's so over.'

'We might require some family counselling to get us through this difficult time,' he says and he laughs, hysterically.

Anna stares at him, thinking, *Bruv, how can you even think there's still something here?*

Anna looks down at Jamal who has tears in his eyes and is hunched in the foetal position on the floor.

'You're both going down for this,' Anna says.

'Says who?' Blakemore replies. 'Patterson will have caught up with your lot by now and found the USB. And anyway, there won't be a building left to save by morning. Your mum and I are in the clear, and you are about to be the daughter of a very rich couple. It's over.'

'It's far from over. We have a video on a phone,' Anna says. 'Of you and your NextGen mate killing Sim. You're going down for murder. And I'm not your fucking daughter!'

Blakemore screams and lunges towards her.

2.16 a.m.

Taran is waiting for Patterson to fire the gun. He grimaces, like he really wants to pull the trigger but can't quite work up the courage to do so. He looks as if he might hyperventilate. He breathes in and out, in and out.

'Come on, do it,' Taran hisses.

Patterson pauses.

'Did you hesitate like this before you murdered Sim?' she says. 'Did you even think about it? Did you think about who he left behind? Who would mourn him? Did you think about what his death does to our community? Do it, you coward.'

She closes her eyes. She is tired.

She steps back behind her wall of ice.

Patterson starts laughing. First, a chuckle, as if to say, *Oh, isn't this funny*, then into full-on hysterical side-splitting laughter.

Taran opens her eyes.

'You think I'm gonna kill a teenager? I am not that heartless,' he says. She doesn't believe him. 'You think you're going to die for this? Oh, Taran, honey, no. You gave me what I wanted and it's done. The evidence is gone. I am plain sailing. Literally. Like, properly literally. Cos I'm getting on a plane in the morning, and I am heading for Miami. First thing I'm going to do is buy a boat, and you won't hear or see from me ever again. I'll be the one sailing around the Florida Keys, living large. Fishing, probably. Listening to podcasts, partying, living an easy life.'

'Why did you kill Sim?' Taran says, the ice wall melting again as tears flood her face. 'Why did you take him away from me?'

'Sim Francis tried to make a bad situation even messier. It wasn't easy. Any of this. Getting NextGen to win the contract to own this area and do something worthwhile with it. So many things in the way. Like a community member trying to buy up the building for the youth club so it can stay open . . . I sorted that. I made Colin Johnson so disreputable that no one would ever consider giving him a Community Asset Transfer to work with kids. No way. He's gone. And then the area's reputation. No probs. Station an officer to look the other way while open dealing is going on. Especially one who's worried about where his parents are gonna live when this place disappears. No problem. Then, throw a concert, bringing back a local hero who moved away. Not my taste but fine. All the lovely NextGen billboards we had knocked up and placed on all the security barriers. Sonic branding they call it. Easy. All this is easy. I am earning. I am making a killing to ensure this deal goes through. Because the council is severely in debt and the mayor needs to create jobs, and here is NextGen Properties, willing to make both of those problems go away. Get rid of the current residents. Promise regeneration. You're so close to the city centre. Makes the area desirable. When the new builds are here, those buyers, well – they'd better be loaded. But then along comes Sim Francis with evidence that's going to stop all this happening? There is a lot of money at stake, a lot. He's just another dead body in an area that needs to forget the dead bodies, I'm afraid. He's gone. And that's just progress.'

'You're evil.'

'I'm just a guy who likes earning money, Taran. It's that simple. It's not that deep. And the funny thing is, all your shenanigans running about the building, setting off the fire alarm, making a lot of tired people so annoyed that they're gonna act up to the police, well, you're doing wonders for NextGen. You know estate agents don't even come round here looking for opportunities. Scared of being mugged. Ripe for mass regeneration. They call it a no-go zone. And all your mucking about with police, causing a riot and all the rest of it, well, it just goes to show what sort of area this is. And those contracts are getting signed in the morning. Goodbye, Firestone House. Make way for the next generation.'

'You just told me what you're up to,' Taran says. 'I can go to the papers.'

'Will you?'

'I will.'

'Who would believe you?'

Patterson turns off the phone light, plunging the underpass back into darkness.

She hears him walk away.

She cannot move. She's going nowhere. Not when she knows that here, somewhere, lies Sim's body, and he died for nothing. She could not even save his memory.

She cries for him.

For herself.

For the people who live around here.

It's useless. It's all useless.

'Sim,' she sobs. 'I let you down.'

2.22 a.m.

Taran emerges from the other side of the underpass, in case Patterson is waiting for her the way she came, and walks slowly back towards the courtyard of her building. She is immediately hit by the change in atmosphere since she left it.

She sees three angry residents shouting and running towards a police van.

There is a rumbling noise all around her.

The armoured police stand dumbly, seeming unsure how to handle a crowd about to erupt, despite their training. Inciters rush towards the phalanx of riot shields. The police hold firm. These inciters look young. There is hesitation. Waiting for an order. Waiting for the go-ahead to do something. They respond to orders. Not cacophony.

The shouts start.

'Fascists.'

'All cops are bastards.'

'Fuck the law.'

'No justice. No peace.'

Taran doesn't quite know what to do.

As the crowd bursts forward into the path of the riot police, Taran can feel the atmosphere is one of unity against a system. They move, unified, all together, ready to defend their community against people trying to ruin it.

As the crowd moves, taking advantage of the pause of the police, a spotlight on top of the riot van is turned on, shining down on to the courtyard. A beacon of blinding white light flares, and hits the people.

Steaming into the courtyard come ten more police officers, all in riot gear, shouting for the crowd to calm down, stand down, stop moving, stand still. There is someone in charge – she holds a megaphone and bellows for calm assertively.

There is chaos.

Taran feels movement next to her. Wearing his hood up and breathing heavily as if he is in pain is her brother.

'You cool?'

'No,' she says. 'You?'

'Patterson clocked me good. And I went down long enough for him to chase after you. But then I chased after him. All I can say is – thank god for his phone light, and thank god you charged up earlier, cos,' he says, holding her phone up, 'I got all that shit on video, fam.'

'That's my phone,' she says.

'Yeah, you dropped it when you ran.'

Taran punches her brother on the arm in joy. He smiles.

2.32 a.m.

The officers form an impenetrable riot wall that pushes the crowd back towards the front door of their building. Using force and their shields, they try to calm the unrest. The residents continue to try to push out for freedom, out of the kettle.

People shout and scream. Relentless screams. At first it was about being let back into their flats, but now something has changed. The atmosphere has brought up other issues. About heavy-handed police, about the community wanting its voice to be heard, about fairness.

The silhouettes of the officers in their riot gear – faceless shadows, monsters – are frightening. People try to push the parents with young children deeper into the centre of the kettle, away from this mass of attacking shields.

Someone tries to shoulder-barge an officer out of her way as he gets too close to her, but she is met with a baton to the neck, a wild powerful swing.

A mum holding her two-year-old kid rushes forward to check her struck partner. Taran knows them. Ellie and

Sarah. Ellie is pushed over and a quick baton hit is aimed at her legs, three strikes. Her kid, frightened, screams as she cuddles herself into her mum.

An old Pakistani woman walks forward, standing between the mum and child on the floor and the policeman.

'You should be ashamed of yourselves,' she shouts. 'Let us back in our homes. We have children. These are all our children. Stop it. We're frightened.'

A barge from a shield knocks her backwards and she falls into the crowd, falling on to her bad hip as she connects with the ground. Taran remembers her name: Shazia.

Shazia's daughter, Shabana, rushes to her mother's aid, but is kicked in the back by the advancing line of police. She falls on top of her mother.

Everywhere is chaos.

Ellie and Sarah; Shabana and Shazia; Mo, Ahmed, Paul; Uncle Terry; Alice and David; Chloe, Cody and Rizwan . . . Every resident.

They all have names.

They all live here.

2.22 a.m.

Anna is ready for Blakemore as he lunges towards her.

'Give me that video,' he screams.

Anna ducks and sidesteps in time for Blakemore to stumble and fall out of the van. As he recovers, Anna grabs at the baton he has dropped. He jumps back into the van and grabs at her shoulders. He swivels her around until he has her in a strong chest hold, his fists clasping each other. Anna struggles – at first his grip is too tight but then she manages to whip her fist up to his face and she stuns him in the eye. He briefly lets go.

Anna turns to run but Blakemore recovers.

He grabs at her hair and twists it till she falls down to her knees.

'Get off her,' Jamal yells.

'Do something, Jamal! Mum?' Anna says, as Blakemore pulls at her hair once more.

With his free hand, Blakemore searches through Jamal's pockets, but finds nothing and kicks at the ground. He searches Anna's, breathing close to her neck, almost touching his forehead to her cheek. She feels violated as his searching fingers make impressions on her body. Anna swears he is smiling. She pulls her body away from him as far as she can but it's no use – his hands are everywhere she has not invited them to be.

She holds herself together, arms tight to her body, legs crossed, chin on chest, hands on her lap. Finding no phones on either of them, Blakemore grimaces at Jamal and pulls at his collars. He holds him close then pushes him backwards, clattering Jamal into the side of the van. Cynthia gasps. Jamal doesn't complain. Instead, he looks at Blakemore, square in the eye. He smirks. Anna wants to smirk too. She hears her mum protest but neither of them can help their defiance. Blakemore pulls Jamal up once more. Jamal doesn't flinch.

'Stop,' Anna says, desperately. 'Stop hurting us. I know where the phone is. I have it.'

'No, you don't, darling. Stop covering for your boyfriend. Neither of you have phones.''No,' Jamal says. 'We don't. But someone else does.'

'Who?' Blakemore demands. 'Who has the phone?'

'Excuse me,' a stern voice interrupts. 'Inspector Blakemore, can I have a quick word please?'

Anna looks, so does Jamal.

It's Mayor Susan Ross. Standing there. By herself. No bodyguard, no personal assistant. No minder. In jeans and a sweatshirt instead of her usual blue suit.

She looks around furtively.

'Inspector Blakemore,' she says again. 'Hurry up. And bring Cynthia with you.'

Anna looks at Jamal.

Jamal keeps his eyes on Mayor Ross, staring her out.

2.32 a.m.

Not wanting to get caught in the kettle, Taran and Hari move as quickly as they can, trying to avoid eye contact with anyone. They duck through the crowd, holding hands tightly, looking for Anna and for Patterson and for Jamal and for Blakemore.

None of them are to be seen.

Taran is worried. Where is Anna? Jamal must have found her by now. Where are they?

The riot police have successfully pushed everyone back against the wall of the building. People are trying the doors to get in, but two officers stand in the way, stopping anyone from entering. There isn't enough room to kick in the glass, but people are trying, hard. The doors are shaking on their hinges.

But the riot line is still pushing, flatter and flatter, till no one has any space to move.

Taran thinks she sees Blakemore outside a police van. She pulls Hari along with her.

An officer blocks their way. Hari pushes at the officer till he moves. The officer looks at Hari, and Taran tries to tug him away. The officer asks Hari to identify himself.

'Leave me alone, pig,' Hari says.

The officer pushes his baton into Hari and Hari falls to the floor. Protesting, Hari kicks out at the officer as he approaches.

'Calm, bruv,' Taran shouts out. 'Calm.'

Taran steps between her brother and the officer to try to stop things escalating. The officer threatens to hit Taran with his baton too so she drops to the ground in defeat.

'It's OK,' she says from the floor. 'We mean peace. This is all a misunderstanding.'

'Stay down,' the officer bellows.

'Fuck you,' Hari says, standing up.

The officer pushes at Hari again, more violently this time.

'What do you think you are doing to my children, officer?' A shrill voice.

Mum is home.

2.32 a.m.

Anna hunches at the end of the van, listening to the conversation between her mum, Blakemore and the mayor.

'Martin, this is fucking chaos,' the mayor says, angrily.

'We got the job done. It just got a bit complicated.'

'Complicated, I'll say. We're in the middle of a riot,' Susan says. 'A riot! Do you know how this looks?'

'Patterson – you know, the one NextGen sent to work with me – he's a loose cannon. He's been . . . look, I'm no snitch, but let's just say, I anticipated this all going a lot calmer than it has, OK?'

Anna looks at Jamal. He gestures over to the counter where Blakemore put down his keys and his wallet. As quietly as she can, Anna picks up the keys and fumbles with them until she finds one that should unlock cuffs. She sorts Jamal, then he returns the favour, and Anna savours the cuffs coming off at last. Jamal rubs his wrists. Anna kisses him. He smiles.

'I've missed you,' she says.

'I've missed you too,' he replies. 'What do we do now?'

'Just listen,' Anna says.

Susan Ross is saying: 'If this deal doesn't go through, the promises on which I was elected are ruined. You know that, don't you? I promised more affordable housing . . .' Anna rolls her eyes at Jamal. No way these new builds will be affordable. 'I promised more jobs. A cut in crime statistics. And more social mobility. These NextGen developments do all of that for me. All of it. We need the deal to go through. Or my job is . . . You . . . you were employed to—'

'Respectfully, I was employed to uphold the law,' Blakemore says.

'With the list of crimes you've committed, Martin, I don't think now is the time to give me sass. Cynthia, have you spoken to Mr Digby? Is he angry?'

Anna strains to hear her mum. Her mum who has let her down, sold her out, and is partly responsible for her dad being in jail.

Cynthia whispers, 'He is not happy. He expected this to be sorted by now. The riot's all over the local news.'

'When did you speak to him? Get him on the phone.'

'I left it in the van,' Cynthia says.

'Go get your damn phone then,' the mayor says.

Anna and Jamal move silently away from the door and pretend to be cowering.

Cynthia enters the van and rummages for her phone in her pockets.

There is silence. Anna can feel her mum looking over at her.

Cynthia leaves the van, and Anna and Jamal shuffle back to their vantage point to listen.

'Why are you calling me? It's the middle of the night,' says the distorted voice of a man. She must have put him on speakerphone.

Anna knows that voice. She spoke to him earlier when she took Blakemore's phone.

There is no doubt that, whoever thinks they are in charge at the moment, this is the person they actually report to.

'It's Susan,' the mayor says.

'Susan? I told you to not call me, especially not with all this chaos going on. Have you seen the videos of the riot? On Twitter? On Facebook? I have. It's everywhere. Shut. It. Down.'

Anna smiles. There will be people tweeting about this, live-streaming, Facebooking, doing InstaStories, vlogging. Hundreds of residents of a significant tower block in a major city have all been thrown out in the middle of the night, and now there's riot police involved. This. Does. Not. Look. Good.

'Sorry, it—'

'Why not let these damn people back into their homes?' the man on the phone says. 'We're after the contract, not a panicked midnight evacuation. This is not the order of things.'

'Sorry,' the mayor says again. 'We decided to—'

'I don't want your excuses. My man on the ground has told me that any evidence of nefarious involvement in this deal from my company no longer exists. So I expect us to be signing contracts in six hours' time. Now, let me go to sleep. I'll let you sort out the mess however you wish. Doesn't matter to me at this point. As long as the contracts are signed before nine a.m. tomorrow, I'm happy.'

Anna feels sick. Everything has been to keep this man on the other end of the phone happy. To ensure that he gets exactly what he wants: a lucrative contract with no complications. Her dad was mess. Sim was mess. The USB stick was mess. Taran, Hari, Jamal, her, they were mess. And now it has escalated. The people are in the street, and tensions have risen because it's the middle of the night and they can't go back into their homes. They know something is wrong. Silas has been beaten up by an officer of the law. Roberts has been floored by his own colleague. All to clean up a mess, a mess that doesn't even register for this man on the phone. That is the power that he wields. This is beneath him, somewhere low on the ground. Anna has never wanted to take someone down. But the small detail in the phone conversation that niggles at her – the evidence no longer exists – that means the USB and the videos clearing her dad are now lost. But she knows he is innocent. And she will do everything in her power to prove that he was set up. If that USB stick is gone, there must be other ways. She will do everything in her power to get her dad out of prison.

Anna jumps down from the van. Jamal reaches out after her but she shakes his arm off. She feels him follow her.

'Mayor Ross, how dare you?' she shouts.

The mayor turns to her. So do Blakemore and her mum. Mum holds up a hand as if to say, *Stop*.

'You were there, at my dad's trial – your *friend's* trial. And you knew he was innocent. All this, so you could sell off some land to a property developer and make good on some unrealistic election promises around redevelopment. You promised affordable housing. How much will it cost to live here? You grew up around here. And now you're selling us out? What about us? Where do we go?'

'Cynthia, please tell your daughter not to interrupt what she doesn't understand,' the mayor asks.

'Excuse me,' Anna says, balling her fist in anger. 'Don't talk to my mum. *I* am talking to you. Talk to me.'

Blakemore tries to grab at her arm but she backs away from him.

'You gonna hit me again, Blakemore?' Anna says. Blakemore stops and looks at the ground. 'Listen, murderer,' she continues. 'You need to shut up. I'm talking to the mayor. How dare you?'

Anna sees the mayor flinch as she gazes at Blakemore.

'Murderer?' the mayor says.

'Your man here,' Anna says. 'He murdered Sim Francis. We have it on video.'

'Martin,' the mayor gasps. 'What have you done?'

Blakemore turns and runs.

2.41 a.m.

Taran has her arm around her brother's shoulder as her mum squares off against the officer. She is in her nurse's outfit and is carrying a book. She folds her arms around it as she speaks.

'Inspector, these are my children. Why are you attacking them? You know they are both under eighteen? This makes you liable for striking a minor. Actually, two.'

'Mum,' Hari says. 'Mum, you're amazing.'

'Taran-Hari,' she says, in her catch-all name for both of them, 'let me talk to the officer. I will deal with you shortly.'

Hari buries his head in Taran's arms.

'You stink,' he says.

'I know,' she tells him. 'Bro, I think we're going to be OK. You still got my phone?'

'Yeah. How so?'

'If you can get Mum's phone and put her hotspot on, can you text CJ and tell him to upload the video of Sim? And can you upload the video you took? The one of Patterson and me in the underpass? To Twitter? And Insta?'

'You want to put the videos up now? With everything else going on? Shouldn't we wait – give everything some time to settle down?'

'The people need to see it. Especially now.'

'Taran, look around. They have other things on their mind. It's only gonna make this worse; more people are gonna get hurt. Riot police are here. We're at fever pitch. Those videos go online, people will be angry. Kids are out here. Babies, toddlers.'

'Hari, bruv, I'm telling you. We have to do it. People have the right to see it and be outraged by it. Look at all these people about to lose their homes. What did Sim die for? Do it. Upload it. Hashtag "JusticeforSim". Hashtag "RageisBack". Go. Do it. And text CJ.'

Taran watches as her mum walks away from the officer and towards her and Hari.

Their mum is glaring at them. Taran isn't worried. Mum's instant reaction to everything is to assume they both messed up.

'Are you OK?' she asks.

Taran nods. She nudges Hari.

'Mum,' he says in that whiny voice that he uses to get Mum to agree to anything. 'Can I borrow your phone? I ain't got credit and I want to make sure Jamal and Anna are all right.'

Their mum hands the phone over and Taran keeps her talking so Hari can do his thing.

'How was work?' Taran asks, with more enthusiasm than is needed for such an innocuous question.

'Darling, what's been happening tonight?' Mum asks.

Taran wants to tell her everything but she needs to keep focused on the task at hand. Mum can find out tomorrow. Right now, she needs to be distracted.

'Don't worry about this, Mum,' she says. 'We got this.'

'Taran, darling, you look exhausted. You have bruises on your face, your hair is missing, we have been locked out of our building and I find you and Hari causing trouble with the policeman. I want to know what is going on here.'

'Mum, it's cool. We weren't doing anything. They were being rough with us.'

Taran can feel the residents' shouting and screaming and anger become a constant and frenzied hum. There is no way this will end well.

'Taran,' her mum says again. 'I am tired. Tell me. What is going on?'

At that point, Hari nods, as if to say, *It is done.* The video is online.

Finally.

'Taran!' her mum says again, more frustrated now.

'Mum, just know that everything you hear about us tonight, know we did it all for the community. Yeah?'

'I . . .' her mum begins, but Taran-Hari are already running off, heading for the crowd.

2.47 a.m.

However it starts, Taran thinks, *it's got to be loud.*

She screams, from the bottom of her lungs. She screams the loudest she has ever screamed.

She screams till her voice is dry and cracking her throat. She screams till the tickle of her vocal chords feels like twanged guitar strings. She screams until there is a hush. A silence.

Even the line of riot police stops, just for a second, before returning to their pushing and their shoving.

She has the attention of her people.

It's got to be loud.

'PC Blakemore, badge number four three one four. Remember that badge number. Remember that when later on tonight or tomorrow you find out that Sim Francis, one of us, has been found dead. Murdered by PC Blakemore and a man from NextGen Properties. They beat him to death. NextGen Properties want us gone. They're buying the building tomorrow. Sim had evidence to stop the sale, so they killed him. They have chased and beaten me and my friends. When you hear about these crimes, know that it is one of your officers, a person sworn to protect you, who is responsible. You know why? NextGen want us out of here. Mate, we're sat on prime real estate.'

For a second, Taran thinks she sees Sim in the crowd, wearing his long puffa that she hated. She stops. Just for a moment. Checks herself, finds her voice again. She sees Ellie and Sarah. Sarah has a thumbs up pointed at Taran.

'Open Twitter, Instagram, right now – hashtag "JusticeforSim". There's a video. Then you'll see what happened to him. And for what, so our ends can become posh flats? It's disgusting. Justice for Sim! Hashtag "JusticeforSim". Check it now!'

'Taran, stop it, you don't know what you're saying.' Patterson steps into Taran's back and pushes her forward, wrenching her arms from around her sides and pulling them behind her. He snaps handcuffs around each of her wrists. She smiles and leans back into it, like she doesn't care.

'This man ain't no policeman. He's NextGen's hired murderer,' she shouts. She looks people in the eyes as she is led away from the crowd. They immediately go to their phones. She can see people pointing and staring at their screens. Their faces are illuminated with white glare as they access the video. The murder of Sim.

'Justice for Sim. Justice for Sim. Justice for Sim,' Taran begins shouting as she is pulled away.

Consternation is growing. People are talking. Starting to panic. To worry. To get angry. People are looking around.

Patterson shakes her to shush her but it does no good. She gets louder.

'Justice for Sim. Justice for Sim. Justice for Sim.'

People in the crowd join in with the shouting – individual stabs of percussive noise that grow into a din.

People are furiously typing on their phones. Hopefully retweeting it. Sharing it. Reposting it. Whatever they need to do to get the message out there.

Shouts and screams from the ground swell; there is a cacophony of outrage everywhere.

Taran can see police in the riot line turn to each other and whisper. Probably saying, 'What the hell?' She smirks.

She watches as more people around her start watching the videos. And people are glancing up from their phones, looking mad as hell.

Connections are made. There is a chaotic pulse in the air in which no one quite knows what to do.

As Taran scans the crowd, Patterson lets her go. She turns around to face him. He has his hands on his head, eyebrows raised, almost like he's worried and for the first time tonight has no idea what to do.

Taran smiles. *It has started*, she thinks. *And it is loud.*

2.47 a.m.

Anna and Jamal chase after Blakemore. *He's not getting away with this*, Anna thinks. Now it's all happening. Now they are able to get closer to the truth. Now, she finally believes, her dad can be free.

Blakemore runs straight into the outstretched arm of Roberts and is clotheslined to the floor.

Anna and Jamal stop running. Roberts holds a hand up to them both as if to say, *Don't worry, I have this now.*

Roberts bends down and efficiently turns Blakemore on to his back and up to sitting. Anna sees Roberts wincing with pain, but that doesn't stop him handcuffing Blakemore and pulling him up to his feet. Roberts smiles at Anna and Anna, not knowing what to do, gives him a goofy thumbs up. Blakemore stares at the ground.

'Steve,' Blakemore says to Roberts. 'Please . . .' He stops himself from saying anything more. Maybe he knows that there's nothing he can say right now to redeem himself.

Roberts walks Blakemore back to the van. Anna and Jamal follow.

'Where's the mayor? Where's my mum?' Anna asks, exasperated.

'What do you mean?' Roberts asks. 'Was the mayor here?'

'She's been getting cosy with NextGen,' Jamal says. 'We heard her chat to some NextGen man on the phone.'

Roberts handcuffs Blakemore to the bench in the van and shuts him inside, then he runs off into the crowd.

'Where you going?' Anna shouts.

'Back in a sec,' he says. 'Need to speak to the commanding officer. See what's happening.'

Anna notices the din of the crowd rising. She starts to hear the shouts.

'Justice for Sim. Justice for Sim.'

'Listen. They're shouting about Sim!' she says.

As she approaches the crowd, she sees people with their phones out. All watching intently, pointing. Angrily. At whatever is on their screens.

Then it dawns on her.

They're watching the video of Sim's death.

People are watching the video, making the connection, feeling the energy of their anger. They push back, as one. Batons fly as police officers, waking out of their confused stupor, respond to the push-back in the only way they know how.

Someone throws a brick. Anna watches it arc through the air. It falls on the other side of the line of riot police, somewhere near the entrance of the building.

Another flies, landing closer to Jamal. They move to one side and study the crowd.

The riot shields get closer together till you can't see the police officers behind them.

The mayor is standing on the other side of the phalanx, with a megaphone, begging for calm. Her voice is lost amongst the shouts of loss and frustration emanating around her.

Anna and Jamal edge closer to listen.

They spot Roberts, standing near the mayor. He darts his eyes at Anna. She nods at him.

'Calm down, please,' the mayor shouts. 'It's been a long night. We want to get you back into your homes at the earliest convenience. However, the authorities are declaring the building unsafe.'

Anna looks at Jamal. 'No,' she says to him. '*She's* doing it. She's stopping us from going back into our homes. She's closing it all down. And they have no idea . . .'

Anna, channelling her best friend's energy and fearlessness, rushes forward and pulls the megaphone from the mayor's hands.

'Your mayor is involved!' she shouts. 'Your mayor killed Sim!'

'Don't be ridiculous,' the mayor hisses, and makes a grab for the megaphone.

Anna, remembering that chorus Taran has been rapping for weeks – 'However it starts, it has to be loud' – raises the megaphone to her lips again.

'The mayor is selling off our building to property developers. We will be moved, to god knows where.'

The mayor gasps. Then she remembers herself and grabs at Anna's hands, trying to get the megaphone from her. She pushes it so it bashes into Anna's mouth and Anna drops the megaphone in pain. The mayor stoops to pick it up but Anna puts her foot on the mayor's back and pushes her to the ground with all her might.

'You're under arrest for assaulting a minor,' she hears. And Mayor Susan Ross is put in handcuffs by PC Roberts.

2.55 a.m.

Taran spies Roberts arrest Mayor Ross. She switches her gaze to Patterson who is watching the same thing. He lets out a slow breath.

She allows herself a smile.

'This is what happens when you try to tear people from their homes,' she says. 'They don't go quietly.'

Patterson smiles.

'You know what your problem is?' he says. 'You think this is still your home.'

'How does your boss feel about your quiet little job now being a trending topic online?' she asks.

Patterson pulls out his gun. Taran recoils. Hari is suddenly by her side, his fists up.

'Time for you to leave our home,' Hari says.

Patterson is laughing.

'I said, it's time for you to leave,' Hari says. 'It's over. OK? This is the end of it. You can shoot me. You can shoot Taran. But that'll be two more murders on your hands. You gonna shoot a teenager? No. I don't think so. Time to leave.'

Patterson gestures at Taran. 'Like she said, I already have nothing to lose.'

'Then take responsibility for what you've done,' Hari says. 'For all of this; for killing Sim; for putting innocent people in jail; for making hundreds of people homeless.'

Patterson takes out his phone. Taran wonders if he's calling Digby again. She is trying to work out how easy it would be to disarm him while he's distracted by his call. The gun is still firmly pointed at her brother. Patterson's hand is tensed and his arm is locked. No, Taran decides. If the gun were pointed at her, she would risk it, but not Hari. Not her brother.

'Hello,' Patterson says into the phone. 'Mr Digby. Look, I've run into a spot of trouble. I need . . . What do you mean? No, I can't just sort it out. That's why I'm calling you. It involves Susan. She's been arrested. Can you hear me? Mayor Ross has been arrested! Yes, I know. Look, I need . . . No, I cannot fucking sort it out myself. Hello?' Taran cocks her head quizzically. 'Hello?' Patterson stares at his phone.

He looks at Taran and Hari and he laughs.

'You know, I was nearly out of this miserable country. Everything in this country is shit. Everything. I was gonna spend my money on a cabin in the Everglades. Live out my days fishing. It was gonna be perfect. You know, in Miami, they have over eight hundred parks. It's the only US city surrounded by two national parks: Biscayne National Park and Everglades National Park. I love the outdoors.'

'What are you talking about, bruv?' Hari says.

Taran doesn't like the look in Patterson's eyes. She can see it. He doesn't have any cards left to play. He doesn't have anything left to lose. He trains the gun on Taran now.

'You ruined it all. My perfect plan. It didn't have to go down like this,' he says, soberly.

Taran flinches. She can feel Hari edging forward, about to pounce.

'Don't do this,' she says.

'Oh,' Patterson says, 'I already did it. Look.' He turns to face the building she calls home. 'After all the media coverage on tonight, and the riot, it'll never be the same. You know that, right? It will be primed for redevelopment. You know, you caused the riot too. You let off the fire alarm. So you caused this. All I wanted was that USB. You did my job for me better than I could. I can see the headlines now: "Riot in Estate, Fourteen Injured". The picture of this building will burn in people's memories for a while. You know why this area is so desirable? It's close to the centre of the city and yet you all just stay here – you don't help its prosperity. You don't deserve to be here. You need to be further out. Let the people who will enjoy the proximity to all the bars, clubs and restaurants pump money back into the city; let them have this space. You can just have your own little enclaves on the outskirts. It's selfish to hog the prime real estate. So, I have helped stop it; I've helped the city. I'm a good person.'

'You're a wasteman,' Taran says. 'When all this is done, no one will know your name, except as a murderer.'

Patterson tightens his grip on the gun and points it at Taran's mum. Then at Hari, then back at their mum. Taran steps in front of her.

'If it's anyone you want,' Taran says. 'It's me.'

'Taran, beti, stop,' comes her mum's voice. Out of nowhere.

'You don't get it,' Patterson says, a strange look on his face. 'Whatever happens, I did what I set out to do. I won.'

His voice sounds calm, ethereal, like he's not even here.

Hari jumps towards Patterson. Mum screams, 'No!' Patterson trains the gun on Hari and then, as Taran makes a desperate grab for Hari to pull him back, puts it under his own chin and fires.

The sound is lost amongst the din of the crowd but Patterson falls to the floor instantly. Dead.

Hari hugs Taran, shaking. Taran doesn't know how to react until she sees the blood congealing around Patterson, heading to her trainers. And she feels winded.

Taran's mother pulls them both into her chest, shielding them from the scene. She rubs at the back of their heads. Taran can feel her heart beating fast. Like she has always done, she wipes her eyes and nose on her mum's scrubs.

She feels at peace, finally, in her mum's arms.

3.00 a.m.

Anna straightens. Her eyes don't leave the mayor. Roberts stands behind Susan Ross, holding her by the cuffed wrists. The mayor protests.

'I'm placing you under arrest,' Roberts says again.

Susan Ross squares her shoulders. She seems taller to Anna. As if she has suddenly remembered herself.

'Do you know who I am?' Susan Ross says to Roberts.

'Yes, ma'am. I'm arresting you for assaulting a minor . . .'

'Watch what you say, officer. I can have you stripped of your badge before you even get me to the station. Now, you listen. There is a riot happening and my officers, your loyal brothers and sisters in the force, are trying to quell it. This is not the time. And you,' she says, looking at Anna, 'any accusation you wish to make, you'd better think very carefully about what you want to say.'

'You're complicit in all this,' Anna says. 'You took our area and you agreed to sell it to NextGen. And look at what has happened? People have died; people are out in the streets in the middle of the night, cradling their kids from riot police; you tangled up my mum in it all.'

'I don't think you know what you think you know,' the mayor says.

Roberts pulls the mayor away, and leads her towards the van. Anna watches them go.

She feels Jamal place his hand in hers. She suddenly feels at peace, with his fingers intertwined with hers.

'Anna,' she hears, and turns to see her best friend running towards her.

3.05 a.m.

Taran runs to Anna and hugs her. She punches Jamal on the arm for running off then hugs him too. Hari daps his friend and hugs Anna. They all pile in on each other, hugging and smiling and crying.

'You OK?' Anna asks.

'Yeah,' Taran replies. 'You?'

'Yeah, cool. Where's Patterson?'

'He's dead,' Hari replies, and shakes his head in a way that says, *Don't ask any more.*

'Blakemore?'

'Arrested,' Jamal says.

'My mum,' Anna says, her voice wavering. 'She was part of . . .' She bursts into tears.

'We're here,' Taran says. 'We're all here for you, whatever happens next. We are all together. We are all safe. Whatever NextGen want, they ain't gonna get it.'

'Look around,' Anna says. Taran notices the change in her voice. She sounds harder, more confident, more in control. 'This riot is gonna get worse. I can feel it. Listen. Did you hear our mayor trying to calm everything down? You know she was part of it, right?'

'Our mayor,' Taran says. 'I still can't believe it. She ran on an honesty campaign. Honestly . . . I can't even . . .'

'Yeah,' Anna says. 'She conspired with NextGen. She has blood on her hands, innit.'

'She's only been arrested for assaulting a minor though,' Jamal says. 'Roberts just took her away. She'll be out again soon as.'

'One thing at a time, Jam,' Anna says. 'We've got justice for Sim. Next we get my dad out. Then we properly go after the mayor. After that, NextGen. This doesn't end. No way. We're only getting started.'

'Innit,' Taran says. 'Every step is a journey.' That was another one of her dad's favourites.

'We know what's behind us, we don't know what's ahead,' Hari says, and Taran feels a tear slip down her cheek.

The friends all break their hug and form a line, their arms around each other.

'Taran-Hari, darling,' Taran hears. She turns. It's her mum. 'I am going to find an all-night cafe to get us some teas. Then you can tell me exactly what happened. But first, tea. It sounds like we have all had a long day.'

Taran laughs and watches as her mum heads off in the direction of the high street. She could do with a cuppa.

Some random copper is shouting through a megaphone, 'Stop!'

But you can't stop this, Taran thinks.

The crowd, all residents of Firestone House, rush forward as one – young, old, men, women, this racial group, that religion, this disability, that upbringing – all as one, they charge at the police. They free themselves from the kettle and burst through the riot shields. Some run to the front entrance of their building, trying to intimidate the officers standing in the way of the door. Others run to the police vans to trash them. Others continue to tussle and push with police. In anger.

In the rush, in the middle, Taran thinks she spies a familiar bald head. The man turns to her. Is that the famous lop-sided grin she loves so much? Sim?

It can't be.

It's CJ. He is grinning and shooting a celebratory finger gun at her. Beaming. Justice for his brother. CJ is at peace.

Anna nudges Taran and points at the man standing next to CJ. Taran slowly recognises him. She freezes.

It's Rage.

CJ is whispering in Rage's ear and gesturing to them, to the four of them. Rage looks directly at Taran. He bangs on his chest at her and nods respectfully, appreciatively. He hugs CJ.

Taran holds on to Anna and cries.

Rage walks towards the crowd, unafraid of the anger around him. He is calling for calm, his arms outstretched, his raspy voice booming across the area. 'Calm,' he calls. 'Calm.'

Something is about to change, Taran thinks. *This is just the start.*

And the din is echoing in her ears, crackling like a rap track, bouncing along with booming kick drums, scattershot snares and a bass so low, it's breaking through the concrete.

Because however it starts, it has to be loud.

DAY 76

11.06 a.m.

Taran holds Anna's hand as they wait expectantly. Both of them have been up since 5 a.m. Anna snores when she sleeps and it's been keeping Taran awake. She doesn't mind sharing her room though. It keeps her from feeling alone.

Mum has gone in search of caffeine. It's nice of her to give up her day off for this.

Jamal wanted to come today but Anna said she wanted Taran with her. She didn't explain why. She told Taran she didn't know why, exactly. And Jamal didn't push her. So he has gone with Hari to London to visit Brunel University instead.

The last ten weeks have been chaotic and they have been slow. Nothing out of the ordinary. Things take a long time when you're waiting for legal proceedings to happen. Mrs Johnson has been texting Anna, from Birmingham, with train times and her credit card details, begging her to book a ticket, sending apology after apology. Anna has ignored every one of them now. She turned eighteen a couple of weeks ago. And on her birthday, she bought a new sim card, with a new number.

They see Roberts every morning. He's been helping with Anna's dad's case. He's moved home with his mum and dad, planning to go to uni to study law. Even CJ's been helping, though he claims he's forgotten everything from the semester of his degree. Roberts told Taran he's been a lot happier since he left the force.

Susan Ross managed to get out of the charge of assaulting a minor. But she didn't manage to save her job. She resigned amid a scandal about bungs and fraudulent city contracts. The story even made the national news. There's been no word of Blakemore. There's been no word of NextGen either. They've backed off from Firestone House, but the Waterbridge House contract is still going ahead, despite the fraud case around Susan Ross. According to Roberts, there's a clause buried deep in the contracts that protects NextGen in cases where they have 'broken ground'. Which Roberts says basically means they've started demolishing the building. Clever. Taran doesn't really understand the ins and outs but she gets it. The people who wield the most power inevitably get away with it.

Who'd live here? she thinks. *I would.*

She looks at Anna. Anna stands tall, fidgeting, shaking her leg.

'Thanks for coming with me, T,' she says.

'It's long,' Taran says, smiling. 'Not long.'

'Life is long, it's not that long,' Anna repeats, quieter, taking the words in.

'There are a lot of procedures, boxes to tick. This whole thing comes with a ton of paperwork.'

'Will we be all right?' Anna asks.

'What do you think?' Taran says, laughing. 'Whatever happens, all of us – we're always there for each other. No matter what. OK?'

Anna nods. She clenches Taran's hand harder as she hears the door open.

'Darling, aren't you a sight for sore eyes?'

'Dad!' Anna shouts, running to Mr Johnson. He beams.

Taran smiles as they embrace.

She breathes.

Acknowledgements

Thank you to Emma Goldhawk, the brilliant editor who was able to wrestle this manuscript into what it is. When I set out to write my first YA, I thought I would make it easy on myself by doing a thriller (I've never written a thriller before), set in real time, with multiple narratives, in a single location. Easy, right? Thanks to Emma for ensuring it became this book you hold in your hands.

Thank you to Julia Kingsford for being there at every turn.

Thank you to Jamie Coleman who, when he was my agent, suggested I write for teenagers as he felt I would have something interesting to offer. Also, thank you to all the young journalists I mentored at *Rife* magazine who said similar things.

Thank you to Kate Tempest and Dee Dhanjal for use of their words.

Over the years, I've had encouragement from James Smythe, Musa Okwonga, Tanya Byrne, Irfan Master, Juno Dawson, Catherine Johnson, Katherine Woodfine and Laura Dockrill about writing YA. Thank you to you all.

Thanks to Mariam Khan for fighting the good fight for more representation in British YA. You know, out of the hundreds and hundreds of YA books published the year this is published, fewer than ten are by British writers of colour. That needs to change. We need more. If you're a PoC writing YA and are looking for places to put your work, check out The Good Journal. If you're looking for representation, look up The Good Literary Agency.

Keep going. We need you.